FIRST I.

THELMA RUE
AND THE TOXIC TONIC

WAYNE POWERS

A LADIES AUXILIARY MYSTERY SERIES

DEDICATION

TO ALL MY WONDERFUL GUEST AT THE SALON! I COULDN'T DO THIS WITHOUT YOU! AND TO MY PARTNER LOUIS! THIS IS FOR THE LONG HAUL!

WAYNE POWERS

Chapter One

HAD I KNOWN THE SUNDAY before Easter would turn out like a nightmare before Christmas, I would have never gotten out of bed, much less went with Pearl White to open the church. This has been our usual Sunday morning ritual since I took over as president of the Ladies Auxiliary close to seven years ago.

Until now, the worst trouble we had ever encountered were stray bulletins left in the pews from Wednesday night service, many of which were crammed into the hymnal depositories, or errant chairs out of place in the Sunday School rooms, all of which I cannot tolerate. You wouldn't leave crumpled-up trash or papers like that around your house unless you were a redneck slob, much less leave chairs all over the place in your home.

What would newcomers think had that been their first visit to St. John's Baptist Church, seeing papers strewn about the sanctuary or chairs out of place in their respective Sunday School classes?

That's why Pearl and I elected to open the church and make sure things were in order every Sunday morning. Plus, we did it to take some pressure off Pastor Fairchild and his wife, Gloria, from having to do it themselves before church services commenced.

That Sunday, things looked exactly like they normally did. Pearl went her way toward the Sunday school rooms and I roamed about the sanctuary, making sure everything was spotless, ensuring no bulletins or peppermint candy wrappers were left behind. I was making my way to the pulpit to dust when I heard the most awful scream I had ever heard from Pearl.

I ran back to the Sunday school room as fast as I could in my chunky heels.

When I reached the top of the ramp leading to the Sunday school rooms, I noticed the lights were on and saw that Pearl had fainted and was lying on the floor. Thank the Lord, I had insisted they put premium carpet down instead of that cheap indoor/outdoor carpet that would have worn out within a year.

For the life of me, I couldn't fathom what would have made Pearl scream and faint like that. She had been a nurse at the Barnville Regional Medical Center for over thirty years before retiring and had pretty much seen it all.

Then I began to worry that it was her heart. Just two months prior, she had stints placed in two of her blocked arteries due to a heart attack. She told me afterward that she had never realized just how bad she felt before until she experienced better circulation after the surgery.

Crouching to the ground, I pulled my dress up and placed her head in my lap. Her white hair glowed against the turquoise-blue pattern of my dress. I feared I would put a hole in my stockings, but at this point, Pearl came first. I could buy more stockings; I couldn't buy a best friend.

I patted her face, "Pearl, honey . . ." I kept repeating in a low voice as I stroked her face, trying to rouse her. After what seemed like hours, she finally opened her eyes.

"Pearl, are you okay? I've already dialed 911 and there's an ambulance on the way. You just be still. I've got you."

Pearl shook her head as she slowly pulled herself up off the floor. She stayed on the carpeted runway of the ramp and sat beside me.

"Oh Thelma, you're not going to believe this." She got up before I could interrupt.

"Please don't tell me it's your heart, Pearl. I can't take it." I started getting up off the carpet. It took me two tries. Getting old ain't for the light of heart!

"Thelma, no!" she exclaimed, as if I was dumber than a box of rocks. She continued, "It's worse than a heart attack. Look in the Sunday school room." She pointed her bony finger with her dipped nails to the last Sunday school room on the right-hand side of the wing. In front of us was the back door, which was put in to meet building codes. It was supposed to be used as a fire escape in case fire ever blocked this wing of the church. We could get out the back door, which opened onto a grassy area about three feet wide before becoming woods behind the church.

I didn't know what to expect to see that would have made Pearl faint. Reluctantly, I peered into the room and saw the dead body of Triston Stylz splayed over the metal chairs with his long, curly, blonde hair falling almost to the ground like stringy spiderwebs. His neck was turned in a way no neck should ever be turned and his mouth was opened with a grimace that laid bare that the last minutes of his life were painful ones.

I felt a coldness running up from my feet to my legs, and then spreading through the rest of my body. My knees started to buckle, and suddenly I had to brace myself against the doorjamb to stay upright. I'd be back on the floor if I hadn't gripped the doorjamb so hard.

The next thing I felt was Pearl as she silently grabbed my shoulders.

I screamed for dear Jesus!

She scared the living you-know-what out of me!

"Pearl, if there wasn't already one dead body in this church, you'd be next! You scared the living daylights out of me!"

"Oh Thelma, I'm sorry," she proclaimed as I looked back at her. My body had started to acclimate to the body and the room it contained. It didn't feel like a normal Sunday school room right now and never again would. You could *feel* the grasp of evil that had been in this room and extinguished the life that lay before us.

I'm not normally one to panic like I did, but when you see the dead body of your hairdresser laid out like Jesus taken off the cross, what else would you expect?

After getting ahold of ourselves, we made our way over to his body. Had he been alive, his neck would have been killing him, but it looked as if someone had beaten him to the punch.

I was breathing heavily. Lord knows I smoked cigarettes, but my lungs had constricted, making me feel as if I had COPD. I must confess, this wasn't the first dead body I had seen. However, it was the first I had come upon in church without a casket to adorn it.

I looked at Pearl. She had a dent smashed into the back of her white hair where she had teased it to give it some volume. She was wearing a long rosette-laced, peach-colored dress that bellowed out below her knees and white Mary Jane kitten heels with T-straps. I know she bought the dress at Rose's because I was with her when she bought it. The only thing that upset me about the dress was that she had found it first. Myra, our other closest friend, was wandering around in the larger section while we shopped. All three of us knew that with the money Myra had, she would never buy her clothes from a place like Roses. Myra usually bought her clothing from small boutiques in Barnville where they served mimosas as you perused the expensive stores. I know I'm stalling. But give me a break. It's not every day you find your hairdresser dead in your church.

"What do we do Pearl?" I clipped, as I lightly nudged her closer to his body. She was the nurse, after all. I had worked at BellSouth most of my life and fixing phones had nothing to do with raising the dead.

Pearl looked over Triston's body, grabbed his hands, and looked at his fingernails. They were a reddish color, much like the rest of his skin, which was off from his normal complexion. In life, he'd had the most beautiful alabaster skin and with his long, natural blonde, curly hair framing his face, he was one of the most beautiful men I had ever seen. He was so pretty he could have been a girl. He had dainty features, but nothing about his demeanor was dainty. He was larger than life. Or had been.

Pearl ducked down to his opened mouth, which was now in a constant state of grimace. She lightly sniffed inside his mouth but was careful not to inhale too much like I would have. At the time, I had no idea what she was doing.

"Pearl, what in the world?" I had declared in whispered tones. Why in the world was I whispering? He couldn't hear me. Bless his heart.

"Thelma . . . " she had said in exasperation with me as she deliberately took her time looking over his body. I stood there, dumbfounded.

Finally, I could no longer take being in the dark. "Pearl, what is it?"

"Poison, I think. It looks as if someone killed him with some type of cyanide."

"Cyanide?" I had questioned her judgment, which I knew she would take umbrage. She had been an ER nurse for most of the thirty years she practiced,

and like I said, she had seen pretty much what the worst humans could do to one another, and also the worst they could look just before death took them into another zip code.

"Look at his fingernails and his complexion. They're redder than they should be at this point. He's probably been dead for about four to six hours, depending on the dose of cyanide they gave him." Pearl politely laid his hand beside his body, his wrist flailing toward the floor, moving back and forth. Not that he would mind. He was deader than a doornail.

"Pearl, we need to be careful if you think somebody might've killed him. Pick'll have a fit if we mess with his crime scene. You don't think that he and Arty could have been making some products from his line and this could have happened, do you?"

"No. I don't. And if it did, I'm sure Arty would have immediately called an ambulance."

I had agreed. I had to sit down. The room had started spinning. Who in the world would want to kill Triston Stylz? The only thing he was guilty of was making women look good and feel good about themselves and their hair. I put my hand to my forehead and closed my eyes. I could feel a kicker of a headache coming on.

Pearl came and sat beside me, and rubbed my back. She's been my best friend since we were in the first grade. We were both mill villagers since our parents worked at the mill. Shortly after the mill shuttered and moved to Brazil, Richard Whitmire purchased the mill and turned it into condominiums with huge, black-mullioned windows and various retail stores below them. The top two floors were owned by Triston and Arty, who had joined them by taking out walls, making them into huge, loft-like apartments. Triston's Apothecary and Salon was one of the retailers below, along with a wonderful diner simply called A Meat & Three, a nail salon called Get Nail'd, a steak house called Southern Sizzle, and a place to purchase the most expensive wallpaper known to man called Perfect

Patterns Wallpaper and More. More must have been about the price.

The Mill Village had a huge revitalization and the homes our parents had lived in had appreciated substantially in value. Thankfully, Pearl and I never had to deal with siblings since we were both the only children our parents had. So once they passed, we moved into their smaller homes. As we got older, we decided that we didn't need mausoleums to roam around in. We wanted to be where the action was and in Sunnyside, it's normally at the Mill Village.

As I was coming out of my stupor, Pearl and I started hearing the police, firetrucks, and ambulance sirens. A few minutes later, Perkins 'Pick' Lawson and his right-hand detective, Hansen Mulvaney, known around the town of Sunnyside as Handsome Mulvaney, were standing at the top of the landing where the ramp brought them down into the Sunday school wing of the church.

Chapter Two

PICK WALKED DOWN THE RAMP to meet us in the room where we now stood. Pearl and I watched as he and his deputy came our way. I had never noticed how bowlegged Pick was or was becoming as he aged. His skin was like tanned leather, his eyes deeply set, and he had wrinkles around them and layered, dug-out marks on his forehead. He hadn't aged well, and you could tell he didn't believe in moisturizing or eating, for that matter.

Although most people in Barnville would call Pick a redneck, he would wear that moniker like a silk scarf proudly displayed around his neck. He was who he was and didn't apologize for it. That was one reason people loved and trusted him.

You could tell Pick was slowing down, and since the town of Sunnyside was in Barnville County, he was our sheriff as well. Pearl and I had grown up with him and his brothers in the mill village. He had come a long way from Sunnyside.

Behind him, Hansen Mulvaney walked bolt straight with his dark jeans and a starched white shirt adorned with cuff links and expensive cowboy boots. His hair was the color of cinnamon, and he kept his beard trimmed and coifed. Hansen had a square jawline showcasing his pure masculinity and ruggedness that permeated all around him.

We could hear the sound of car doors closing. We soon found ourselves surrounded by Barnville's finest: the CSI team, the paramedics, the fire department (although once they had figured out this was a murder scene, they would leave), and the coroner of the Barnville County Medical Examiner's Office.

My body felt a sigh of relief, which I had not realized I had hung onto. Finding a dead body does something to you that I still can't explain. Maybe you'll understand one day. Hopefully not.

"Thelma Rue and Pearl White. Look at you two," Pick had said. It had been awhile since we had seen one another. The town of Sunnyside didn't have a sheriff's department for a reason. It was a treasured place by almost everyone who lived here, and the specialness of the town was that it was somewhat contained within itself. We had only one grocery store, but could always make a trip to Barnville if needed. Many did because they wanted to keep the quaintness of Sunnyside. Everyone who lived in Sunnyside knew it was a precious commodity.

"Everything changes, but stays the same. You still carrying toothpicks in your mouth." I shook my head and smiled. Pick had a calming sense about him. Not that I had forgotten about Triston, but I knew that Pick would make things right somehow. He and his team would find his killer. Thank the Lord.

"Now they're cinnamon flavored," he'd said, taking the toothpick out of his mouth. "Pearl, look at you. Still the stunner." Pick again removed his toothpick as he took Pearl's hand and kissed it.

I know, believe me! I wanted to tell them to get a room. But it wasn't the right time or place.

They have been at it since high school. Pick's been widowed for awhile, so who knows what could happen between these two? I could see the slight smile on Pearl's face and that vacant look she gets when she's around Pick for any length of time.

Hansen, standing behind Pick, simply said, "Ladies." This was all he needed to say to most women, in that deep, raspy voice of his, to make panties fly.

"All right, what do we have here?" Pick finally asked after googling at Pearl for a few more minutes. We both stepped away from the door and as Pick entered, he whistled, giving us the impression that something was afoul.

Duh, I thought.

But that was Pick being Pick. Hansen came in behind him and looked around the room, moving from one spot to another, getting different angles of Triston's body splayed out over the metal chairs. They both put on black nitrile gloves before touching anything.

Pick immediately went over to the body after his whistle died down and, as Pearl had done, picked up his hands. This wasn't Pick's first day at the rodeo, and like Pearl, he had seen it all, too.

Pick looked at Hansen as he came closer to the body. "You thinkin' what I'm thinkin'?" Pick asked Hansen. Hansen studied the body for a few more seconds, bent down, and lightly sniffed in Triston's mouth. "Smells like almonds and is that cherry too?" Hansen looked back at Pick. Pick looked at Hansen as if he had something to say, but didn't. He simply did the same thing Hansen had done sniffing into the grimaced mouth. "You're right. There is a hint of cherries," Pick said quizzically.

Hansen agreed with a slight nod.

At the top of the ramp, we could see a little lady in scrubs, with a name tag on her white doctor's coat, making her way down the ramp. Birdie Goodwin was always stylish and when Covid hit, she allowed her colored hair to grow out white. Now she had the most beautiful white hair, cut into a pixie that she could style a thousand ways, and believe me when I say a thousand, I mean it. Her hair is different almost every time you see her. I suppose she's not into signature looks. Birdie was also a member of our church and a member of the Ladies Auxiliary.

"Well, I suppose this means that church is called off," Birdie had said to me and Pearl, as we both hugged her. She had been coming to St. John's for years, but because of her job, had only become a member of the Ladies Auxiliary over the past two years. She would soon retire from her position as coroner, but when was anyone's guess, even her own as she had told us. She'd changed her retirement date at least four times that I knew of.

"Excuse me girls," Birdie whispered as she entered the room, donning her gloves. Pick was twirling his toothpick around his mouth. I often wondered how in the world he did that. Believe me when I say it's not easy. I've tried it and 'bout choked myself to death!

After Birdie said her hellos to the boys, she got down to business, shaking her head, as she took in Triston's last seconds on this earth. I'm sure she knew, from the look of his skin and from the sniff she did immediately before looking at his hands and fingernails, what had happened to him.

They weren't as red as they were when Pearl and I had found him, but with Triston being her stylist as well, Birdie also knew his skin looked like pure white marble.

"One thing's for sure. Whoever did this not only knew what they were doing but also knew the amount of pain it would cause as the poison metabolized in his body," Birdie said to no one and everyone at the same time.

"So, you think it's cyanide, then?" Pick asked her.

"No. I don't," Birdie had said, looking into Pick's deep-set eyes. "It looks and smells like bitter almond oil. That's where the top notes of cherry come from. Then, of course, you have the almond scent indicative of cyanide."

"Bitter almond oil?" Hansen questioned. "I thought that was safe and used in many products, from cooking to styling aides."

"Bravo, but no star," Birdie corrected him, "but you're very close Hansen. What you're referring to is sweet almond oil, used in various ways and means, but if I'm right, and we'll know once we have the tox screens, I think Triston was poisoned with bitter almond oil and it's a terrible death. Bitter almond oil contains a compound called amygdalin."

I could see that Pick and Hansen were looking at the grimace on Triston's mouth and both seemed to be pondering just how bad his death had been, especially toward the end.

"What I don't understand is why would anyone do this to this poor boy?" I asked incredulously. I could tell by the way his neck was positioned and the set of his mouth that he had suffered something awful. What I couldn't get my head around was why.

Triston was the sweetest person you could meet. He had a very successful salon and product line. The shopping network channel, KDP, offered him a thirty-minute spot between more prominent lines, and he had completely sold out of his products in twenty minutes, with people wanting to be placed on waiting lists.

"I've been asking myself the same question, Thelma," Birdie responded.

"Oh, come on now. Surely he had made some enemies as successful as he was," Pick proffered. However, those of us who knew Triston couldn't come up with a name of anyone we thought could do this to him.

Listen, I'm sure things happened in the salon, and a few years back some stylists had left Triston's salon, but once gone, those chairs were filled the next time Pearl and I went in for our cuts.

We always went together and afterward would have pedicures. I never bothered with manicures because with all the work and cooking I did at the house, manicures never lasted anyway, and I know Pearl felt the same way.

Triston wasn't the gossiping type like a lot of stylists. If he heard anyone in the salon gossiping about someone, he cut them off and asked them to please change their conversation. This was a rule he had not only in the salon but one he lived by. If he didn't have anything good to say, he didn't say anything at all.

He was also so busy not only doing his job behind the chair, but his salon had six stylists not counting himself; two or three apprentices to help shampoo hair; and then his husband Arty, who managed the place. He also had receptionists at the front desk who scheduled appointments, checked people in, and took their money once their service was over. Arty was the literal glue that held everything together.

"Pick, please tell me Arty already knows what's happened," I had exclaimed, remembering poor Arty as I was meandering in my head about all the people who worked with Triston on a daily basis. "The last thing I'd want to happen is him finding out that someone murdered his husband over the phone."

In a small town like Sunnyside, where everyone knew just about everyone else, gossip spread like wildfire. Lord knows we'd use the "gossip hotline" if we needed to change the dates of the Ladies Auxiliary meetings or if we needed people to bring certain things for that night's meeting.

Believe me, you tell one person who runs their mouth and the next thing you know, I'm fielding calls about who needed to bring what.

I would rather die than Arty hear about this over the phone. That would not only be tacky as tarnation, but cruel to boot.

"Don't worry Thelma, I had Susie on it the minute we got the 911 call from you earlier," Pick had reassured me.

"But what did she tell Arty? We didn't know what had happened to him," I quickly asked in return.

"We knew we'd be running onto the scene not knowing anything before we got here, so I told Susie to go over to their condo and sit with Arty explaining that something bad had happened to Triston, but we were still in the phase of figuring out just what had happened," Pick had replied.

"He had already called earlier this morning since Triston didn't come home last night after a meeting Triston told him he had. Of course, with Triston being an adult, we couldn't do anything for at least twenty-four hours," Hansen added.

"I'm glad he didn't hear it from the streets!" Pearl uttered as she started to sit down in one of the chairs. But before she could, Pick told me and Pearl we needed to leave the room and allow the CSI team and Birdie to do their jobs. There was enough cross contamination in the room from where we had touched the body and Lord knows what else we had touched.

Pick then asked us to come up front where he and Hansen could take our statements. Susie Bright, another one of Pick's homicide detectives, finally arrived, giving the awful news to Arty. My heart ached thinking about that poor boy. They had the world at their fingertips. Who would do something like this? It was more than I could handle. I was also starting to worry about Pearl. She had just had a heart attack less than two months ago. I know they put stints in and supposedly fixed everything up and placed a bow on top, but I could tell this was draining for her and me, too.

"Pick," I said to him as Pearl and Hansen headed into the sanctuary, "I think Pearl may need an ambulance to give her a good looking over." Pearl looked as if the life had been sucked right out of her. Of course, I ain't going to win no beauty pageants myself. "There really ain't nothing Pearl could tell you that I can't."

"Yeah, I agree. The last thing we need is for Pearl to wind up back in the hospital," Pick conceded.

Once we all got to the sanctuary, Pastor Fairchild walked through the church's two front doors. He didn't want to get in the policeman's way, but I could tell from the looks of him that this was his church, and he wanted to know exactly what was going on.

"I can't believe we forgot to call him," I had said to Pick, hoping it was out of the pastor's earshot.

"No worries, Thelma. Once you called the 911 dispatcher, we called Pastor Fairchild and asked him to call church services off for the day. We surely couldn't have everyone showing up thinking it was going to be a regular Sunday service."

"Thank the Lord somebody had the brains to call him. Here I'm the president of the Ladies Auxiliary and I should've been the one to call him immediately after I called 911." I was so exasperated with myself.

"With what you and Pearl witnessed today, I was happy you had the foresight to call 911."

"Some good it did for Triston!" I clenched my dentures until I could feel the metal scraping on my back tooth that held them in place.

I was heartbroken over finding Triston like that. No one should have to die the way he did, I thought to myself.

From the looks I got from Pick, it seemed as if he could read my mind. I have to say in all the years he's been sheriff, Pick's kept both Barnville and Sunnyside safe. That's why no one ever opposed him when he ran for sheriff. They knew their money would be better spent starting fires in fire pits instead of being used for campaign money that would be lost forever.

"Pastor Fairchild, I am so sorry I didn't think to call you, but with all that's been going on, I'm glad my head is still attached to my body." I felt so defeated, looking him in his eyes.

I was the president of the Ladies Auxiliary. I should know better.

Pastor Fairchild had always looked to me to be another hand of the church. I took pride in doing my job and upholding the standards of St. John's Baptist Church. However, finding a dead body, and a person I knew at that, in one of the Sunday school rooms was a good enough excuse if there ever was one. At least that's what I told myself.

Thankfully, he looked as if he understood and gave me one of his hugs. I needed that more than I thought I did. I could see the sun glint off the wooden pews.

"Hello, Sheriff Lawson." Pastor Fairchild held his hand out to shake Picks.

"Howdy Pastor." Pick started hitching at his belt, making sure his pants were in place. I suppose it was because of the weight he had lost. "Sorry we had to hijack your church service today," Pick had said, as he took the pastor's hand into his and shook it vigorously.

"Don't be sorry. What we're sorry for is this poor boy and his family," Pastor Fairchild said sympathetically.

"Yeah, finding someone dead is hard enough on any family, but to know they were murdered is something entirely different," Pick said to the pastor.

"Well, he and his family have our deepest sympathies and prayers," the pastor had said wholeheartedly.

"I have a feeling we're all going to need those prayers, Clayton." Pick placed his hand on the pastor's shoulder.

"I have to say, I've been a pastor of three different churches over the past thirty years, give or take, and one thing's for sure, we've never found a dead body in one of our Sunday school rooms," Pastor Fairchild had added.

"Pearl, that reminds me. The Auxiliary needs to get some food over to Arty's. The last thing he'll want to do today is cook. He probably won't be hungry knowing him, but he's got to eat something," I had said. I also needed to remember to call Myra before we left the church.

"Well, I would hope that he ate some breakfast. So that'll give us a little wiggle room before he needs something else to eat." Pearl looked at me with a little more confidence than earlier. I could also tell she had gone to the ladies' room to fix her hair because that indentation she had in her teasing when she fell out was pulled back into perfection now. As a woman, you always carry around a teasing comb if you like a little body in your hair. It's as southern as apple pie.

I looked at my watch and it was already a quarter past eleven. Good Lord, time flies when you find a dead body! I wonder if Pick feels that way, or is it just because I'm a newbie?

I had slam forgotten that Susie Bright was in the room until she spoke up. "Once I heard about what happened, I got on the phone with Myra and told her everything. She was going to come to the church, but I told her that they wouldn't let her in since it was a crime scene. So she told me she would call some members of the Auxiliary and have some food sent over to Arty. She even said that she would schedule members for different days, so he'd have enough food for the whole week."

I had forgotten that Susie and Myra were kin in some way that you could only justify in the South.

"Susie, thank you for doing that. That takes a huge burden off my plate. Things need to be organized and I really appreciate it." I smiled at her. That was one thing I could check off the list, at least for today, regarding food for Arty. I'd still like to go over and check on him, though. I'm not sure when his family will be able to get here.

Myra was also one of my and Pearl's best friends. Usually when you see me and Pearl, you see Myra, too, except when we open the church up each Sunday. Myra is a late riser and barely makes it in for the afternoon service, much less Sunday school.

Myra differs completely from Pearl and me in so many ways. First off, she has more money than God himself and if she could have paved her streets with gold, I'm sure she would have done it by now.

But it ain't her fault that every time she marries a wealthy man, he dies on her. She took it hard when her last husband, Henry, passed from a stroke. At first, it seemed he was going to come out of it with some heavy rehabilitation, but soon after the stroke, he suffered from what they called dysphagia. I think that's what Myra called it. Anyway, every time they tried to feed him something, he would aspirate it, and shortly afterwards, he came down with pneumonia. It didn't take long after that and he was gone.

I feel sorry for her. But even with her bad luck, she was a millionaire many times over after the death of her first husband, who we all affectionately called Daddy Warbucks. Course it ain't funny no more. Only thing I'll get if Charlie passes before me is the money he has in his 401(k) and savings he had placed in mutual funds when he was still working at the paper mill down in Barnville.

I don't know what I'd do without Charlie, which makes me think about Arty even more and what he must be going through. I feel sick to my stomach.

Pastor Fairchild told everyone he just wanted to show his face to see if there was anything he or the church could do.

Pick stepped in, walking the Pastor back to the front door from which he had entered, making sure he didn't touch or contaminate his crime scene any more than he already had. Pick wasn't even sure if the CSI team had had a chance to check the front entrance for fingerprints yet, although he knew it would be fruitless. There would be fingerprints on the front door handles, but he doubted that any of them had to do with Triston's murder. I had heard him say so to Hansen in private or what they thought was private.

I could tell from the way Pick was speaking to his deputies and Hansen that he felt the murderer was already three or four steps ahead of them, and with the way Triston was murdered, we all knew this person would do anything to take out anyone that got in the way. It takes someone with a very dark soul to watch a man die the way Triston did, and I'm more than sure Pick knew if he didn't find the killer soon, they may kill again.

Chapter Three

AFTER PASTOR FAIRCHILD LEFT, Pick and I pushed Pearl into getting checked out by two of the paramedics who were in the parking lot. More teams of paramedics showed up, but once they realized the person was dead, they all skedaddled out of there to help people who really needed to be rescued.

They gave Pearl an EKG to check her heart and thankfully, everything was okay. It had only been two months ago that Pearl had a major heart attack and with the scare she had at the church, neither Pick nor I was going to allow her to leave without getting fully checked out first.

Fortunately, they said she was perfectly fine. Even with the fall she had taken, when she had fainted outside the Sunday school room, they told us she was perfectly okay to go about her business as long as she didn't have any headaches or show any other signs of a concussion. Thankfully, she didn't. She's got a hard head like me.

Pearl wasn't happy with me or Pick, but she would have made me do the same thing.

Once they gave her a clean bill of health, we assembled in the parking lot. I told her I needed to check on Charlie. I had called him earlier during all the commotion and he wanted to come and get me, but I insisted that I was fine and would be home once Pick and his team had taken our formal statements. Of course, Pick took Pearl's statement. Seeing the sparks fly between the two of them, I finally told them they needed to go ahead and get a room at the Hotel 9. That didn't go over too well! Pearl was furious that I had said this. She told me privately that there was nothing between her and Pick.

Yeah right!

Charlie was at the door, patiently waiting, when I pulled into the garage. The first thing he did was give me a big hug and a kiss, making sure that I was okay. Had Pearl been there, she would have told us to get a room, but Charlie knew just how much of a toll that morning had had on me.

"I'll be okay," I had reassured him. He smelled so good. He had just gotten out of the shower and had used a body wash I had bought for him at Walmart that had scents of Palo Santo, which is some kind of wood that was supposed to relax you. I don't know if he felt relaxed, but under different circumstances, it would have revved up my engine. But I was too pooped to do anything but throw myself into a chair in our kitchen. He had heated the pot roast and potatoes I had cooked in the instant pot my daughter Amber had given us for Christmas. He ladled two heaping spoons full of the pot roast in a bowl for me, microwaved a couple of biscuits, and made me a cup of iced sweet tea. I had been running on pure adrenaline since we had found Triston, and now, coming off of it, I realized just how tired and hungry I was.

"What did Pick have to say when he got there?" Charlie had asked as he sat in the chair beside me at our round kitchen table.

"He pretty much did exactly what Pearl did. He went over to Triston's body and lightly smelled his mouth and thought that he had possibly been poisoned with cyanide or something that would work like it."

"Cyanide? How in the world would they have known that?"

I took a spoonful of the pot roast and savored the bite before I answered him. "Well, you could tell his skin had this reddish look to it, and his hands and fingernails were pretty red, too. Triston's complexion normally looked like alabaster, and when they lightly smelled his mouth, which had the worst grimace I've ever seen, they said it smelled like almonds and cherries." Tears started running down my eyes. Charlie gently wiped them away with his fingers and went to get me a Kleenex. I blew into it.

I was so shocked by everything that I hadn't cried at all for Triston. It's not like he was a stranger. He had been doing my hair for almost ten years. Charlie knew just how much I loved my appointments with him.

"I can't believe anyone would do this to him," Charlie had said as he was making himself a cup of coffee.

"It's the craziest thing I've ever seen, but if that's the way he died, it was a terrible death," I said in a shaky voice. I took another spoonful of the roast beef and used the biscuits to sop up some of the juice. It was good if I said so myself.

Charlie had eaten an hour earlier when I called him. I told him to go ahead and not wait on me since I had no idea when I'd get home. I took stock of the kitchen. Charlie had cleaned all the dishes that were in the sink. He was always good at helping me keep the house clean. I had a wonderful husband and then I thought of Arty and how he must be feeling right now, and I just burst out crying.

"Oh, come here, sweetheart." Charlie moved his chair closer to mine, and I held onto him for dear life. I wouldn't know what to do if something happened to Charlie. We had been married for close to forty years and I loved him more now than I did all those years ago when we first met.

I was with Pearl the first time I saw him, and I told her that I was going to marry that man. We were at some bar. I don't think she believed me at first, but he had asked me out for dinner one Friday night and that was all she wrote.

Our daughter Amber married a French man named Henri Lefevre. They got married and now live in Paris with our granddaughter Lucie. Henri's job was in finance and when they met, Henri lived in New York City, where Amber was doing her rounds at Bellevue Hospital to become a nurse. She had always wanted to live in New York City since taking a trip one year in high school with her art class.

Now she was thousands of miles away with my beautiful granddaughter, Lucie. Lucie was so beautiful with her bright green eyes and curly blonde hair. Lucie had just had her second birthday party. We talk every week and I've finally figured out how to do Facetime, thanks to Myra. So, now when Charlie and I talk to them, we can see them too. Thinking about my family made me sob even more, realizing just how lucky I was.

After I was cried all out, I dabbed the Kleenex around my eyes. The mascara I was wearing was supposed to be waterproof, but I didn't put too much faith in something I bought at Walgreens for four dollars.

"I'm such a lucky woman and sometimes I just take it for granted." I had looked into Charlie's eyes.

He sat there holding my hand. "We all do. It's called being human, and I'm the lucky one waking up beside you every day," He had replied.

"I know, but after what I saw today, I'll never take you, Amber, Henri, or our beautiful Lucie for granted again," I said and promised myself. Life was so short, and we had not had the fortune that many grandparents had of watching their grandbabies grow up. Ours was an ocean and a day's flight away, but at least they were healthy and happy. That's all a mother could ask for, and to know that her daughter found someone as special as Henri was a plus. He was so handsome, and his accent and those blue eyes would make any young girl envious. He was a gentleman, though, and had no idea just how good-looking he was. Course Amber was always a knockout and believe me, she knew how pretty she was.

"I'm sorry I'm such a mess."

"You're my mess, sweetheart," Charlie soothingly said. "With all you've been through this morning, I'd think something was wrong with you if you didn't have a good cry. I know how much Triston meant to you."

"I know and all I can think about is poor Arty, and how he's alone now in that big ole loft at The Mills."

I pushed the food away from me. I couldn't eat anymore, but was surprised I had almost eaten all of it.

"Thelma, please eat a little more for me," Charlie coaxed.

He was so sweet and brought another bowl to me, and before I knew it, I had eaten another whole bowl. "I guess I was hungrier than I thought."

"You've been running on fumes since this morning." I looked at him and he smiled at me with that grin of his that showed the dimples in his face. I placed my hand on his face and told him just how much I loved him.

"I love you too, sweetheart," he'd said, placing his hand on top of mine.

I looked at the clock on the kitchen wall over by the sink. It was almost three o'clock.

"Lord, where does the time go?" I said, getting up from the table and taking my plate over to the kitchen sink where I put some dish liquid on it and washed the bowl and spoon. I placed them in the drying rack. For a minute I just stood there thinking of all the things I needed to do, but all I really wanted to do was to cuddle up with Charlie on the couch and take a nap.

Before leaving the church, I texted Pearl and Myra and told them I would call them after I got a bite to eat and changed my clothes. Then we could all go and see just how Arty was holding up. I dreaded seeing him.

I hated leaving Charlie, but he understood and told me to go and see how Arty was holding up. This had been an emotional morning, and I knew it would be an emotional afternoon and night as well.

Myra told me that she would meet us at The Mills since she lived outside of the mill village in the über community of Sheradon Lakes. Myra's home was probably bigger than at least five or six homes in the mill village. The homes in the mill village were built for the mill workers. Most had two bedrooms on the left-hand side of the house, with the living room and kitchen on the right. "Shotgun-style houses" was what my mother had called them years ago. My and Pearl's houses looked almost identical in regards to the layout of the homes, but everyone put their own personal touch by adding carports, screened porches, or adding another bedroom onto the back of the homes.

I picked Pearl up. I lived at the end of Thirteenth Street, and she lived in the middle of Twelfth. She had a small porch on the front of her house. There were hydrangeas in huge containers on both sides of the stairs that led to her wooden porch, which in southern fashion, was painted haint blue along with the porch ceilings to keep the haints or bad spirits away from the houses.

Pearl had changed into a peach-colored chenille jumpsuit. As it was still spring, you could never really tell what the temperatures would be at night. In Sunnyside, one thing that was always unpredictable was the weather. Last year at Christmas, I remember wearing shorts around the house. It was close to sixty-eight degrees for three or four days before finally chilling down for the Christmas holidays.

Pearl got into the passenger seat. She had a basket that she had put together with some of her famous fig preserves, some wheat crackers, a bottle of white wine, and two different kinds of cheeses.

"That looks nice Pearl." I wish I had thought of bringing something to Arty's, but after lunch, I had called and made sure there was a spread already.

"Thank you, but really, it's nothing much. I made the preserves last summer when the figs were perfectly ripe, so they should be good and sweet by now. I had the cheeses that I had bought for myself, and to be honest, I had never even heard of these types of cheeses so I thought that with a nice bottle of wine and some crackers, it would be something small we both could give Arty together. You know I hate going to anyone's home empty-handed. My mother always made sure we had something when visiting someone's home." Pearl had placed the basket between her feet. The car continued to chime until she fastened her seat belt.

"I'm so thrown off, I can't even think straight. Thank you for doing that, Pearl."

"Well, you know no matter what we bring, Myra is going to make sure that he has everything he needs, even if it means calling her caterer." She looked at me with conspiratorial eyes.

We both loved Myra, but with the money and the connections she had, Pearl and I would always come up lacking. So we allowed Myra to do what Myra does best. She's always willing to say that we all three had been in on the gifts she gave, the platters of food she had made, or the most gorgeous flower arrangements she had delivered for someone at the drop of a dime. I'm so thankful she's one of our dearest friends. She truly was one of a kind, and we loved her dearly.

Being that The Mills was just up the street from my and Pearl's house, it didn't take us more than a few minutes to get there. We parked the car in a space close to the building. Normally, we'd have had to park toward the back of the parking lot, but with it being Sunday, a good many people probably went out to eat after Sunday services or drove into Barnville for brunch.

"Let's do this," I looked at Pearl. I hated we had to see Arty after finding out the most horrible news he would probably ever hear in his lifetime. Being the president of the Ladies Auxiliary, I knew it came with the job, but this differed from going to see someone whose husband had died from a heart attack. Triston had been murdered in cold blood and left in one of the Sunday school rooms at the church. The whole thing was unconscionable.

"Let's go." Pearl started getting out of the car. I followed, making sure to lock my car with the key fob. As we walked away from the car, I made sure that my dress was not riding up my pantyhose. For some reason, my pantyhose had too much electricity in them and my dress kept wanting to ride up, causing it to stick to my pantyhose. I did the best I could and pulled the dress down, praying it would stay as we walked into The Mills.

As we entered the foyer of the building, there was an over-the-top arrangement of some of the most exotic flowers I had ever seen. Even Pearl let out a "wow" when she saw the flowers herself. After a more opened space outside of the foyer, there was a flank of elevators toward the left of the walls. In the middle of the room stood a huge wraparound mahogany desk with someone always behind it, making sure that the people who lived in The Mills were greeted warmly when they arrived home to their sanctuaries, but also making sure they didn't have surprise guests show up unannounced at their doors. Behind the desk was Tony Manelli. We had gone to school with Tony, and he also owned a condo in The Mills. He made his money selling cars. His family owned Ford Motors and Phillip Manelli Cars, which carried more elitist vehicles like BMWs, Teslas, and Porsches.

Tony walked from behind the desk and met us at the bank of elevators.

"Thelma, Pearl." He tipped his white hat to us.

"Hey Tony," I had piped up, hoping this wouldn't take long. Tony was one for gossiping, and I couldn't blame him. Even though he had been brought up with money, his parents had made sure he had both feet on the ground, which was why he went to public schools with us.

"I can't believe this about Triston. I heard that it was you and Pearl that found him." He had looked at us with a wet mouth, hoping we would feed him some good gossip that he no doubt would share with everyone who came into the building. Arty was going through enough without everyone in the building talking about him behind his back. But no matter what we said, we both knew that with Sunnyside being so small, word travels faster than the speed of light and time.

"We certainly had a fright." Pearl looked at Tony. I could tell that she didn't want to give up more than that, so I jumped in.

"Tony, it's been a terrible Sunday. We're going to go up and check on Arty to see how he's been holding up. At this point, that's our main objective."

"Oh, sure. I can definitely see that. Myra's already here. She came in about thirty minutes ago with a spread you wouldn't believe."

I would definitely believe it and was thankful she was so generous.

I pressed the up button on the elevator again, trying to make it come faster. The elevator doors, clad in gold, and the small tables that flanked them, probably cost more than my diamond ring. There were gold table lamps with no shades and Edison bulbs, which glowed against the marble tops of the tables. Even though the Edison bulbs gave off an old-fashioned feeling, they had a modern touch without being gaudy. The tables also had small bud vases with yellow English roses that were just opening—probably put out fresh this morning.

Thankfully, the elevator dinged.

"Nice to see you, Tony. Tell Nancy we said hello," And with that, we stepped into the mirrored elevator, and Pearl pressed the button with the letter *P* on it.

I would hate having an elevator as the door to my house. Call me old-fashioned, but I always wondered if just anyone could go straight up to their apartment.

"Just a second." Tony climbed in with us. He took a keychain from his pocket and put a small golden key into the lock beside the letter *P*. Then he jumped out of the elevator and wished us a wonderful day.

The Mills wasn't that tall. The penthouse comprised both the fifth and sixth floors since they purchased the apartment below them. They had merged the two floors with a stunning flight of stairs that you could see immediately after stepping into the open-concept lofts they had decorated and called home. The elevator automatically went to the sixth floor, where they had a huge open-room concept that served as their living room, with the kitchen to the left. The apartment was huge and had old, mullioned windows. It was as if the sun was created just for this space. It was perfect for all the flowers, plants, and trees they had scattered throughout. They even had lemon and olive trees in giant terra cotta antique containers. They had bought the olive trees while visiting Athens, Greece, one year, and had them shipped home to Sunnyside with white-glove delivery. I had never seen a container the size of the one they had the olive trees in. One had a cracked lip, but it made it look even more appealing. If the rich lived like this, then I needed to figure out a way to come up with some money, and fast. But if I'm truly being honest, what in the world would Charlie and I do in a space as vast as this? I know they had to have a full-time maid to keep a place like this clean because if you didn't keep up with the dust daily, you'd have a mess of a place with cobwebs and dust bunnies floating around.

Arty met us at the elevator, clad in black jeans and a black cashmere sweater with a funneled neck. He wore black Gucci slippers that clacked as he walked toward us to give us both hugs. His eyes were bloodshot from crying.

"Thanks y'all for coming over. I don't know what I'd do without you and all the wonderful ladies from the Auxiliary." Arty hugged Pearl and she held him to her intimately. Then I hugged him as hard as I could, desperate to keep him close.

Bless his heart.

"I hope you have everything you need regarding food and drinks." I looked over at the kitchen counter and table.

"Thelma, what with all the ladies brought in this afternoon and the food Myra brought, there's no way I'll ever be able to eat it all. I'm afraid most of it will go to waste, and I don't want that." Arty seemed truly overwhelmed. Can you blame him? First, God only knows who murdered his husband. Then he gets bombarded with loads and loads of food one person could hardly eat, much less a family, no matter their appetite. I'm sure he isn't even hungry, considering all he's learned about Triston today. I know I wouldn't be.

"It's okay, sweetheart. We'll take some home with us. I asked the ladies to get some food ready for you and well, with the number of members we have in the Auxiliary, they all wanted to do as much as they could to take any burden off you."

Arty bowed his head, put his hands to his face, and started crying. I brought him to me and hugged him as tight as I could.

"We've got you, sweetheart. Anything you need, you just let me know. I'll make sure you have anything you need," I had whispered to him. He was short for a man, I would say five feet six inches. He planted his head in the crook of my neck. I could feel the tears running down my shirt, but I didn't care. This poor man had lost everything he loved in one of the most horrible ways. It had to be the worst day of his life.

As he cried into my neck, Myra had stepped away from the kitchen area, which was blocked by the giant olive trees that touched the thirteen-foot ceiling. *I'd hate to have to prune them*, I thought as Arty was crying against my shoulder.

I patted and lightly rubbed my hands up and down his back, letting him get it all out. It was obvious from his red eyes that he had been crying before we got there, and I'm sure there would be many days ahead before the crying would finally stop. You get to a point where you just can't cry anymore. You're literally cried all out.

"Come on, let's get you to the sofa." I led him to the huge L-shaped sofa that fit perfectly into the designated "sitting" area they had carved out, which is where they spent most of their time reading, talking, playing games, and watching TV. I could see a table near the window with one of those five-thousand-piece puzzles Triston loved to piece together. He had told me that when he got home, and after they ate and watched a little TV, he would fiddle around with the hardest puzzles he could find. He told me it kept his brain working optimally, and with all they had going on with the salon and product line, he'd feel like a wreck. He needed something to keep brain fog from taking over. I agreed. Trust me on that! It just gets worse the older you get. That's why you keep it at bay for as long as possible with brain twisters, like the undone puzzles Triston would never finish.

Arty allowed me to lead him to the avocado-green velvet couch where there was already a box of Kleenex. I took a couple of tissues and handed them to him. He took the tissues from me and wiped his eyes, sniffling a bit.

"I'm sorry." He looked at me as he wiped his eyes.

"Sorry? Sweet thing, you don't have a thing to be sorry for. We're here for you," I clarified. Both Myra and Pearl sat on the couch, surrounding him with as much love as we could give him. Myra looked at me and shook her head, feeling sorry for him. We all did. Pearl had placed her hand on his arm for reassurance.

I looked up into the kitchen area and could see that every countertop was overflowing with food from macaroni pie, lamb chops, fried chicken, deviled eggs, potato salad, a whole ham, and about a hundred more things including Skitter Limpkin's ten-layered chocolate cake. I'd definitely take that if he wasn't going to eat it. It's one of the most coveted cakes in Sunnyside. Pearl had laid her basket on the glass coffee table in front of the couch.

Arty sat there, his head bowed as if he were looking into his lap. This event had completely wiped him out. I wondered if he had anything he could take to help him rest. I had some Xanax in my purse.

"Do you have anything to help you get some rest, Arty?" I grabbed both of his hands so he would look at me. He lifted his head, sniffling back a torrent of tears.

He shook his head that he didn't. "No, we don't normally have any problems sleeping?" he sheepishly replied, wiping tears away from his eyes before they could run down his face.

"You have to be tired?" Pearl questioned him, getting down on the floor so she could look up into his face. She used to be a nurse and when you're sick or not feeling good, it's nice to have Pearl around. She had gotten me, Charlie, and Amber through many sick nights and days.

"I'm exhausted, but I can't sleep in our bed. I don't know if I'll ever be able to sleep there again." He had begun sobbing, as I handed him more tissue.

Myra got up and found a throw blanket on the other end of the couch and a couple of comfortable-looking decorative pillows. She made a makeshift bed on the couch. I reached into my purse, pulled out my bottle of Xanax, and took out a two-milligram pill. I take the strong ones, what with my nerves and all.

"Arty, have you ever taken a Xanax?" I had the pill in my hand, making sure he could see the long rectangular-shaped pill in my hand. Myra went into the kitchen and brought back a glass of iced water.

He whispered that he had taken them before. I didn't want to give him anything that could be potentially dangerous or something he was allergic to.

Myra handed him the water and I gave him the pill. He threw his head back and swallowed the pill. He had definitely taken a two-milligram Xanax before, seeing the way he threw his head back. That's the only way to get them down. The last thing you want with a two-milligram Xanax was to try to get it to go down dry.

Then we told him to lie down and rest some.

"Here you go Arty, Myra found you a blanket and some pillows." Pearl helped him lie down and pulled the blanket over his body. He grabbed my hand as I was standing over him. "We're not going to leave you, baby. You just lay there and get some rest. I promise we'll be here when you wake up."

Arty didn't hesitate. It was as if he just needed someone to tell him to rest. He lay his head down on the huge couch and within five minutes, we could all hear heavy breathing. I noticed he had glasses on the end table. I didn't know he wore glasses. You learn something new every day.

We all went over to the kitchen area of the apartment. Their master bedroom was upstairs right off of the kitchen with a powder room outside the bedroom. I'm sure they also had a master bathroom suite inside the bedroom, too. The other three bedrooms are in the downstairs apartment.

"Lord, look at all the food," Pearl had whispered.

"I've got dibs on Skitter Limpkins' ten-layered chocolate cake." I didn't want them to get any ideas.

There was food spread all over every counter, as well as the kitchen table. I glanced around the room, amazed by the food offerings from the members of the Auxiliary.

We're always there when you need us, come hell or high water.

We were trying to whisper as much as we could, but I kept hearing a scratching noise that sounded like it was coming from the bedroom.

"What in tarnation is that scratching noise?" I glanced into the dark bedroom, but still couldn't dial in on what was creating the noise.

"Well, apparently Arty's aunt passed away a couple of months ago and left him something in her will," Myra had a grin on her face like a dog eating cat shit.

"What is it?" Pearl also turned to the bedroom. Her eyes were filled with wonder, like a child waiting to watch a magician pull a rabbit out of his hat.

Myra led us to the bedroom and told us outside the door that we needed to be quiet. We didn't want to wake Arty up. That's probably the first time he sat down to rest since last night when Triston didn't come home from his so-called meeting. Arty knew then that something was wrong, but the police couldn't do anything because Triston was an adult and it hadn't been over twenty-four hours since he went "missing," which I thought was hogwash. They've been partners going on about twenty-six years. It would feel the same if Charlie didn't come home one night, and I didn't get a phone call explaining what was going on. Surely the police could do something you'd think.

Myra didn't turn the bedroom lights on, but opened the blackout curtains that hung on the far wall across from the enormous California king-sized bed. Covering the bed was the most beautiful burnt orange linen duvet and sheet set. Even the sheets were the same color, but a deeper rust orange that matched perfectly with the duvet. They had white accent pillows that looked bohemian chic, with burnt orange accents.

Because the windows were the same windows that were in the mill when it was running, they were huge and allowed enough light in as if you had turned the lights on. The black mullioned windows were like steel bars that wouldn't allow anything in that wasn't supposed to be there.

I could see a blanket covering what looked like an ornate Chinese bird cage. It was three times the size of Amber's parakeet cage she had had as a little girl. She loved her parakeets, and I loved hearing them sing. Although, after reading Maya Angelou's book, *I Know Why the Caged Bird Sings*; I wanted to let them loose, but feared that they only knew how to eat the bird seed we gave them and left them in their cage. They didn't know how to forage for their food since they were raised in a cage.

I suppose we all have some type of cage or other, whether we admit it or not.

Once Myra took the blanket off, I thought I would die!

"Hello . . . hello," said a parrot with the most beautiful plumage of feathers in varying shades of gray. It was a stocky, medium-sized parrot with a tail as red as a barn door. Myra smiled at us as the bird kept saying hello.

"Hello," Pearl put her fingers to the cage. The bird was so fast that he almost bit the tip of her finger off with his massive beak. He had the beadiest, yellow eyes I had ever seen, with white feathers surrounding them, making the yellow of his eyes pop even more.

"Lord have mercy!" was all I said, as I looked at Pearl caring for her finger that had almost lost its tip. It was bleeding a bit, and I went into the bathroom in search of a Band-Aid and some toilet paper. I instructed her to run her finger under some soapy water. After she did, I wrapped the toilet paper around her finger and then placed two bandages over it. They had a huge medicine cabinet in the bathroom that looked like something out of *Garden & Gun*. They had a shower with a pebbled floor that I'm sure felt good under your feet as you showered. The shower had rain shower heads and jacuzzi-type nozzles that sprayed heavy hot water on your skin, giving you a massage and shower at the same time. I'd never get out!

I couldn't help it, but I had to open their medicine cabinet.

You can learn a lot about how people live by seeing what's in their medicine cabinet.

I didn't find any medication, but they were still young. Triston surely didn't need anything where he was at. God bless his soul. I didn't see much of anything in the medicine cabinet, except for four bottles of ClearSight eye drops. Lord, they must have eye problems. But with Arty wearing contacts, I'm sure his eyes got dry from time to time. That's why I couldn't wear contacts. My eyes stayed dry the whole time I had them in. That and trying to put something in your eyes wasn't an easy thing to get used to. I suppose if you were young when you transitioned to wearing contacts instead of glasses, it might be different, but not when you were in your late fifties. That's when my eye doctor thought it would be easier for me to wear contacts. Easier my foot. I took them things back within the week and got my money back. Changed eye doctors too! I had never had trouble seeing out of my glasses, and I only really needed them to see far off, like while driving. But I did like seeing, so I got used to wearing glasses after living for fifty-something years without them. Doctors really know how to make you feel old.

Myra waved me and Pearl out of the bathroom, but I had to see their tub. It was a Japanese soaking tub that could fit both me and Charlie, and still have room for another person. What I wouldn't give to have something like that. I was brought up as a bath person, so it was hard taking showers instead of baths. I only used the shower when I was in a hurry.

Myra finally came to the door and asked us to come back into the bedroom. Lord, that woman needs to pray for some patience. Pearl and I relented and went back into the bedroom.

Myra had her head near the bird's cage.

Myra smiled at me and Pearl like this was the most normal gift someone would leave after they passed. A beady-eyed parrot that liked to talk.

"*Lord have mercy*," was all I thought.

"Hello Chipper," Myra smiled and cooed at the bird. Pearl and I locked eyes.

Chipper. What in the world!

"So, his aunt left this in her will for Arty to take care of?" I had asked to see how much info Myra had gotten from Arty. Now, I *had* seen it all.

"Yes. Before she passed, she had been looking for another home for Chipper, because she knew he would outlive her. He's an African Gray parrot and they can live up to sixty years." Myra craned her neck forward toward the cage.

Chipper was so observant that he, too, craned his neck forward and chirped, "Cracker? Chipper wants cracker." He held his wings out, then turned his head 180 degrees and started preening the feathers behind his head.

"I done seen it all now." I watched as Myra pulled out a box of treats sitting on the table next to the birdcage. With his neck turned all the way around to his back, all I could think of was *The Exorcist!* He would scare the hell out of me. I wouldn't care if *my own Mama* left that bird to me. I'd have to find some other sucker to take it off my hands.

Myra pulled a small cracker, apparently made for parrots, out of the box, and gave Chipper the seed-covered cracker.

"Thank you, bitch," Chipper said, after grabbing the cracker with his beak. I guess that's the thanks you get for feeding a bird like that. I had never owned a bird like this. Of course, I knew some people loved exotic birds, but after hearing this bird call Myra a "bitch" for giving him a cracker, I wanted to see just how far I could twist his neck!

"I know what you're both thinking," Myra said, coming to his defense. "But when Chipper lived with Aunt Essie, apparently she liked to watch *Jerry Springer* and *the Maury Povich Show*, not to mention she had a potty mouth, and you know how those shows are. Pure white trash."

"I think it's time for Chipper to go back to sleep." I grabbed the blanket, about to put it over his cage. But Myra stopped me.

"Thelma, he hasn't had any time with hardly anyone since last night. Arty told me he adored Triston and would walk around the house perched on his shoulder or his fingers." I looked at Chipper's nails and there was no way he was going to play piggyback with me.

"Please tell me you're not going to take him out of his cage." I looked at Myra as if she had lost her ever-loving mind.

"Lord no. I don't want him to wake up Arty. Bless his heart, he didn't sleep at all last night. He was in pretty bad shape when I got here." Myra looked back to Chipper, cooing at him.

"How long have you been here?" I wanted to know. Pearl seemed intrigued by Chipper and was probably thinking she would love something like Chipper to keep her company.

I looked at Pearl. "Pearl, don't you get any ideas." I raised an eyebrow at her.

"Oh, come on Thelma, you can't tell me he isn't the most beautiful bird you've ever seen," Pearl said in response. I knew it.

"Yes, he is beautiful, but he called Myra a 'bitch' after giving him a treat. That's not what you say when someone gives you a treat."

"I don't care, I still think he'd make for a wonderful pet." Pearl had her face set and was clenching her dentures like she does when she gets her dander ruffled.

"He says things a lot worse than that," Myra had told us. "But I still think he's adorable."

"He needs his mouth washed out with soap." I crossed my arms over my chest. I didn't want to have anything to do with Chipper. Myra cooed at him, blowing his feathers. Chipper seemed to really like that.

"When I first got here, Arty had him out and Chipper was riding on his shoulder all over the apartment while the food was coming in." She was too enthralled with Chipper, the parrot.

"So, what time did you get here" I asked again since she got distracted the first time I asked.

"Oh, it was a little after ten thirty. Right after Pearl called me and told me what had happened, I immediately got on the phone and started calling the ladies and they started coming over, bringing what they had cooked for their Sunday dinners, no more than thirty minutes after that. Many said they hadn't eaten out in awhile, and a good hamburger or fried chicken from The Shake Shack would be a great diversion." Myra was like me and Pearl. If she said she was going to do something, she did it.

"Thank you so much, Myra. With what all me and Pearl had going on at the church with Pick and his team, taking our statements and fingerprints because we had contaminated the crime scene, we could never have acted this fast." I put my hand on her shoulder to show my appreciation for a job well-done. She placed her hand on top of mine.

"I'll say this. I'm so glad for once I wasn't with y'all. I didn't want to see Triston that way. Now I can remember him the way I always did, with his beautiful curly, blonde hair swaying in the wind. He had the most beautiful skin. Almost like marble. I swear I know women that can't grow their hair as long as he had his and to top it off, it seemed so appropriate for him." Tears started welling up in Myra's eyes. I know her mascara wouldn't run down her face if she started crying. She had told me and Pearl about some mascara that plumped your eyelashes while also being waterproof. The only thing was that it was thirty-two dollars.

I would never pay that much for a tube of mascara, no matter how plumped it made my eyelashes! It'd have to plump more than my eyelashes.

Pearl barely wore any makeup, so I know she wouldn't buy it either; but like I said, Myra has more money than the whole town of Sunnyside. I don't know how much money she has for sure, but she does hang out with some bigwigs in Sunnyside's and Barnville's high society circles. That was mostly from her making friends with her ex's friends and their wives. Her last husband owned almost all the stores in downtown Barnville, and when he sold them, I'm sure he got a pretty penny for them. She hung around these people with ease, but I have to say, most of the time, she was with Pearl and me. I think they bored her to death, because at heart she was from Sunnyside and will always be from Sunnyside, no matter how much money she has.

Myra cooed a little longer and told Chipper that she would take him out later and play with him. Chipper looked at her with his beady yellow eyes and said, "Fuck off asshole," to which Myra had laughed and couldn't stop. This, in turn, infuriated Chipper, who was moving from one side of the cage to the other on his perch, saying, "Fuck you bitch, fuck you bitch."

I couldn't believe what I was hearing from this bird! *Help me Jesus*, was all I could think to keep from wringing its neck.

Chipper would make great company for Arty when he was alone and would give him something to do with keeping his cage cleaned and all. Course, he had enough money to have someone else to clean it for him. But I couldn't put up with that cursing. If he had learned to curse, he could unlearn it.

I had had enough, and I looked at that beady-eyed bird and told him, "Stop it!" I pointed my finger at him. He stopped moving back and forth, from side to side in his cage, and just stared at me with eyes like daggers. If he could have gotten out of that cage, it would have been just like Hitchcock's movie *The Birds*. Except he would have been a dead bird. But as soon as I thought it, I wanted to kick myself.

Arty was in the other room sleeping and this was the only creature he had at night to talk to now. I doubted Chipper called Arty or Triston bitches, even though at times they could be just as bitchy as the rest of us. My heart ached for that poor boy and what he must be going through. Thinking about what he would have to go through in the future was almost more than I could take. Then I started tearing up. Although I had waterproof mascara on, I knew it wouldn't hold up under the ugly cry, and I had already washed my face after leaving the church and cleaned the black around my eyes. I looked like a raccoon when I got home. Thankfully, Charlie is sweet and didn't say a word about it.

I also didn't want Arty seeing me like this here, so I sucked it up.

Myra put the blanket back over Chipper's cage with him chirping sadly. "Chipper sleep now. Chipper sleep now."

Please do, was all I could think.

We left the bedroom and followed Myra downstairs to the other apartment. I had only seen it once when it was under construction. It was just as huge as the apartment upstairs. The only difference was that it had three bedrooms, so the open concept was smaller than the one upstairs, but still like a palace compared to my house.

Myra took us into a bedroom that had a Jack-and-Jill bathroom that served two of the bedrooms. I looked at the huge king-sized bed with a large, gray fabric headboard. The linens and duvet were a gorgeous deep-chocolate color that I didn't think I would have liked, but in this apartment it was beautiful. I saw, standing up near the bed, Myra's Louis Vuitton luggage.

"I'm going to spend the week with him. He told me that during the day, he would be at the salon making sure things ran smoothly there. Bless him Lord, but he told me in tears he had no idea what he was going to tell Triston's clients." Myra was shaking her head. I could tell she had just gotten a new touch-up color. Her hair is naturally dirty blonde. But Myra, being Myra, went with a warm copper color and had her hair cut in a short bob that was long enough on the sides so she could put it behind her ears. She wore her bangs cut at a slant on the left-hand side so that they fell in perfectly with her other hair. She looked amazing. She always did. Come hell or high water, Myra was going to maintain her looks. To hell with growing old gracefully. She was going to fight it all the way. Botox and all. Thank Jesus she hadn't started plumping her lips like so many women do now. They look like duck bills instead of lips, especially when they are two inches away from your mouth.

"I'm glad you're staying with him. It's going to be a hard week, especially when all the shock wears off," I said, looking around the bedroom and into the bathroom, where I had moseyed. "Ohhh! Look at that claw-foot tub!" I couldn't believe it. It was definitely an antique, in pristine condition, and looked so comfortable I wanted to climb in and start running hot water.

"I know!" Myra squealed a little. I thought she would be used to luxury items like this, but I also know that Myra had a nice bathtub with jacuzzi jets, but it wasn't an antique claw-foot tub like this. I wondered how old it was because it looked brand new, but I knew better than to think it was new. Triston and Arty loved antiques.

"Thelma!" Pearl wrapped her arm around mine, pushing me to the side so she could get a good look.

"I can't wait to take a bath tonight with a glass of white wine," Myra threw her arms in the air as if she had just booked a stay at the Taj Mahal.

"You better not get drunk around Arty." I turned to Myra to let some air out of her tires.

"Thelma, you know me better than that. I'll have just one glass of white wine with my spa bath. Arty had already taken some bath bombs down for me." She looked to the counter where two lavender-colored balls sat wrapped in cellophane.

"Bath bombs? What are they?" Pearl and I went over to the counter that had two sinks and plenty of storage. We were looking at the medium-sized balls sitting on the counter. I picked one up and smelled it. Oh my goodness, it smelled just like pure lavender. "Pearl, you have to smell this." I put the lavender ball into her outstretched hands and her eyes got big. She shot her eyebrows up in admiration.

"Can I stay too?" Pearl asked.

Myra and I both said at the same time, "No!"

Chapter Four

TWO DAYS HAD PASSED, and we still hadn't heard a thing from Pick or Birdie. Birdie had told me at the church, before our official statements were taken by Pick and Hansen, that it would take a couple of days or more to process the tox screen, but I was getting restless.

Myra had called earlier and told me that Arty had called everyone into the salon that previous Monday for an early morning meeting before clients started showing up and asking all kinds of questions. Arty could answer most, but like us, he hadn't heard anything from Pick or Birdie either.

Myra told me that Arty had assured everyone they were not closing the shop and that things would run pretty much as they had when Triston was still with us. Arty had run the salon anyway, so he knew everything he needed to know to run the salon and the product line.

Arty had told Myra that he had gotten a phone call from Twilight Woods, the goddess of the KDP shopping channel. She wanted to come down and talk with Arty about their expansion with KDP. She assured him that she knew the line just as much as he and Triston had, and she could sell it herself on the shopping network unless Arty wanted to come on air with her and talk about the products like Triston had. Myra had told Arty she would be more than happy to go on air with him and help sell the products if he wanted. Arty was more of an introvert though and I couldn't see him leisurely appearing on television selling any type of products. Triston was a natural star. There was no doubt about that. He could sell "shit on a stick," as my daddy used to say about some of the car dealers in town.

She was coming into town this Friday and staying over the weekend, so they had time to strategize. I'd love to be a fly on the wall for that meeting. I'm sure he'd have their lawyer with him to go over the contracts she would surely bring. I also think that the days of Arty and Triston making the products themselves were over. I'm sure Arty could make every single product, but he would have to teach someone else just to keep products in the salon and that would be a full-time job by itself.

Myra had asked him about it already, and Arty had told her that he had decided to allow KDP to recreate the products in their labs. Since they were going to be selling them on the KDP shopping network channel, he wouldn't ever be able to keep up with demand. He also told Myra that Triston had been leaning that way more and more lately.

I hadn't had the chance to get back over to Arty's, but I'm sure after running the salon all day, he would be dead tired when he came home. He had been putting on a good face in front of everyone, but Myra said she could hear him crying during the night in his room, with Chipper trying his best to make him feel better. I had no idea that parrots were that smart. But after doing some investigating on Google about them, evidently they're very smart for being a bird. And compassionate, too. Who would have thought?

Myra said he would come home, take a quick shower, and come out in his Gucci pajamas and Gucci slippers, with Chipper on his shoulder. Evidently, he and Chipper were becoming fast friends, and I was so happy for Arty to have Chipper during this horrible ordeal he was living through.

It was going on about four o'clock when I got a conference call from Pick and Birdie.

What in the world, I thought when Pick told me that Birdie was on the line too.

"Pick, I have to say I'm a little shocked that I'm speaking to both of you. I hope me or Pearl didn't mess anything up at the church." That was the only thing that might explain why they both would be on the conference call. Charlie was still at his part-time job at the Ace Hardware store in Barnville, and I was in the kitchen fixing myself a cup of coffee.

"We both thought it would be the easiest way to tell you what we have to say," Pick said cryptically.

This was definitely not a normal phone call.

"Okay. I'm all ears."

"We figured as much. That's why we both thought that talking to you would be the easiest way," Birdie spoke up while Pick was quiet for once.

"First, I'm going to let Birdie talk to you about everything we found at the church and elsewhere." Pick sounded more like himself. Maybe he had to switch out toothpicks. I don't know, but this seemed like it was going to be a weird phone call. I could tell right from the start. One that could change everything. That much I was already sure of. I had known Pick and Birdie for so long that I knew this was just odd. What did he mean by elsewhere?

"So, to start, I wanted to tell you the results we got from the tox screen we did on Triston. They came back with deadly levels of bitter almond oil in his system. That was the cause of death. Someone poisoned him, but it's not that cut and dry. For starters, we found bitter almond oil in his and Arty's penthouse, and also at their salon when we went in with search warrants for both places."

"When did you search his home? Myra's been there all week and didn't say anything about a search warrant."

"That's because we did it during the day, when Arty was at the salon, and Myra must have gone home or was running errands. But when we found out what the true culprit was, we knew exactly where we needed to look, so to be honest, we didn't go in and search their whole place. We just concentrated on the small room where they created the products. And we found a bottle of bitter almond oil there and also some at the salon."

"Do what?" Thank the Lord I was already sitting because if I had been standing, I'm sure my knees would have gotten wobbly.

"Yes. We found a small bottle of it in both places. But to be fair, I knew we would find it. I also had an idea we would find it at the salon too, because I know personally, that they kept a lot of their essential oils at the salon, as well as oils they would've used during the creation of some of their products."

I stopped Birdie. "So, when did y'all search the salon, and why did y'all need a search warrant?"

"We waited until they cleared out and did it after they all left late last night. We didn't want to cause a scene during the day and interrupt their workday. We were in and out because I had told Triston about how dangerous that bitter almond oil was. Now it smells amazing, but when he first came out with his Japanese Cherry Deep Conditioning Treatment, he put a tiny bit of the bitter almond oil in the treatment. But it was negligible. The amount wouldn't have hurt anyone and when I say anyone, I also meant him and Arty, as well. When he purchased the oil, he called me up and told me why he wanted to use it. I understood the reasoning, but I also told him that I would show him the proper amount to use so that he didn't hurt himself, Arty, or anyone else using the product. He agreed with me, which is why he called me in the first place because he knew how toxic it could be in certain dosages. Then we found another bottle of oil that smelled similar but was made from crushed cherry pits, making the bitter almond oil obsolete. So, he stopped using it. When we went in for the search, I knew exactly where they would be. We were probably in each place, maybe ten minutes at the most."

I lit a cigarette and took a long drag from it. "So, did he kill himself? Please don't tell me that's what you think." It would kill me to know that Triston had taken his own life. But if he did, how in the world did he end up in the church? I took another drag from my cigarette and put it in the ashtray on the table beside my coffee. I took a sip of my coffee before it got too cold to drink. I don't do iced coffee!

"Cut to the chase, Birdie. What are you going to tell me that's going to blow my lid? Because I can feel it coming on." But it wasn't Birdie who answered me. It was Pick.

"Are you sitting down, Thelma?"

"Perkins Pick Lawson, if you don't tell me what you called me for, I'm gone blow a gasket now."

"Okay. Once we found the two bottles of the bitter almond oil, we had to put that in the report and apparently, we have a leak in one or both of our offices," Pick explained. I could tell he was chewing on the toothpick, which was never good. He didn't chew on them unless he was upset. Most of the time, they just stuck out of the right side of his mouth, and he liked to twirl them when he was thinking.

"Don't tell me someone at the paper is going to write some exposé about Triston killing himself. Because I can tell you both, he wouldn't have killed himself." I picked up my cigarette and filled my lungs and hoped it would help calm me down. I got up from the kitchen table with my coffee, went over to my purse, and pulled out my Xanax bottle. I knew I would need one by the end of this call. I slugged one down and returned to the table with the prescription bottle still in my hands.

"No, that's not what we believe, either." Pick was trying his best to ease into what he was going to say.

"Well then, what's the deal?" The Xanax wouldn't hit fast enough. My doctor prescribed them for me years ago when

I was having panic attacks. Since then, I could use them as needed after he titrated me off the pills. But lately, I could feel the panic attacks coming back on. Having Chronic Panic Disorder was no picnic.

"The point is that we're going to have to rule his death as accidental," Pick said, put off and with a note of anger in his voice.

"Do what? How in tarnation did he get in the church? He didn't even go to our church. Surely, someone else could have slipped that into one of his Cherry Cokes!" I made exclamation marks when I said cherry coke, even though they couldn't see me do it. I kept thinking they could see me since it was a conference call. But conference calls differed from FaceTiming. Triston had always been funny about his Cherry Coke. He wanted a real coke from Mexico since they used real sugar. Then he would use real maraschino cherry juice poured into the coke and would top it off with two cherries. Sometimes three if he was being daring that day or needed a sugar boost.

"I know, Thelma, I know. Believe me, I'm madder than a rattlesnake about this, but somehow it got back to the mayor that Triston had the bitter almond oil in his possession, and therefore he wanted this ruled as an accidental death."

"You mean to tell me that 'Moon Pie' Hubbard is the one that shut this investigation down?" I was so mad I could have spit nails.

"Yes," Pick said.

"Thelma," Birdie chimed in, "The town charter gives him the authority to do it. It was the way to give a safeguard against a runaway police department."

Then it hit me like a bolt of lightning. I had just seen one of his billboards the other day when I went to the grocery store. "So, what you're really telling me is that he doesn't want a murder case during an election year. Is that it?"

"Yes," they replied at the same time.

"You've *got* to be kidding me!" I was so upset, I could feel my face turning red. I knew my blood pressure was probably through the roof. Lord, what are Pearl and Myra going to say when I tell them?

"I wish that were the case. But Thelma, my hands are tied. He's my boss even though I'm an elected official, just like him. He is my check and balances."

"And who is Moon Pie's?" I could see Moon Pie Hubbard sitting behind that overlarge desk in his office. I could see his round face and his chins jiggling around like Jell-O, as he found the perfect way to tell Pick he had to close this investigation.

"He doesn't find it odd that he was splayed out in one of our Sunday school rooms. How did Triston accidentally do that?" I said, spitting into the phone. "That weasel of a man is going to hear it from me. I'll get the ladies to protest with huge banners in front of his office."

"Thelma, that is one reason we called you through a conference call," Birdie said, trying to de-escalate the conversation. "We were wondering if the Ladies Auxiliary would investigate his death." Birdie said this nonchalantly, like we were all deputies and hired private detectives in our spare time.

Praise be to Jesus for that Xanax. It started calming me down. Because when she said that, I thought of opening the bottle and taking another one!

"Birdie, we're not investigators. You and Pick both know that." I looked down at my cigarette and it had burned itself out. I took the last swig of coffee I had left. It might as well have been iced as cold as it had gotten.

"That's why we think it'll work," Pick said convincingly.

"Just hear us out, Thelma," Birdie explained. "We're going to turn everything over to the Auxiliary. Everything we have, you'll have. And if you need anything, you'll get it from us or people in our offices that we can trust to keep their mouths shut. I know when some of my colleagues heard about this, they were not happy at all."

"You reckon?" I said bitterly.

"You'll also have me for anything you need me to run down." It was obvious from the sound of his voice that Pick was twirling that toothpick around in his mouth. For the life of me, I still don't know how he does it.

"So, y'all want the Ladies Auxiliary to investigate Triston's murder, but if we need anything, we can count on both of you for support from both of your offices?" My head was spinning, but I knew when the Ladies wanted something done, they didn't stop until it was done. No one thought we could raise enough money to take all twenty-three of us on a five-night Caribbean cruise until we did it, and we have the T-shirts to prove it.

"You do. But there's a catch." Pick sounded reluctant.

I rolled my eyes. The more I thought about it, the more I knew we could do it and keep it under the radar. Our group doesn't have leaks. Not if I tell them it's top secret and the punishment would be expulsion from the group if they told anyone else that didn't need to know.

"What's the catch other than your offices have leaks like a spaghetti strainer?"

"Thelma, I can't tell you how important it is to only tell people you completely trust. We can't have this getting all over Sunnyside or Barnville. It's also for your safety and the safety of every lady in the Auxiliary too. There's a killer on the loose and my hands are tied. But that doesn't mean me, or Birdie, can't help. We just can't let our offices know about what's going on and can't officially help, but what we do on our own time is none of Hubbard's business."

"I'll be able to give you a copy of the coroner's report about Triston's death. And since I'm a member, I can also explain the report so everyone can understand it in layman's terms."

"So, we're not out on a limb by ourselves, is what you're both telling me, right?"

"Right," they said in unison, like a choreographed dance.

I got up from the table and paced the kitchen floor, thinking to myself. This would be a huge undertaking, and could I really trust every one of my ladies? I knew I could. Most of them went to Triston and when they found out what Moon Pie Hubbard did, he may not have his job come this election year. We were going to find out who did this to Triston if it was the last thing we did and put Moon Pie Hubbard out on the street of

Barnville. He didn't deserve to be the dog catcher of Barnville and Barnville County, nor Sunnyside, much less the mayor.

I promised myself that. He would lose his job this election year.

I thought about it and then relented. I knew we could do anything we put our hearts into. Plus, we had some smart cookies in the Auxiliary.

"Okay then. I suppose we're in. But I have to talk this over with them, too," I said to Pick and Birdie with as much confidence as I could muster. I trusted them with my life. I better because Pick was right about one thing. There's a killer on the loose and until he's caught, nobody in Sunnyside is safe.

Chapter Five

WHEN I GOT OFF THE PHONE with Pick and Birdie, I sat down at the kitchen table. The first thing I did was take out a notebook and write down the names of anyone I thought could have gotten away with this. I have to tell you the list was very short.

Very short!

I had no idea who could have done something like this. But come hell or high water, we were going to find out. I ripped out a page of a notebook I keep by the landline phone. Yes, we still have a landline. I'm old and like talking into a real phone that ain't smarter than me. I have an iPhone. Amber gave me and Charlie our own for Christmas a couple of years ago. She told us it was time we got into the computer generation. I rolled my eyes at her. She didn't like that. But after a few lessons from her and the YouTube videos she showed us how to find, we figured the phones out, which gave us the wonderful FaceTime we have when we call them. But I still want a landline just in case something happens to those towers. And I'd love to know where they were. I hadn't seen one Verizon tower and believe me, I've looked all over Sunnyside for them! They must be top secret because they were well hidden.

I thought about who would do this to Triston. Who would know about the bitter almond oil? I looked at the name on the page I had written on. I could only think of two people who could do this, but I also knew he couldn't have done it. Or could he? I cringed when I looked at the name I had written: Arty.

They always say that when something happens to a spouse, the other spouse is always at the top of the list. But I didn't believe Arty did it. Yet, there his name was on the very top of the page. I could have written the names of everyone Triston worked with at the salon, but I didn't know them very well. But I know some of the other ladies could help me fill in the blanks.

First, we had to get Arty off the top of the list. I wanted to know what time he called the police last night. I also wanted to know the timing of the death. However, it couldn't have been too long before we got there, because he still had that reddish tint to his skin, which would have faded. Rigor mortis had already set in, and I think it starts about an hour or two after you pass.

I'm writing all these questions down because Birdie could tell us about a closer time with all the equipment and expertise she had. Thank the Lord she was part of the Auxiliary, but we had to be extra careful that her involvement didn't get back to Moon Pie Hubbard. I could just slap his big ole round face, telling them they couldn't investigate Triston's murder. Saying it was accidental.

Accidental my foot!

All he cared about was looking good for his constituents. I know when his constituents find out that he ordered Pick and Birdie to rule this an accidental death, they'll see just the type of person he is. Just like Boss Hog of the old Dukes of Hazzard TV series. He looked just like him. All he needed was that white suit and a bolo tie to wrap around his fat neck if he could find one that would fit.

I lit another cigarette. I had to calm down. After taking notes, I started pacing the kitchen floor and was going to run a path into our new parquet wood floors if I kept this up.

So, I sat back down at the kitchen table after I poured myself some iced sweet tea. I needed to lay off the coffee. It had too much caffeine and when you get my age, it can mess with your sleep patterns. I never had trouble sleeping like Pearl did. She had to go in and they did all types of sleep studies on her. She has to wear a CPAP machine now. They told her after the sleep studies that she had sleep apnea. Of course, she knew exactly what she had before they even told her. Her doctor was someone she knew very well when she worked at the Barnville Regional Medical Center.

I don't know how she could get used to that mask. But if you ain't getting no sleep, I suppose you'll do what you need to do. Thanks be to Jesus, I don't have that problem. My problem is having to get up about two times a night to go to the bathroom. We keep night lights on so we can see if we need to get out of bed during the night.

I suppose the next thing I need to do is call and invite Pearl and Myra over and spill the beans.

Wonder what they'll think when they realize they're going to be PIs and not even get paid for it or get to carry around a gun like the Charlie's Angels? Course, I always was packing a gun. I had a permit to carry and all. I could hit the side of the wall, and if I was lucky, take one of those suckers out if they were coming straight for me. I was trying to pump myself up. If I kept going like this, I might turn out like GI Jane and shave all my hair off. But I'd look more like Brittany Spears spiraling out of control than Demi Moore with a six-pack of abs.

All I could think was "Jesus wept"!

Pearl got here about ten minutes before Myra. Myra's always late. But after all these years, me and Pearl have learned there's no reason to get upset because nothing is going to change Myra. It's too late for that. Myra Frankfurt Pembroke Armstrong would show up when she was ready to show up. Sometimes, I admired her for it. She was herself, unapologetically, but when you were holding other people up, it became a problem. For our auxiliary meetings, I would always tell her to be there ten minutes before the meeting started. That way, she'd be on time.

Yes, I can be sneaky!

Pearl and I sat at the kitchen table. Charlie was at the barbershop, which meant he would sit around before and after getting the little hair he had cut off gossiping with his other buddies. Men always say it's women who gossip, but believe me, he always comes home with some juicy news about someone who had cheated on his wife, or who was getting a divorce after thirty years because of gambling addictions.

Lord, what's this world coming to?

I didn't want to tell Pearl anything about the investigation until Myra got there. I could tell she knew something was up, but Pearl was as patient as Job. Something I wished I had more of. But I've always been told, by people who pray for patience, to keep your mouth shut. Because one way or another, God would hear and answer your prayer for patience, and try you in ways making you wish you had kept your mouth shut and not asked for patience. I know better than to even contemplate that prayer. There are a lot of things I ask God to help me to be a better Christian, but I wouldn't touch patience with a ten-foot pole.

Pearl was telling me about her visit with Arty yesterday, explaining how he had Chipper out of his cage and was walking him around the loft on his shoulder or letting him walk around by himself on the couch. Pearl said he didn't curse one time with Arty. But when she went to pick him up, he chirped, "Not you bitch. Not you bitch," which mortified Pearl, as well as Arty. She said that Arty told him that he was a bad boy for saying things like that. Arty told Pearl his aunt had a "potty mouth," and she cursed all the time, which is who he learned it from. That and watching Jerry Springer and The Maury Povich Show. I just shook my head, sipping on my iced sweet tea. Pearl said she wanted water, so I fixed her a glass of iced water.

We both could hear Myra pull up in front of the house. I went to the front door and could see through the transom window that she was driving her BMW. I wondered where her Porsche was. Honestly, I think she's too old to be driving a Porsche around, but it does have all the bells and whistles you could ever want and more from a car. The Italian leather seats are heated in the winter and cooled in the summer. It drove so smoothly that it was like you were flying until you hit a pothole. Sunnyside's roads have a lot to be desired.

Myra had just had her hair blown out at the salon. She always had them blow it out at least twice a week. Sometimes three times a week, according to what she had on her social calendar. Triston didn't blow anyone's hair out. He had his assistants do it for him and he would come in at the end and fluff it with his hands to perfection, then finish it off with some of his Shellac hairspray. I have to say, I used to be a White Rain girl until I used his fancy hard-hold Shellac. It smelled amazing for one thing, and it held all day long.

Myra was wearing a russet cashmere tunic that popped against the white cashmere jumpsuit she was wearing. Her hair looked perfect. It had enough body with just the right amount of bounce. Katie Smith was the girl she always requested for her blowouts. Course Katie was in her fifties, so I suppose "girl" wouldn't be the right word. That's what Myra always called her, her blow-dry girl.

I let her in the house. We hugged and made our way into the kitchen, where we sat around the table. The kitchen table and our recliners in the den were really the hub of the house. With the mill village houses being smaller and usually only two-bedroom shotgun houses, the den doubled as our living room.

I asked Myra if she wanted something to drink, but she pulled a Mountain Dew out of the bag she was carrying. I was surprised she'd placed a Mountain Dew in her purse, but I suppose that's why it's oversized. I would have spilled it all over my purse and my white clothes, but Myra could wear white to a dirt bike challenge and come out without a spot of mud on her white clothing. I would look like Pig-Pen trailing dust in my wake with mud all over my clothes, face, and hair.

She took off her cashmere tunic and placed it on the far side of the table. I suppose wearing a cashmere jumpsuit could put off some heat, and even though it was spring, you have no idea what the temperatures would be like from day to day. One day, they will be unseasonably cool, the next unseasonably warm. We've never really had what most refer to as a spring season. It seems to go from winter to summer pretty fast in Sunnyside, South Carolina.

Pearl and Myra hugged each other before Myra got comfortable at the table. Then we got down to business. They knew this was something big for me to call a meeting during the day. Normally I would just call them, but this was so important that a phone call wouldn't suffice.

"How's Arty been doing, Myra?" I asked to break the ice. Myra had just taken a swig of her Mountain Dew, one of her favorite drinks. I keep telling her they will give her kidney stones if she keeps drinking them. She obviously doesn't listen to my advice when it comes to her health. Pearl is too sweet to say anything she thinks will ruffle someone's feathers. Pearl sat back in her chair and crossed her arms around her chest as if she knew she wouldn't like what I had to say. I've stalled as much as I could. They sat there, just looking at me, waiting for me to spill the beans.

Damn it! I hate this!

"Okay, I've got something to tell you both that you cannot share with anyone else. I want to have a meeting with the other Auxiliary ladies, but before I do that, I wanted to run this by y'all first." My mouth suddenly was dry. I hated telling them this. It was wrong. Pick and his homicide team should be handling this. Not a bunch of retired ladies that didn't have any experience investigating a murder. Sure, we had Pick and Birdie in our corner, and they would explain things that we may not understand, but I was reluctant to get them too involved with both of them being under Moon Pie Hubbard's chubby little fingers.

Pearl pulled her favorite cardigan tight around her chest as if she was suddenly colder, and I hadn't even told them anything yet.

"I got a call from Pick and Birdie this morning," I finally said. They both moved in closer to make sure they could hear every word.

"And there's a minor snag with Triston's murder investigation. Yes, he was murdered. They both were sure of that. So, they had a warrant to search Triston and Arty's apartment and salon, and they found two bottles of an oil called bitter almond oil."

"What do you mean, they searched their house and salon? I've been at Arty's loft every day this week, and they never came by while I was there." Myra took another sip of her Mountain Dew.

Pearl couldn't get anything out. Her mouth hung open like a mailbox door.

"They had search warrants for both places and searched during times that you and Arty weren't at the loft and made sure the salon was closed before searching it. They were looking for the bitter almond oil. That's what they were after." I took a breath and lit a cigarette, making sure I blew the smoke in the opposite direction from where they were sitting.

"When the tox screens came back, Birdie said that it was the bitter almond oil that killed him. She thinks someone may have slipped it into one of his Cherry Cokes that they make for him at the salon. She did find cherry juice and maraschino cherries in his stomach as well. But he drinks them everywhere he goes, so it could be anybody, but I think it's got to be someone close. I don't think it's Arty if you're going to ask me that."

"So, do they think someone at the salon did it?" Pearl held tight to her cardigan. I thought if she pulled it any tighter, she would have ripped it at the seams. Myra didn't say a word, but her mouth, hanging wide open, said enough.

"I can't believe they searched the loft and the salon too. Nothing looked out of place. It smelled the same. I don't know what to say!" Myra couldn't believe they went into the loft and searched it since she had no idea they had been there.

"Except they knew what they were searching for, and Birdie knew they would find it, because she had known that Triston had used the bitter almond oil in one of his products initially, until later finding a substitute made by crushing the cherries pits giving the oil much the same smell without the toxicity," I said taking another drag from my cigarette. "So, like I said, they found the bottles of the oil in the loft in the room set up for making the products. Then they found another at the salon. Birdie knew they would find them. Triston had used the oil in a very negligible way. She had told him the exact amount to use in a twenty-five-pound batch of his Japanese Cherry Deep Conditioning Treatment that he used and sold."

Myra's hand went straight to her mouth.

"I have that deep conditioner at the house. I also have them use it on me at the salon. The smell is amazing, and it leaves my hair so silky. I had no idea I could have died from using it." Myra gripped her Mountain Dew bottle until I thought she would blow the lid off and clean my ceiling with it.

"Thelma, they're not trying to say Triston killed himself, are they?" Pearl asked, even though I had told them less than five minutes ago that they thought it was a murder. She definitely wasn't Miss Marple. Of course, they hadn't heard the worst part yet.

"No. They both think it was a murder. Plain and simple. Think about it. Why would Triston try to kill himself? He had a loving partner of twenty-six years, a profitable business, and was in talks with the KDP Shopping Network to sell their product line on air and that's a big deal."

"I don't get it. What are you trying to tell us, Thelma?" Myra was getting impatient. I couldn't blame her. I would be the same way. I took another drag, held it in my lungs to help keep me calm, and then blew it up in the air. I had stalled long enough.

"Okay, so someone from the police station and/or the coroner's office called and told Moon Pie Hubbard they were calling it a murder and since this is an election year, he decided that since they found the bitter almond oil at his home and salon, then it had to be an accidental death. And he expected it to be written up that way. He's Pick's boss even though Pick's an elected official. According to Pick, the mayor has the right to tell him what to do. I'm not so sure about Birdie's position, but it puts her in a tough spot. The last thing she needs is to be on Moon Pie's bad list. Moon Pie doesn't play around. He shifts his weight around and gets what he wants or heads roll. Or he could make their jobs a living hell." I took a swig of my iced sweet tea, but the ice had melted, weakening the sweetness of the tea.

"They're just going to do nothing!" Myra was furious. Her natural color was a dirty blonde, but she had the temper of a real redhead.

"That's why I asked y'all to come over. So we could talk."

"Talk about what, Thelma? Moon Pie has already tied their hands. There's nothing they can do. I can't believe this." Pearl sat back in her chair. She was clenching her jaw. I could tell she could spit nails right about now.

Myra looked like she was coming undone. She had pulled up the sleeves of her white jumpsuit. I'm thinking that her cashmere jumpsuit was getting hotter by the second. She had nails put on yesterday and started tapping the table with them. One finger, two fingers, three. She only did that when she was mad. It drove me up the wall, but I had to keep the peace. I hadn't even told them everything yet.

"They can't do anything. But we can," I finally said. They both furrowed their brows and looked at me as if they had just let me out of The Bull Street Medical Facility, which around these parts was considered the looney bin.

"What are we supposed to do?" Myra asked, shaking her head like she had lost it. Pearl wasn't doing any better. Any minute now, and that cardigan was going to become a straitjacket.

"Pick promised me that they would help us with everything. Pick would quietly run interference at the police station, while Birdie would give us everything she had from the autopsy report and anything the CSI team had found at the church, which I'm guessing ain't much, but I could be wrong. I think they were so shocked when Moon Pie shut 'em down, they didn't know what to do. So, they did the next best thing and asked if the Ladies Auxiliary would investigate. Think about the ladies and all the connections we have all over Barnville and Sunnyside."

"Thelma!" Myra shouted, then realized how loud she had said my name and stopped speaking for a few seconds before starting again. "We're not trained to investigate diddly-squat."

"I disagree, Myra. I think that if we do this right, we could start talking to anyone we want to. The investigation is closed, so they couldn't say we're interfering with an ongoing investigation."

Pearl finally asked what she had been wondering, "So if we get in over our heads, will they come save us if need be?"

"That's what they told me, but they also said we had to make sure that whatever we do, it doesn't get back to Moon Pie

Hubbard. I smell a rat where he's concerned, but that's nothing new. He's always been a slimy Boss Hog type, if you ask me."

"I agree. He doesn't care. If he were here, I'd wring his neck if I could get my hands around it." Myra did a mock choking with her hands.

"I agree with Thelma; something's not right where Moon Pie is concerned." Pearl had finally loosened her grip on her cardigan. Although it was pulled out of shape once again, maybe it's made with those new fibers that stretch back into place like the ones made in China or Taiwan.

"I don't know how many ladies on the Auxiliary to tell. I'm worried that if we tell everyone, what we're doing will get around."

"I agree," Myra said, looking at me and then at Pearl.

"So, who should we recruit?" Pearl asked.

"We have a few people with mouths like steel traps. And we also have some that would leak like a spaghetti colander." I picked up my notebook from the table beside my ashtray. I looked at the cigarette I had been smoking, which had burned itself down and cigarettes ain't cheap.

I had written down six names of ladies in the Auxiliary I thought would work perfectly, but I wanted to see how close the three of us came to naming the same people. I tore two pages out of the notebook and handed each a sheet and a pen.

"I want y'all to write down six people you would trust with your life. There's a murderer on the loose, and they could be right under our noses. We have to have people we know won't say a word to anyone, not even their husbands." I looked at my trusted friends, who were more like sisters to me. I needed them to know just how high the stakes were. It could truly mean life or death.

When they both finished writing the names down, I took their sheets and put them all three on the table, so we could all see the names of the six people we had chosen. We had all written down the same six names: Skitter Limpkins, Mitzi Woods, Bunny Ashford, Fifi Jones, June Bug Akins, and Babs Johnson.

"That does it then. Now all we have to do is get them together to see what they think about us investigating Triston's death." I wasn't surprised we had all selected the same ladies. We had known these women all our lives and knew they had mouths like trapdoors when needed. We could trust these ladies with our lives. One person had already lost their life, and we were entrusted to find justice for Triston since the establishment wouldn't do it for us. My only prayer and greatest fear were that if they all agreed, we'd be able to find the killer without any danger to any of us in the process.

Chapter Six

BIRDIE CALLED ME THAT MORNING and asked to be present at our first meeting with the ladies we picked to be on the investigation.

I told her I didn't think it was a great idea. We needed Birdie and Pick to be at arm's length. Of course, we would expect them to give us all the information they had so far and any that might come in later, and also help us with some inquiries if needed.

She understood and told me that she would bring me all the necessary reports: the autopsy report, the CSI reports, and any reports Pick and his team would've made. She also said she would bring all the evidence documentation they had created before Moon Pie Hubbard put the kibosh on the murder investigation. I told her the names of the six women we'd handpicked to help find Triston's killer, and she concurred.

"Thelma, I think y'all picked the perfect ladies for this. However, they have to know that this could put them in danger if it ever got out that they were snooping around and trying to figure out just who this killer could be. This isn't going to be easy, but I think with all the prudence and connections with the various women on the panel, this could work." Birdie sounded more upbeat. I could tell a sudden weight had been lifted from her shoulders. It wasn't like Birdie to give up on something like this, but she had no choice.

"I know Birdie, but we can count on you and Pick when we have questions about what we find that might be relevant to the case, right?" I wanted to make sure nothing had changed since we last spoke. We didn't want to go out on a limb without their help and expertise.

"We'll do everything we possibly can to help, but you know there will be times our hands may be tied." Birdie sighed heavily. "I still can't believe Moon Pie Hubbard shut us down. It just doesn't make sense to me. I've thought about it and thought about it, and if we could find the person responsible for Triston's death, it would be a win for him, too." I had known Birdie was frustrated. I could see her sitting behind the enormous green metal desk government officials use in small offices without windows. I pictured her clad in her white doctor's coat and under it the green scrubs she wears to work.

You would think in the coroner's office that the furnishings would feel homier considering people had to come and identify the bodies of their loved ones. I couldn't imagine having to go into a morgue to identify my baby Amber's body. I had to stop going down that path. I was beginning to get chills.

"Let me know how it goes," Birdie said, upbeat.

"You know I will. According to how long the meeting lasts, I may just talk to you in the morning."

"That sounds good, Thelma. One last thing. Please, please be careful. This killer could be anyone and until we find him, I'm afraid none of us are safe." I had never heard Birdie sound so scared before. It surprised me at first, but I had to admit she was right.

Now that we had spoken, I called and asked all our handpicked ladies to meet at the church at 5:30 p.m. I didn't explain why we were meeting. I just told them it was top secret, and with that, they knew I wasn't playing around. Although I knew we had chosen well, I was dreading this meeting. However, I truly believed we could do anything we put our minds to. At least, that was what I kept telling myself.

///////////////////////////////////

Pearl and Myra showed up at the church at 5:00 p.m. that April evening. The days were getting longer as spring was turning into an early summer. Flowers were blooming around the church's parameters. Yellow daffodils were coming up out of the ground along with crocuses with shades of purple, white, and yellow. They usually bloom much earlier than a lot of the other flowers. The Ladies Auxiliary had planted the flowers along the edges of the church, giving it a bounty of color that would put smiles on even the most downtrodden. I could smell the hyacinths when I got out of the Cadillac. This year, we even planted pink ones along with our normal blues, whites, and purples. I shut the car door, aware that I was there by myself. It was the first time I had been at the church alone since finding Triston's body. I have to say it was a little creepy. I had just gotten off the phone with Myra, who was bringing Pearl today. They had been over at Arty's as I sat all day and mulled over this meeting. Probably one of the most important meetings we would ever have as the Ladies Auxiliary, even though we were immersed in the church.

We still had our say on things as much as the deacons did. The Ladies Auxiliary all thought we were important enough to keep ourselves ready to plead our case, on what we thought needed to be done to the church, to Pastor Fairchild, and all twelve deacons. Do you think the deacons would have planted all those flowers? Yeah right, and I'm Florence Nightingale.

I walked slowly up to the side door of the church. The graveled parking lot sounded off like Captain Crunch cereal. If men knew how hard it was to wear high heels in a graveled parking lot, they would have had this parking lot paved already. Cheapskates. The Ladies Auxiliary was going to do some fundraisers this summer to help raise money to have the parking lot paved. Even if they put blacktop and some tar on it, it had to be better than gravel. Of course, it was usually the men making all these decisions. Let them wear high heels, they'd change their tune. Myra and Bunny wore the most expensive high heels I had ever heard of. They both had high heels, with those red bottoms, called Jimmy Choos. I thought the Choo part was a play on the word shoe, but they soon told me that Jimmy Choo was a fashion designer known for his shoes, especially his high-heeled shoes with red bottoms. One day I thought about getting out some good glossy fingernail polish and painting the bottoms of a pair of my chunky heels red just to see what they would say, but when I went online and saw the type of shoes Jimmy Choo made, I knew I would never get away with it. Not to mention the polish would probably chip off in this gravel pit. I liked my chunky heels because they gave me more support than regular high heels, plus I never felt like my feet were in vise grips around my arches when wearing them like I did with normal high heels.

I'd bet you ten to none that Myra would be wearing her Jimmy Choos along with Bunny Ashford.

Pearl and Myra traipsed into the church like wet cats. I could tell they were not happy that this investigation had been slid under the rug. I felt the same way, but now we had a job to do and I had to rally them into doing it.

"Howdy, ladies," I said optimistically.

"Hey, sweetheart." Pearl hugged my neck.

Myra used the time to place her bag on the table beside me so that we were the triumphant threesome at the top of the table, which was the normal way we sat. I could already tell Myra was ready to fight. She had a lot of money and knew all the right people in all the high places here and in Barnville. If she wanted Moon Pie Hubbard out, she'd find someone to replace him and fund it herself to make sure her candidate of choice would win the mayoral election.

"Hey, Darlin'." She hugged me after Pearl. She always smelled like Chanel No. 5. It was her fail-safe scent and smelled amazing on her skin. For some reason, I couldn't pull off the scent, but Myra saddled herself in luxury, and it saddled itself to her.

Pearl was wearing her beige cardigan that had miraculously pulled itself back together. Myra had on a long caftan that was cinched at her waist so that you could see her hips and busty bosom. And those were real. That was one thing she didn't have to pay for. She had had a busty bosom since we were in high school, much to the delight of half the football team. She was never indecent or promiscuous, but she did like to lead the boys on a bit until they tired of it and went to look for some other floozy that would put out.

"All right Thelma, what do we need to help you with?" Myra asked right away. "I talked to Birdie today who said she had to stay away from this meeting, but that she had given you some things we would find interesting."

I pulled the large folder out of my Barnes and Noble tote bag. I had gone to the library and paid to have all the reports copied and stapled and assembled into individual packages. That way, no one had to share; everyone had copies. I stressed that these copies were for their eyes only.

"First, we have got to make sure they understand the stakes of this investigation. Almost everyone went to Triston or someone else in his salon. So, we have to make sure they know this could be dangerous since a murderer is still on the loose, and we still have no clue why anyone would want to kill Triston. Then we have to make sure that it doesn't get all over Sunnyside that *we* are investigating Triston's murder."

"Okay. Got it." Myra had stopped at the Starbucks that was built between Sunnyside and Barnville. She knew that Pearl and I didn't particularly like their coffee or cappuccinos.

We grew up drinking black coffee. Preferably Maxwell House, but if you need your coffee, beggars can't be too choosy. She sipped on the hot concoction, her pale brown lipstick staining the cup's lip.

Pearl sat to my left and grabbed one of the stapled reports I had placed on the table. Myra leaned over and grabbed one, too. They both started reading in silence.

Myra peered over the pages in her hands and said, "Well, most of this we already knew." She picked up her cappuccino and took another sip. We knew because of my conference call with Birdie and Pick.

"I didn't say we had a smoking gun." I looked at Myra, then at Pearl. "This is going to be the hardest thing we've ever set out to do, not to mention how dangerous it could be if someone found out we were the ones investigating this." I couldn't stress enough how dangerous this was for all involved. I didn't want to end up like Triston. The grimace he had on his face still haunts my dreams.

"Pearl and I were talking about that on the way here." Myra sipped on her cappuccino. She had changed her nail polish to a festive purple.

"What do y'all think the others are going to say?"

They both just shook their heads.

"I think we picked the right people for the job," Pearl said, starting to play with her cardigan. I'm surprised since she stretches it out so much it still holds its shape.

"I agree," Myra said, looking at the documents I had copied. It was the coroner's report, the police report, the CSI findings, and the things they didn't find, and everything in between. Something might be the clue to solving this case or might just be a lost avenue of inquiry. Or could at least lead us to another clue and then on from there. But the documents were flimsy. It was hard for me to believe that, if the police were investigating this, these pages would be what they would use to start their investigation. But I also knew it could be a gut instinct about any of these things that might be like a dog with a bone and lead to something that could crack the case wide open.

"It's not much to go on, as you can see," I admitted.

"I'll be honest, Thelma. It's more than I thought they had to start with," Pearl said.

"For example, if you look at the CSI findings on page 6, it reads, 'The back door to the Sunday school wing was wiped clean of prints, while the other doors had many fingerprints you would expect to see in a busy church. Therefore, the back door was probably the door used to bring the deceased's body in and display it in the Sunday school room as if on parade for the church to see.'" Pearl read from the police report. She had gotten her reading glasses out of her purse, and while I know the glasses were cheapy's from the Dollar Shop, I thought they looked good on her face. The shape and black color of them gave her face more interesting angles.

"I noticed that too. Another thing it says is that it had to be a man who killed Triston because they would have had to bring him into the church from the back in the dark. And both of you know how woodsy the back of the church is, especially this time of the year," I noted.

"I wouldn't go back there if someone paid me to," Myra said, tilting her head back to drain the last swig of her Starbucks cappuccino.

"But don't you think we need to?" I asked them both. "Think about it. Whoever did this probably brought him in from the back. I think once the other ladies get here, and we talk about the stakes of this, as well as get a count of who will stay and who may want to leave, that we go to the back and see if we can find anything back there the police might have overlooked. After all, this is our church. Granted, we don't ever use that door much, but don't you think if something isn't right, we'd be able to spot it before they could?"

"You've got a point, Thelma." Pearl had started pulling her cardigan tight across her chest. As she wasn't as blessed as Myra and me when it came to boobies, she would have stretched that sweater inside out by now.

"Pearl, you are going to stretch that poor cardigan out of shape." I finally said it. It was her favorite cardigan and as much as I would love to see her in a new one, she loved it dearly. She had found it years ago at one of the church bazaars.

"Oh, I'm doing it again. I caught myself doing it the other day when things got a little stressful."

Myra snickered. "Pearl, if you keep it up, you won't be the only thing that's stressed," she said, mentioning the cardigan.

Pearl placed her hands on top of the table. She put the reports to her right and placed her reading glasses on her left.

Myra had strewn everything on the table. She also took her reading glasses out of her Louis Vuitton purse and placed them haphazardly beside her cup of cappuccino.

No sooner had I looked at my watch for the time than the ladies started coming into the church. I told them to come in through the side door that leads to the sanctuary or the back of the church, where we always have tables ready for use. In the earlier days, we had used this area for our Sunday school rooms and had one class in the church's sanctuary.

Skitter Limpkins and Mitzi Woods were the first ladies to enter. Skitter had turned her left foot wrong and was wearing a boot on it. Her hair was the most beautiful white color, but she never did anything with it. I doubted she even took the time to comb it. It looked clean but disheveled, and it looked as if she had taken a nap earlier as she had a lump on one side while the other side stood out in wisps. She was by far the oldest lady in the Auxiliary, but she was as sharp as a tack. Nothing got by her without her knowing about it. At eighty-six years old, she could run circles around most of us and did.

Mitzi had turned eighty this year, and much like Skitter, who was one of her closest friends, she also acted much younger than her age. She kept her hair dyed pure black, straight out of a grocery store box. She had worn that same dull black shade for years. It made her face look pasty and much too white. If they ever needed an older Morticia Addams and were looking for an actress in Sunnyside, Mitzi would surely get the part. Like Morticia, she had stringy long hair that went below her shoulders. She was always so pleasant, and like Skitter, was a hoot to be around. They had both seen and done it all, and if they hadn't done it yet, they were surely going to do it before leaving us all.

I smiled as they came in. You couldn't help it. They had that contagious energy everyone wanted to be around.

They moseyed over to the table, Mitzi walking slower, making sure Skitter didn't try to overdo it as she would do if left to her own devices.

"Hey Thelma, Myra, Pearl," Skitter said when she finally got to the table. She sat down next to Pearl. Mitzi threw her large, black pocketbook, large enough to fit a pile of laundry, down and sat down beside Skitter.

"How are you two doing today?" I asked, as a formality.

"Fair to middlin'." Skitter piped up first. "If it wasn't for this dang boot, I'd sure be doing better."

"Well, next time that'll teach you to wear a steady pair of gardening shoes or at least your tennis shoes when you go out to garden, instead of your bedroom shoes," Mitzi responded to her best friend. They were like two married kids.

"Hush it. That didn't have a thing to do with me twisting my foot. If it wasn't for that darn messed up gutter, I wouldn't have turned my ankle like I did. It made a hole in the yard like a crater after the rain we got a few nights ago. I have to admit, I wasn't paying any attention, though. I was too busy trying to plant my zinnias."

"Well, you need to be careful. You're lucky you didn't break your ankle."

"What are you trying to say, Mitzi? That I've got osteoporosis?"

"Now you know I don't believe that. You're too mean to have anything like that," Mitzi laughed, as she flipped her jet-black hair over her shoulders. Then Skitter got to laughing with her until we were all laughing at the two going at it.

"I swear you two are a mess!" I smiled while shaking my head. I knew this meeting would soon get heavy and was so happy for some levity beforehand. This was one reason we picked these two. They were perfect as they were smart, and not many would pay much attention to them because of their age, and those who didn't see their penchant for noticing things no one else ever did would be doing themselves a disservice.

They were a dynamic duo together, and with the other ladies from the Auxiliary soon to arrive, we had a chance of figuring this out as long as we were steadfast and tight-lipped. Those were the two things we had to do to ensure this investigation was a success. That and the fact that 'they are the sharpest tools in the shed,' as my daddy always said.

We were all laughing when Babs Johnson entered the church by herself, which shocked me. It's funny how women find their dearest friends, and most of the time they are diametrically opposite in their personality, quirks, and many times, social standing. Babs and Bunny Ashford were completely different from each other, but from the first time they met at a church social function, they had become inseparable, which was why I thought it odd that she came by herself. Normally, she and Bunny would have been together. I hoped they hadn't had a falling out over something.

Babs had dark brown hair flipped up in the back like Mary Tyler Moore with olive skin that darkened in the sun as if she were Mediterranean instead of someone from the Bronx. She looked amazing and kept herself up to date with new cosmetic procedures you could attain in some of the best dermatologists' offices in Barnville, Columbia, or Charleston. It didn't matter to her if she had to drive to get the best Botox, dermal fillers, or laser resurfacing. The wonderful thing about her is she never hid it. She would gladly tell you where she had her lips plumped, or her wrinkles erased with laser treatments that didn't have the downtime as other drastic cosmetic procedures. She walked into the church with her black handbag thrown over her shoulder like you would a coat. She came to me first. "Thelma, could you be any more secretive about this evening's meeting?" she said in her thick New York accent. She looked me straight in the eyes as she did to everyone, making you feel as if you were the only person in the room.

"I'm sorry, sweetheart, but I promise when I tell everyone I've invited, you'll understand." She lowered her neck as if she had just bowed to the Queen of England with just her neck. Taking a seat at the far end of the table, she began taking things out of her purse. She found a pen and stationery to write on, knowing I wouldn't have wasted her time.

Then the last three showed up at the same time. Fifi Jones, Bunny Ashford, and June Bug Akins waltzed into the church. June Bug, heavier than the other two, carefully limped to the back of the church.

June Bug was somewhat famous in Sunnyside for the cakes she made for people all over the state. She baked and created the most extravagant cakes that not only looked beautiful but tasted just as good as they looked. People called her from all over to have her create their wedding or anniversary cakes, as well as the most elaborate birthday cakes. She loved doing it for the younger ones. June Bug had never grown up herself, so she loved nothing more than creating the most audacious cakes for children.

When Lucie, my granddaughter, turned one, I asked June Bug if she would make a cake for her first birthday party. It had been so long since I had had a birthday party for Amber; I had no idea what to ask her to make. Amber was no help because she didn't think it mattered since it was Lucie's first birthday party. I thought being a year old was significant. I had a birthday party for Amber when she turned one.

I thought it mattered, and June Bug knew it, even though I didn't go on and on about it. She had made the most gorgeous cake literally around a Barbie doll. The cake was formed like a doll wearing a full gown, with the gown's bodice around the doll's torso. When I saw it, I was blown away. I couldn't figure out how June Bug had created such a dramatic cake. The dress had frills in white icing and the rest of the dress was a soft pink with fondant at the top and cake that masqueraded as the dress. It cascaded toward the bottom, making the dress bell out.

It wasn't until we were about to cut the cake that June Bug took the knife from my hand and started cutting along the bodice of the dress that I realized what she had done. As the doll would have no support after cutting, she removed the barbie's head and torso she had cut in half and placed it on the counter in case I wanted to keep it for when Lucie was older and could see pictures of how beautiful her first birthday cake was. I still have the half-Barbie with no legs in her scrapbook that I've kept since she was born. I want her to know what her first words were, how old she was when she started walking, along with all the highlights of her life. I never did that for Amber and thought it would be a wonderful gift to give Lucie when she was older.

June Bug had bad arthritis in her legs, and on some days, it was almost debilitating. But she never let it get her down and if there was something she thought was more important than her mobility, she would've shown up in a wheelchair if necessary.

"Hey everybody," June Bug said, coming to the table with a sincere smile. She hugged my neck and took a seat beside Mitzi and Skitter.

Bunny Ashford walked in behind June Bug. With her severe bob swinging, she walked into the church's meeting area, which was more like a catchall that was used for Sunday school rooms, vacation bible schools, and a place where the deacons and Pastor Fairchild met. But since we created the Sunday school wing, this area held only a metal table surrounded by metal chairs.

She gracefully glided into the room, her back ramrod straight from all the years as a dancer. She still worked as a dance instructor at her own dance studio. When I approached her about this meeting, I knew it was on a night her dance school was open. I told her that what I needed to say, I couldn't say over the phone. I promised her it wouldn't be a waste of her time, to which she replied, "Thelma, when have you ever wasted anyone's time?"

She had a point. I never asked the ladies of the Auxiliary to meet unless there was something that needed to be addressed, and in certain circumstances, like tonight's, the ladies knew that sometimes the meetings were highly confidential; and unlike the sheriff and coroner's office, we didn't have leaks.

"Good evening everyone," Bunny said, coming to me and pretending to kiss me on one cheek and then the other as if she were French. She went and sat down next to Babs, smoothing her long white collared shirt, which was cinched near the waist, billowing out near her legs, perfect for dancing in. Although Bunny was in her seventies, she could have retired years ago since her husband, Barry, had been the CEO of The Nation's Bank and Trust before retiring with a massive severance package. Together, they were one of Sunnyside's power couples. Like Babs, she took out her pen and a small leather notebook that matched her pocketbook. It looked as if it was a set.

Finally, Fifi Jones pranced over to the table. She had stark white hair, with lavender fairy hair she had allowed someone to add.

Lord have mercy, I thought. Bless her heart, she looked like she had a disco ball on her head. Now all we needed were some bell-bottomed pants and a Donna Summer track, and we could all get up and do a jig to "Last Dance."

Her hair looked like someone had placed purple tinsel over her head and the tinsel was holding on for dear life. I know a lot of women were wearing fairy hair, but it looked as if they had placed too much of it in Fifi's short hair. She had always been eccentric, but as she got older, she became even more so, as if she was trying to take back her youth. She was always the life of any party and had nothing but kind things to say about everyone she knew. If there was malice in her heart, I had never seen it and I've known Fifi for close to thirty years now. She had left Sunnyside and moved to the mountains of North Carolina near Brevard and finally came back to Sunnyside after her husband passed from pancreatic cancer. She came back more of a hippie, that was for sure. Mountain living in North Carolina can do that to you. Still, I can't even imagine what she went through with her husband. One month they had given him his diagnosis, and the next she was burying him at Sunnyside Rest Haven Cemetery. That was an awful time. At least she gave us some levity in a grave situation. You can always count on Fifi to do that.

As she got closer to me, her hair glittered even more in the fluorescent lights, making it look like a flashing disco ball. The weird thing was that she had a short haircut that was no more than two inches long all over her head. I knew she had always worn a pixie cut which suited her thick hair perfectly. But the fairy hair was longer than her real hair and made it look like someone threw Christmas tree tinsel in her hair.

If I had a pair of scissors, I'd cut the fairy right out of her hair.

I got up and she hugged me tightly. She was a good hugger. Then she sat beside June Bug, one of her closest friends.

Now we were ready for the meeting to start. I had a lot to tell them, and I had a feeling they were going to dislike

Moon Pie Hubbard more than they already did for shutting down Triston's murder investigation. That's where we came in though, and I had the assurance of Pick and Birdie that they would be feeding us more information once they got more. So far, we had everything they had. And now it was time to start this meeting, which I prayed would turn into an investigation. With all the clout these women carried in town, I knew we had a better chance of passing under the radar as we tried to find the killer before he murdered someone else (and that could be anyone at this table).

Chapter Seven

"FIRST OF ALL, I want to thank everyone of you for coming tonight. I know that many of you had to change your schedules to get here, and I appreciate that." I looked at each of the ladies around the rectangular table as I spoke. "Now, Myra and Pearl are going to hand you some reports I want you to look over before we begin. But before they do this, I want you to know that what I'm about to ask of you could put you or your loved ones in danger, so if you want to leave the meeting now before we talk about what's going on, I would not blame you at all."

Then I went in for the kill, because I needed them to know this was deadly serious. Serious enough that it could put their lives at risk.

"We all know that Triston Stylz died not far from where you're sitting right now, and this meeting could put you in danger. Now, having said that, I'm pretty sure I let the proverbial cat out of the bag, but I need you all to be clear about what you're getting yourselves into."

I looked around the table at every woman, and each had a stoic look on their face. They were genuine ladies of the

Auxiliary, and when push came to shove, they knew how to shove back.

"Okay then. Pearl, Myra, would y'all please hand out the reports to the ladies on your side of the table?" They passed around the reports, and it was obvious to them that these were official documents from the police station, the CSI team, and the coroner's office. Stapled to each was also a subpoena showing the authorization to go into Triston and Arty's home and salon. I knew this would probably make some of them angry that Pick had gotten a subpoena to search their dwelling and business.

"Now, before we start, I would like for you all to read every report you have in your hands. After you have read everything, we'll talk about why we have these documents and what we're supposed to do with them."

I watched as each read the reports. I heard some collective gasps; some brought their hands to their mouths. A couple pushed glasses closer to their eyes as if they could see them better. They were engrossed in the reports like I knew they would be.

There was also a picture, taken by the CSI team, of Triston lying dead in the Sunday school room. I knew when many of the ladies saw that picture, they would have a visceral experience much like Pearl and I had on that Sunday morning the week before Easter. Needless to say, we didn't have an Easter pageant this year.

Bunny was the first to speak after looking through the materials. "So, let's cut to the chase," she said, taking off her black, big-rimmed reading glasses she had grabbed from her purse after getting the papers. She placed them on top of the reports. She sat straight in the chair with her back never touching the back of the chair itself. "Are we supposed to help the police investigate Triston's murder?"

Once she said it, I saw a lot of other ladies nodding their heads, also awaiting the answer.

"No. We will be the ones investigating," I answered perfunctorily. I could see some clutching at their pearls. Pearl started messing with her cardigan, and Fifi couldn't take her hand out of her fairy hair.

"Say what Thelma?" It was June Bug. I knew I should have just come right out and told them what was going on instead of playing cloaks and daggers, but I needed them to think this through before proceeding. Their lives could be in danger, and I didn't want anyone to die on my watch.

I held up my hand before everyone descended into questioning mode. I'm sure they were confused as to why we had anything to do with this at all.

"The reason we've been asked to investigate Triston's murder is that Mayor George Hubbard instructed Pick and Birdie to rule Triston's death as accidental since they found the bitter almond oil, which Birdie determined had killed him, in both his home and salon. He assumed Tristan had been careless in using the bitter almond oil." I needed a cigarette badly, but I could never bring myself to vape because of the issues those brought. Of course, it's not like cigarettes are any better.

"You mean to tell me that Moon Pie Hubbard told them to stand down, because he says it's an accidental death?" June Bug decried.

"That's exactly right. Since it's an election year, Hubbard told them he wouldn't go into the election with a murder on the books. Plus, with Triston having used the bitter almond oil, it gave Hubbard an out. I think it is underhanded and stinks to high heaven and back," I said, gritting my false teeth. I better not break them. I would hate to walk around toothless. Lord, that would be a look.

"Oh my goodness. I can't believe that conniving asshole. Triston didn't just walk himself into the church." Fifi shook her head, and the way the light played on her lavender fairy hair, it sparkled like stars in the midnight sky.

"So, in essence, is this the only thing we have to go on?" Babs said in her thick New York accent. She used her hands to gesture as she always spoke with her hands as well as her mouth. She also had those long, square-shaped acrylic nails that she liked to tap on the table when frustrated. She reminded me of Myra. She and Pearl just sat beside me, giving me their strength and prayers.

"That and all the questions we can think of. If I didn't think we could do this, I would have told them no. But I truly believe, with the connections we have, we can investigate this just as well as the police can. Maybe better, since no one would see us coming. They would look at us as doughty older women and that could play to our advantage." I'm sure some of the ladies would have taken umbrage to me calling them doughty older women, but it was the truth. Many people would look at us as little old ladies, and we could use that to our advantage.

"You have a point, Thelma," Bunny said, sitting ramrod straight in her chair. Her back still never touched the back of her chair the whole time she sat there. She was sitting close to the edge of the chair so she could maintain her perfect posture, and since she was a dancer and still teaches dancing, she probably had no idea she was doing it. It just came naturally to her.

"So, we really need to be very careful with the information that we have then," Skitter said, looking around the table.

"You've got that right!" Babs said, her New York City accent as strong as ever. She was shaking her head; her Mary Tyler Moore hair, flipped up in the back, moved with each shake. Today, it was teased even higher on top, like Peg Bundy in *Married with Children*. She's worn this style as long as I've known her.

"That was one thing that Pick warned me about. He and Birdie both wanted you all to know that if you decided to investigate, you also had to agree to keep it to yourselves. You can talk to the other ladies in this room, but be very aware of where you talk about this and with whom you talk about it. Preferably, you wouldn't talk about it around anyone. Think about how Triston died. He had an awfully painful death. You can see the picture of the grimace he had on his face. Till the day I leave this earth, I cannot unsee his face like that." I had to punctuate just how deadly this could get.

"What about Arty?" Mitzi volleyed to the table. "Do any of you think that he could have done it?"

Everyone at the table shook their head no.

"I've seen Arty at the salon and there's no way I believe he could have done this. Now he does make those cherry cokes that Triston is so fond of drinking and in the coroner's report, it said that he had coke, maraschino cherry juice, and two cherries in his stomach, which was probably what killed him. Whoever did it made him his drink of choice and put the bitter almond oil in it. But I don't think Arty did it. I could be wrong, but he looks like someone carved his insides out," Bunny said.

"I agree, Bunny," Skitter quickly agreed. "I was at the grocery store the other day and people in the grocery store were talking about Triston's death. I overheard some girls who work at the salon talking to one another, saying how Arty is pitiful and how sad he is to be around."

I agreed. I didn't think Arty did this, but we would be remiss if we didn't check his alibi and talk to him about the night Triston didn't come home from his meeting. Me, Pearl, and Myra would take care of that.

"Why don't we split up into groups, and then we can think of some things that need to be looked into like alibis for one thing? We need alibis for everyone at the salon, too. I'm sure with all the perm solution in those rooms, there's bound to be some friction. Triston was always good at keeping the girls and customers from gossiping in the salon, since he believed if you didn't have anything nice to say, then you don't say anything at all. I also don't think anyone at the salon would be caught up in Triston's death, but we have to start somewhere."

"I think that's a great idea, Thelma," Mitzi piped up. The more I looked at her dyed black hair, the more she looked like

Morticia Addams. She must have picked up the wrong shade of color at the grocery store, because her hair was never this black. It looked almost matte and did nothing for her complexion.

"And one thing they always talk about on the CSI shows is to always follow the money, and with Bunny's husband, maybe she and I, and Babs, could see if her husband could take a sneak peek at Triston and Arty's financials," Mitzi was on to something.

"That's a great idea, but instead of having Bunny's husband do it, let's get Pick and Hansen to run that down for us. We don't want to show our hand to anyone. Remember, we have to use discretion at every point. We already have one person dead. We don't need another." Once you see someone's finances, you can really tell how a person lives from day-to-day.

Mitzi had a great idea. If we could get ahold of their bank statements, we could see their finances and would be able to see if Triston and Arty had received any good sums of money and who from.

"Thelma, I think one thing we could do without raising any alarm bells is to get our hair and nails done at the salon. We could all call and make different appointments for different days and see what the stylists have to say. Surely they have to think something is going on," Skitter said.

"Skitter, I think that would be a great idea and when you go for your appointments, don't force the subject. They'll want to talk and gossip now that Triston isn't there to stop them. I doubt Arty would say anything to them. Bless his heart. I don't know if he should be working at all, but I suppose it gives him something to do."

"I think that's a wonderful idea, but do I have to get my fairy hair taken out? I just got it put in at the Easter Fair in Barnville. They had a huge spread of food at the fairgrounds, of course, and they also happened to have all types of tents that sold jewelry, clothing, and whatnot. They had one with four Asian-looking women putting fairy hair into people's hair, and when I saw it I knew I had to get some, and with my hair being white, I've always wanted to add some lavender to it. And since this hair isn't permanent, I had to get some for myself, so I went with the lavender color. And I love it. Every time I see myself in the mirror at home, I feel like my head shimmers all over. I just love it!" Fifi said fervently, putting her hands in her fairy hair.

At least *she* loved it. Cause she certainly got her money's worth. I've never seen the likes of fairy hair! What will they come out with next?

"Myra, what's the girl's name at Triston's that does hair and nails too? Is it Stacy?" I had asked. Maybe Fifi could have her nails done instead of her hair.

"No Thelma. Her name is Sherry Haster, and she does nails on Tuesdays and Thursdays. I think that would be a great idea, Fifi. Just call and ask for a manicure with Sherry. I know Patricia, who runs the front desk. She can find you an appointment with her. Sometimes with Sherry, if she's booked, it's best to get on her waiting list because something always happens, and she'll have an opening sooner than you might think. But don't wait too long or it'll take forever to get in with her, especially since spring has sprung and summer's almost here. Everyone is doing pastel colors this year for their nails. I saw it in *Cosmo*. I love that soft green color by Essie they showed in the magazine." Myra put her hands out, looking at her nails. I suppose she was trying to picture that light green she liked so much. I wouldn't wear any type of green nail polish. I'm not a leprechaun. I have to say she's always dressed to the nines and never has trouble finding dates. That's for sure.

"I'll do it as soon as I get home, then. I *think* they're open on Sundays?" Fifi questioned to no one in particular.

"They're open every day of the week," Myra told her. She should know as many times as she gets her hair blown out. Plus, she has a standing appointment with Sherry Haster every Thursday at three o'clock in the afternoon for some kind of nail dip that they use now.

I don't do manicures. It's a waste of money for me with all the things I do around the house. I always wind up chipping the nail polish. Every now and then I need a good pedicure and Sherry is definitely up for the job.

"What are we going to call this . . . assignment?" Mitzi asked. She loved to name everything we did, like we were in some *Mission Impossible* movie.

"How about Mission Hairdresser?" June Bug piped up.

"That's great June Bug. So, if we all agree, we'll call it Mission Hairdresser." It was a little on the nose for me, but the ladies knew not to talk about it in front of others, to keep it secret, to keep them safe. I looked around the table and saw all the nods. "Mission Hairdresser it is." It was obvious June Bug liked the name immensely. They say the older you get, the more you regress back to childhood. If that were the case, we'd be close to second graders at this point.

I looked at my watch and it was close to 6:30 p.m., so I asked if anyone had any more questions about what they needed to do. I looked around at the silent table. "Okay, then everyone needs to get into the salon and see just how much gossip you can get from your hairdresser or nail tech. They're bound to know something. Anything and we could crack this case wide open," I said, about to adjourn the meeting. But June Bug appeared to want to say something.

"Thelma, from looking at all the reports, it looks as if the murderer must have brought Triston through the back door. I have a metal detector in my car, and I think before we leave, and the sun goes down, we should all go out back and see if we can't find something the murderer or Triston may have dropped on their way into the church." Who in the world would keep a metal detector in their car? What was June Bug doing for pleasure? Searching for gold? Or would that even be heard on a metal detector? I didn't know. The only gold I had been around was the beautiful golden wavy chain necklace Amber and Henri bought me for Christmas from a jeweler in Paris, and in the middle, it had a garnet heart, which was Lucie's birthstone. I treasured that necklace as much as I did the engagement ring Charlie had given me when we got engaged. My wedding ring is a simple oval-shaped diamond mounted onto a golden band. Its simplicity was what made it so beautiful.

"I think that's a great idea!" I said enthusiastically.

I wished I had thought of it myself. I can't be perfect all the time, though, I conceded.

Just most of the time.

Chapter Eight

WE ALL HEADED TOWARD THE BACK of the church after June Bug limped to her car, her arthritis giving her a fit. She brought the metal detector into the church. I had never seen one and thought it looked similar to the Weed eater Charlie used around the house when he mowed the lawn and kept my flower beds neat and tidy. She held it in her hands like she was a pro.

I had no idea June Bug was into metal detectors. When I asked her about it after she came in with it, she told me that I'd be surprised at the things that you find hidden just beneath a little bit of dirt or a clump of grass. I had to hand it to her; this was a good idea. Though I'm sure the CSI team had combed the back of the church. But what could it hurt? Maybe we could find something useful or expensive. People lost jewelry all the time, but no one was supposed to go behind the church. Maybe with this, we'd get somewhere with this case other than what was in the reports.

June Bug turned on the metal detector and it started clicking. She said the more it beeped, the bigger the piece of metal could be, or the closer it was to the surface. She used the detector for the next thirty minutes. The sun had started going down behind the church. She had found many coins and beer bottle tops, which I thought were odd behind the church. Were kids getting drunk behind our church?

It started cooling down as the sun started descending. Then, suddenly, the metal detector started beeping like crazy. BEEP. BEEP. BEEP, BEEP, BEEP. It sounded like a monitor at the hospital when someone was about to croak.

"What is it, June Bug?" June Bug kneeled on the ground carefully and picked up a necklace. Everyone in the group let out oohs and aahs. It looked brand spanking new and had a beautifully shaped pendant on it. It looked like a Tree of Life pendant that was supposed to represent eternal love. I took a tissue out of my pocketbook and placed it into the tissue. I turned it over and on the back, it had three letters written on it: KMS. I had no idea what that meant. Was it the name of someone? The murderer, perhaps? Had Triston pulled on the murderer's necklace and torn it from the killer's neck? But it looked like a woman's necklace. If the killer was a woman, how did she get Triston into the Sunday school room?

KMS. I was dumbfounded but didn't want the ladies to see me like this, so I wrapped it in the tissue and placed it in the side pocket of my purse.

June Bug started to go over the ground again near where she had located the necklace, and within a few minutes it started beeping again, but this time it was beeping up a storm.

I kneeled down on the ground and saw a key. Something about it made me freeze in place. Time stood still and I felt a chill down to my bones. It was not just any key. It was the key to the back door of the church. It looked like the same key I had just used to open the back door and it also had the letters ACE written on it. It had been a copy, just like mine made at the Ace hardware. Charlie could have made it. I looked in my purse again and took one of Charlie's handkerchiefs out and picked the key up from the ground. I showed the ladies what we had found. I heard collective gasps and saw hands going to mouths. Babs said in her thick New York accent, "Oh my sweet Jesus!!"

Sweet Jesus was right

Of course, this could be a key that had been there forever. This could be one of the deacon's keys that was lost a while ago.

I instinctively knew better. My heart was slamming in my chest as I slid the key into the keyhole. At first, the key seemed stuck, but then it let loose. I turned the key, and it locked the door!

Jesus wept!

My hands were shaking from the adrenaline pumping through my body. It had started turning dark, and I prayed no one saw my hand shaking. The killer could have used this very key.

Obviously, the killer didn't know about me and Pearl opening the church every Sunday morning before it opened for Sunday school. I couldn't believe we had found *the* key that could have potentially opened the door to allow a killer to enter our church and dump Triston's body into one of our Sunday school rooms.

Lord Have Mercy! was all I could think. I stood there frozen on the steps. I didn't know if the ladies noticed that the key had worked until I heard June Bug say, "Thelma, sweetheart, you need to put the key into the handkerchief and put it in your purse. It could have the killer's fingerprints on it." She was right.

I wrapped the key in the handkerchief and placed it in the same pocket as the necklace.

KMS. Was that someone's initials? Or was it just something that was already on the back of the necklace, like ACE was on the key? Who would have had another key made? Who would have given their key out to allow someone to make another key? I couldn't answer these questions, not now, at least.

I needed to call Pick and Birdie and tell them what we had found. But why hadn't the CSI team found them? Were they just sloppy? Surely, they had a metal detector, or did they? These were questions for Pick.

I was still at the top of the steps when I turned and looked at the ladies. They all looked like they'd seen a ghost, as if they knew what we had just found was unheard of. We all knew from the report that Triston had died way before they brought his body to the church. Were they trying to be repentant by bringing Triston to the church? My brain was rapidly firing with thoughts upon thoughts, swirling around like water in a drain.

I found my strength, looked at my ladies, and said, "Okay, now that we have found what we have been looking for, I need to make a few phone calls."

All the ladies said their goodbyes to one another and told me they would all call the salon on different days and make their salon appointments. Some said they needed another appointment, anyway. Many of the ladies had gone to Triston to have their hair done. They knew they were sure to hear some gossip from their stylists, with Triston not being there. That's what we needed to hear. We needed to hear what they thought had happened. I know that Arty had already held a meeting to talk to them to allay any fears that the salon would have to close or perhaps not be open for the foreseeable future. Myra had told me that Arty had said the salon wouldn't be closed at all. He had told her that Triston wouldn't have wanted it closed. He would want his people to make sure that everyone who sat in their chairs left feeling better about themselves than they had before they came in. That's what good hairdressers do, and Triston was the best Sunnyside had to offer.

I immediately called Pick. He answered, knowing it was me. These phones give away too much! Not only that, but that Siri girl was listening to every single conversation we had. Charlie didn't believe me when I told him that, so one night, I whispered in his ear to talk about something we never talked about. I suppose he thought it was funny, so he told me that he wanted to buy me some new lingerie with the frilly bras and the panties that rode up your butt crack. I looked at him like he was crazy. Because one thing is for sure, I ain't wearing no dental floss around to get his jollies off. That's for sure. Then I told him that I had been thinking about the same thing, but I really wanted to buy him a pair of handcuffs so I could cuff him to the bed. Lord knows if I did, I'd leave him lying in the bed for a couple of hours until he learned how to talk to a lady, 'cause I sure ain't going to traipse through my house in one of those outfits. Good Lord, how old does he think I am?

Well, wouldn't you know when we went to bed that night, I had an offer on my iPhone from Fredrick's of Hollywood for some new lingerie. I showed it to Charlie, and he wanted to take the phone away from me so he could look at that frilly filth. I slapped his hand and gave him a look to go you-know-where. But he just smiled that grin he has when he wants to be together. I declare men will always be men until the day they die. Just ask the pharmacists. I'm sure they could tell you that the number of Viagra pills they sell in a month would be enough to keep the whole store open.

It just goes to show how these phones are listening in on our conversations and then they try to give you information they think you requested. If people wouldn't think I was up to no good, I'd get me a burner phone. Then when I called someone, they wouldn't know who was calling. They'd probably not pick it up at all and allow the answering machine to get it.

"Thelma, you there?" I could tell Pick still had that toothpick in his mouth this late at night.

"Yeah, I'm here. Just lost in thought. You'll never believe what we found at the church tonight." I didn't give him any time to respond. I just kept talking. "After we had finished our meeting, June Bug told us about her metal detector. Well, low and behold, she had it in her car. So, she went and got it out and we all went to the back of the church." I had to catch my breath. "And you'll never believe what we found."

"I can't believe you found anything. The CSI team swept that entire area behind the church and even went into the woods behind the church. Of course, they didn't find anything," Pick said, twirling his cinnamon toothpick around in his mouth.

"They didn't do a good enough job then. June Bug, and her metal detector, found a necklace with a beautiful pendant on it with *KMS* engraved on the back. I don't know if that's supposed to be someone's initials or what, but it looked brand new."

"A necklace?" Pick asked. I could tell he had been lying down but was sitting up now.

"And that's not the kicker, Pick. We also found a key. A key that opens the back door to the Sunday school wing!"

"What! And it works?" I sensed that Pick had stood up. Probably putting his jeans on.

"Of course it does. I wouldn't be calling if it didn't."

"Thelma, listen to me. You didn't touch them, did you?"

"Pick, you should know better than that. When I picked up the necklace, I used a piece of tissue I had in my purse. Then I placed it in a side pocket by itself. Then when we found the key, I knew it had to be the key to open that back door, so I got out one of Charlie's handkerchiefs and used it. I picked it up and then climbed the stairs to see if it would fit. It did! The key opened and locked the door."

"Thelma, I'm lost for words. I can't believe my CSI team didn't find those items. They could be very important."

Duh!

"Don't you think I know that? When I saw that key, my whole body got the chills. Believe me, I was the only one to pick them up, and I used something that wouldn't leave my fingerprints on either one of them, because I knew when I saw that key, it may have the prints of the killer on it."

"Let me throw on some clothes. I was getting ready to settle in for the night. Do you mind if I come by your house and take them off your hands?"

"Not at all Pick. I want to see if we can find out anything about the necklace and the key." Adrenaline was pumping through my body so much that I doubted I'd get any sleep. I wanted Pick to have them as fast as possible. Maybe he or Birdie could find some fingerprints and blow this investigation wide open.

"I'll be there in about fifteen minutes." Pick clicked the phone off. I was sure that he was anxious to see the necklace and the key. I just prayed they had fingerprints on them. Plus, I kept thinking about that necklace. I took it out of my purse, still wrapped in the tissue, and placed it on the kitchen table. Then I took out my noisy phone and snapped a picture of it. It looked like it came from Langston's Jewelers in Barnville. Tomorrow, I wanted to see if the girls would like to go to Barnville and find out if they had made the piece or not. I would tell Pick about it when he got here to take it off my hands. I also took the key out of Charlie's handkerchief and took a picture of it, too, with the ACE lettering on it. Of course, they make so many keys at the Ace Hardware in Barnville, that I doubted Fisher would remember making the key. Only the good Lord knows when it might have been copied.

I was so caught up with the necklace and the key that I didn't notice that Charlie had come into the kitchen. When I got home and said hello, he was watching *Gunsmoke* on the TV. He came up to me and put his hands on my shoulders.

I screamed!

"Charlie Rue, don't you sneak up on me like that. You gone give me a heart attack." I slapped him against his chest.

"I'm sorry, Thelma." He kissed the back of my neck. And looked at the items on the table. "Did those come from the church?"

"Charlie, you wouldn't believe it. But yes, they did. June Bug had a metal detector in her car. Don't ask why 'cause I have no idea why anyone would carry around a metal detector. Anyway, we went to the back of the church where the killer had to take Triston into the Sunday school wing, and June Bug turned her metal detector on and found the necklace first, then she found the key, and the key opened and locked that back door."

"Sounds to me like y'all had a productive meeting. I have to say I'm proud of you, Thelma." Charlie kissed my neck again and wrapped his arms around my waist from behind. I could tell he was a little too happy. I pushed him off me. Pick would be here any minute.

"I called Pick and told him what we found, and he's on his way over. I'm praying that they'll be able to get some fingerprints off of them." I wasn't getting my hopes up too high. I had a feeling that this killer was pure evil and wouldn't be so sloppy as to leave any prints, but you never know.

"I haven't seen Pick in years," Charlie said, sitting at the table directly across from the necklace and key. I could see him eyeing his handkerchief.

"Yes, I carry one of your handkerchiefs with me. You never know when they might come in handy." The truth was that I carried one because they smelled like him and now and then I'd pull it out and sniff it. That way, he was always with me. At least that's the way it made me feel.

I went over and turned the porch light on. It was already dark outside, and I didn't want Pick breaking his neck coming to the front door. I went to the fridge and made myself a cup of iced sweet tea. I had eaten before the meeting, but my stomach was gnawing at my backbone as if I hadn't eaten a thing in days. I suppose with all the running around I've been doing with this investigation, it kept me hungry.

I grabbed two pieces of white bread and made a peanut butter and jelly sandwich. I grabbed a paper plate, put the sandwich on it, and went to the table with my tea. I had taken two bites of the sandwich when I heard the knock at the front door.

Charlie got up and went to the door. I could tell he was worried about us doing this investigation. I don't blame him. One person was already dead, and I prayed that it would stay that way. I don't know what I would do if something happened to one of my ladies. I'm supposed to be their leader and leaders don't tell people to run toward a fire, they tell them to run away.

We couldn't run away from this. We had promised Pick and Birdie that we'd stand in their place and do what they do for us every single day, and we all loved Triston and Arty.

I also know that even though none of us believe for one second that Arty had anything to do with Triston's murder, we still needed to get his alibi to cross him off our list of suspects. I have to be honest; the list is brief. The only name I had on my list was Arty, and I still didn't believe he had anything to do with this at all.

"Thelma Rue," Pick came strolling into the kitchen as bowlegged as ever. He had that toothpick sticking out of his mouth, as usual.

"Hey, Pick." I hugged his neck. He sure was skinny compared to Charlie. Charlie used to play football in high school and some in college until he messed his leg up. Now he's got a brand-new kneecap which he says has bionic powers. Yeah right!

"So, these are the treasures June Bug found?" Pick surveyed the necklace and the key. He picked up the necklace first with Charlie's handkerchief. He looked at the front for a few minutes, then at the back. "KMS. Huh, I wonder who this belongs to."

"I'd love to know myself, Pick. If we knew, it might help. Course it could have been back there for a while." Charlie came into the kitchen where all the action was and sat across from us at the table.

"Take a load off," Charlie told Pick. I knew Pick better than that. He wanted to get these items and skedaddle.

"Thanks, Charlie, but I really have to get back to the house. Looks like your wife gave me something to do for an investigation that was already ruled an accidental death."

"That's hogwash if I ever heard it and we all know it is too," I said incredulously. "If I happen to run up on ole Moon Pie Hubbard, he'll wish he never met me. He's going to get a piece of my mind."

"No, don't do that. The less he knows that you know, the better we all are. If he thinks that I told you about this, he's likely to jump the gun and figure out what's going on. There's a reason he's been the mayor so long." Pick was putting the items in a ziplock baggie he'd brought with him.

"I suppose you're right, but when this is over, I can promise you one thing: he'll wish he had never closed Triston's murder!" My face was getting hot. My blood pressure must be high. I have to take a blood pressure pill in the morning and one at night before I go to bed. My face usually gets a little flushed if my pressure is high.

"He'll get his. Being a sheriff all these years, there's one thing I've learned. Seeing people guilty as sin just be able to walk away from some crazy situations. One thing is for sure. Karma is real and the Lord almighty will take care of people like that."

"Preach it, brother Pick." Charlie loved playing around with Pick. Like old times, I suppose. It's hard to imagine we all went to high school together, even though Charlie is two years older than me and Pick.

Pick just laughed at Charlie.

"Thelma, we got to find Pick a woman. That's what he needs," Charlie said, grinning like a opossum eating a sweet potato.

"I have to go now," Pick said and smiled back at Charlie. A woman would settle him down, though. He's been widowed since he was in his thirties when his wife Sarah caught the cancer. I know he's got a thing for Pearl. He wanted to date Pearl when we were in high school, but it never happened, and he married Sarah, who was also in our class.

"Thank you, Thelma. I can't believe my CSI team didn't find these. They are supposed to use metal detectors too. I don't know how these slipped through their fingers." Pick was bothered by the fact that his team wasn't on their A game, especially on a case as big as the murder of Triston Stylz.

Chapter Nine

EARLY THE NEXT MORNING, I drove Pearl and Myra to Langston Jewelers in Barnville, so we could see if they sold the necklace we found. Myra had been buying jewelry from Fred and his wife Jenny since marrying her first husband, the late Holland Frankfurt, who had more money than all three of us could comprehend. When he and Myra started dating, he had a quaint house in Barnville and a decent car. Nothing to write home about. There was nothing about Holland to make one think he was a multimillionaire.

Before he proposed to Myra, he came clean with her about his financial situation. He came into some family money when his father passed away. His mother had passed when Holland was young, and his father never remarried. I can remember the night she called and told me he had proposed, and she had told him yes. Then, to put the cherry on top, she told me he was one of the richest bachelors in Barnville County.

"Get out!" That was what had I said to her. I couldn't for the life of me understand why anyone with that kind of money would live the lifestyle he did. Myra didn't care. She was so in love with Holland, she would have married him if he was flat broke. They would have made it somehow.

When she showed me the ring, I about fell on the floor. It was a four-carat, pavé set diamond ring. The band was encrusted with small diamonds so clear you could see straight through them, giving it a continuous sparkle. The diamond was a cushion-cut diamond with rounded corners, giving it a vintage appeal. It was so romantic and elegant. And boy, did that rock garner some attention. Course, it didn't help that Myra was throwing up her hand to her face every time someone new came near her, oohing and aahing about that ring.

When I saw it for the first time, I was completely speechless. Rings like that were things you saw on *Dynasty*, not in real life. I'm not usually the type to be speechless about anything! I had never seen a ring like it, and to this day, even with her marrying two other men just as rich as Holland, they never could top that ring. Myra still has it in one of her many safes she'd had installed in her house in places you would never think to look for a safe. It was safe to say that her jewelry, and some of her more important papers, were well hidden and secured.

Pearl was riding shotgun, and Myra kept pulling herself to the front of the car no matter how many times I asked her to put her seat belt on. If I hit the brakes hard enough, she could go flying out the front windshield.

"I'm not worried about a seat belt, Thelma." Myra had pulled herself so far forward that she was practically sitting in the front seat. Pearl, so used to it, didn't say a word. It was useless with Myra.

It was a beautiful spring day with the temperatures hovering around sixty-five degrees, but it didn't stop Myra from wearing a turquoise Winslet cashmere cardigan coat with white slacks and a beautiful white silk shirt. Myra always dressed to impress, while Pearl and I dressed for comfort. We both had on blue jeans and regular long-sleeved t-shirts. Of course, Pearl had her favorite cardigan on again. It was about time to put that poor cardigan out of its misery. But it had sprung back into its normal shape. I swear I think she uses it as kids would do their favorite blankets for security. Security from what, I'm not sure.

I was anxious about what we would learn about the necklace. It was a long shot, but there was something about it that screamed Langston's.

As if on cue, Myra asked, "Do y'all think that Fred or Jenny sold that necklace?"

Pearl hadn't said a thing. She wasn't acting like her normal self. It was as if she didn't feel good. Something seemed off and if it continued, I would ask her if she was okay. Maybe she just wanted to enjoy the ride into Barnville in peace and quiet. The scenery is beautiful this time of year, with all the trees donning new leaves and wild daisies pushing their heads out of the ground.

I looked in the rearview mirror at Myra. "I don't know. But when I saw it, something told me it was a Langston piece." They were known the state over for some of the most beautiful jewelry and not everything costs thousands of dollars.

Just most.

"That's what I thought when I saw it last night, too. It brought back a lot of memories of Holland."

"I'm surprised you didn't wear your ring today," I said, looking down at her hand on the middle console. She had her fingernails dipped, and they had a shiny turquoise lacquer to them. They were beautiful. Thank the Lord she didn't listen to *Cosmo* and didn't have green-colored nails. Whoever heard of wearing green nail polish? Don't get me wrong. I know it exists. But for the life of me, I don't know why.

"No. I'm not going to parade that ring around. Lord knows everyone in town would be oohing and aahing over it."

I rolled my eyes. "Ain't that the point?"

"Not for me, it's not. Holland gave me that, and I will treasure that ring for as long as I live," she said rather somberly.

"Touch a nerve?" I asked apologetically.

"Maybe a little if I'm being truthful. I see you and Charlie and other married people who have been together for more years than I was with three men. Sometimes I feel like I was robbed a little. They were taken so young."

Pearl turned to her. "It's better to have loved than to have never loved at all. You've been blessed beyond anything you could have imagined for yourself. And I can see how you feel about your husbands dying young, but at least you have some of the best memories about them."

I felt Pearl was speaking from experience since she never married herself. Sure, she had men trying to knock down her door, but there was always something that stopped Pearl from letting go and seeing where life would take her. I have to admit,

I wouldn't have given half of them the time of day, but Pearl was always the nice, pragmatic one of the three of us. She'd go out with them for about a month if it lasted that long, and then that would be it. She wouldn't see them anymore. I wondered many times if she was just afraid. She had always been one who kept to herself and liked her own company. But I know deep down she wished she had married.

"You're right Pearl. I am blessed to have fallen in love with three of the most handsome men I have ever seen. And it didn't hurt that they had money, too. Of course, after Holland, I had enough money on my own that I didn't need anyone else's. Maybe that's why it worked out with Fairfax and Henry."

"You got to admit they were some handsome devils. And Henry with that Tom Selleck mustache was the most handsome man I'd seen other than my Charlie."

"Yes, he was nice to look at." I knew Myra wasn't just thinking about their faces when she said that. I didn't want to know and I'm sure Pearl didn't either, so I quickly changed the subject.

"Okay, before we get there, I'm going to let you talk to Fred and Jenny, Myra. They know you better than me or Pearl." It was true that I had bought some pieces from Langston's, but they weren't into costume jewelry, which is what I can afford to wear. Today, all I had on was my Timex watch and my wedding ring.

"I think that would be best too," Pearl chimed in numbly.

"Pearl, are you feeling okay today, sweetheart?" I had asked. With the way she was talking, I wondered if she was getting depressed.

"Oh, I'm fine. I didn't get much sleep last night and the car ride is making me want to take a nap."

"A nap. Pearl, it's only nine thirty. You sure you're okay?" I hated to nag her. But honestly, I really *didn't* hate to nag her too much. That's what we did with one another. All three of us.

"I know. I woke up this morning around three thirty and I couldn't go back to sleep. So I got up and turned the TV on, and guess what channel it was on. And I don't remember it being on that channel before going to bed."

"What channel? Don't tell me they got that nasty ole porno stuff on late-night TV like they used to in the seventies before people got good sense."

"Lord no!" Pearl exclaimed, looking at me as if I had just burned her with a curling iron. "It was on KDP and Twilight Woods was selling some really nice cookware. I declare, I almost called in and ordered me a set. That girl's a star."

"She's a star all right and she'll let you know it, too," I replied. There was something about her that made me feel uneasy. Maybe it was the way she sold everything, even when she was carrying on a conversation with you. It was like she was always on air. I can't explain it, but my gut feeling about her is she's a snake. I wondered what Triston thought about her.

"Then I really couldn't sleep after seeing her because every time I tried closing my eyes, I saw Triston in that Sunday school room deader than dead." Myra pulled Pearl in to give her a hug. Pearl grabbed hold of Myra's arm to hug her back as much as she could without getting choked by the seat belt.

"There's something about her I just don't trust. When I saw her that night they had the party at Triston and Arty's after the soft launch, she just traipsed around the place like she owned it. I don't know, but something's off about her."

"You know Thelma, I think you might be on to something. The week I stayed with Arty, she called about three times asking if he had signed the contracts for KDP to take over the logistics of the product line so they could start making them to sell on KDP. Arty didn't seem too keen on signing those contracts." I looked at Myra in the rearview mirror when she said that. That was a turn. But why wouldn't Arty want to sign it? Surely it would have made his and Triston's life easier with KDP producing the products. From what I understood, they would still have ownership of the products, but of course, the pricing would be different. They would have to purchase the products from them for the salon, but I didn't see anything wrong with that. I also hadn't read those contracts. I'm sure they would've had their lawyer look them over to make sure they were aboveboard.

"Did he ever say why?" Pearl looked over her shoulder at Myra.

"Not to me. He was always quiet after he got off the phone with her. I'm sure it killed him every time she called since those products were Triston's babies," Myra explained.

"I would love to get my hands on those contracts. But I'm sure they've had their lawyer look 'em over." Myra just shrugged her shoulders, as if she had no idea. She didn't know any more than me or Pearl, and she had stayed with him for a week after Triston's death. I'm sure that big loft has to be a lonely place to live without Triston being there, even if he had Chipper the cursing bird to keep him company.

We had made our way into downtown Barnville. We had just passed the Barnville welcome sign that read *Gateway to the Lowlands*. Barnville was situated at the junction of US Route 278 and SC Highway 64. It straddled South Carolina's regional divide between the Midlands and what we call the Lowcountry. It's literally the halfway point between the upstate and the Lowcountry. Barnville was also known for producing peanuts, watermelons, cotton, and grains.

I saw the Langston's sign up ahead, got into the left lane, and turned my signal light on. I hated this light. It seemed to stay red forever. Down the road on the right was where the sheriff's department and coroner's office were located. I would have loved to stop by and see Pick and Birdie, but I knew it was too soon. I didn't want anyone to get any ideas of why we would show up at the police station and coroner's office for no good reason. Pick was probably out with Hansen, anyway. Even though Pick was the sheriff and they weren't partners, Hansen tended to tag along with Pick. I'm sure it was on-the-job training in preparation for Hansen to take the reins as sheriff. Pick had been the sheriff for most of his adult life, and I couldn't see anyone else doing his job. However, we were all getting older, and at some point, we realize that it's time to pass the torch to the next generation and enjoy retirement while we still have some life in us.

After what seemed like fifteen minutes, the light changed, and luckily, no cars were coming our way. I turned left into the Langston's parking lot.

"Okay, we go in and Myra, act like you're looking for something to buy. Tell them you have a meeting with one of those boards you're on and would love a new necklace to wear to the meeting. Tell Fred you want a statement piece and show him or Jenny this picture to see if they have something similar. I'm sure if they see it and it was one of their pieces, they may say something about it and who purchased it." I gave Myra my phone and in two seconds, she had sent the picture to her own iPhone. I still hadn't figured that out and probably never would. I'd have to give it to Steve Jobs; the phone took some pretty pictures, but all those apps didn't make a lick of sense to me. You'd think since I worked for Bell South my whole life, I'd know something about phones. But these were little computers. Not phones!

"Sounds good, Thelma." Myra had sat back and started to open the Cadillac's door.

Something was really off with Pearl today, and she was scaring me. She was almost despondent. She sat there, and I finally asked her, "Are you going in with me and Myra?"

She looked at me rather void-like and said, "Of course I am." But she wasn't undoing her seat belt or making any move to get out of the car.

"Pearl, what's going on with you this morning? And I heard you when you said you didn't sleep well last night, but the way you're acting is scaring me."

"Oh Thelma! I didn't want to say anything to you or Myra about what happened last night that kept me up."

"Well, it can't be that bad. You're acting like one of those zombies Charlie watches on the TV, but your brain ain't showing and your face doesn't have huge holes in it." I turned to her. I really had begun to worry. What happened that seemed to spook her so much? Or was she depressed? I'm not Dr. Phil and I can't just go around and diagnose people like he can.

"It's Pick."

"Pick? What in the world does he have to do with you not sleeping?"

Then it hit me. "No!" I wanted to put my hand over my mouth to keep her from seeing the smile forming.

"See, this is why I didn't want to say anything." She crossed her arms around her chest.

"Well, you haven't. So, you've won on that part."

Myra looked in Pearl's window and said, "Are y'all coming?"

I used the window control button to lower Pearl's window. "Myra, could you just go on in? We'll be there in a second."

"Okay. See you soon." Thank the Lord Myra wasn't the jealous type. Often Pearl would clam up around everyone but me. Believe me, I know it's weird, but it is Pearl. Bless her heart.

"Pick came over last night and asked me to go out with him to the Applebee's in Barnville." She was trying her best not to look my way. I was wondering how long it would take him.

"And."

"And I accepted, but I have reservations about all of it."

"Pearl, sweetheart, don't make such a big deal out of it. He's always had a thing for you, and I never understood why you never reciprocated. I knew you liked him."

"That's the problem. I do. But Thelma, I've been by myself for over sixty years, and now I'm just supposed to open up my life and allow someone to come in and turn it upside down?"

"Oh Pearl, he doesn't want to turn your life upside down. He's not asking to move in with you. You may realize that you're better off as friends than companions, or you may not. There's nothing wrong with dipping your feet in the water, and if the water is too hot to handle or too cold to touch, then there's no harm done. You'd have a nice dinner with a wonderful guy. That's all." I was looking toward her with compassion for that scared little girl who still lived in Pearl's mind and heart.

"Putting it that way makes it sound more reasonable. I don't know why my mind kept going so far ahead of things. And he is such a gentleman."

"Pearl, your face is glowing talking about it. I think the problem is that you feel the same way he does, and you're scared to death. You don't think I felt the same way when Charlie asked me out? Of course, we were a lot younger, and the expectations were different. But you don't have to have any except to go to Applebee's and order some baby back ribs." I had smiled at her like a doctor telling her he had to put stitches in her head. Yeah, they are there, but they won't hurt. I was tempted to ask her if she wanted a sucker for her doctor's visit, but I don't think even she could have followed that train of thought.

"You?" She had sheepishly smiled.

"Of course. At our age, we need to get out and live Pearl. Don't waste the time you have left on shouldas and couldas. Go out there and let him wine you and dine you. You might just like it, you know?"

I suppose that was all she needed to hear because before I could say another word, she had unbelted herself and was out of the car, leaving me to look at her back as she got out. She turned back to the car looking like my best friend and said, "Well, are you coming in or what?"

"I'm coming," I said, opening the door. She was waiting for me at the front of the car. I grabbed her hand and held it. I squeezed hers and she squeezed back. Then I knew she would be okay with whatever happened. But I also knew that this meant things were really going to change. Now I was the one getting jealous.

All these years, when I called her to do something, she was always game. But if she and Pick hit it off, like I'm thinking they will, I'll have to be second fiddle to Pick. I was a little saddened and realized how selfish and childish that was of me. Pearl was a beautiful person inside and out, and any man would be lucky to have her. Then I just smiled at her as we walked into the store, holding hands. The bell over the door alerted the Langston's that they had company.

Once we were in the store, she found her stride and started looking at bracelets. She loved to wear bracelets. I'm not a huge jewelry fan. Don't get me wrong, I have a good amount of costume jewelry, but I didn't care if it was the real thing or not. Sure, I loved beautiful stones, but with costume jewelry, I always felt like I could have my bling and wear it, too. I would be scared to wear some of the earrings, bracelets, and necklaces Myra wore all the time. You could buy a car with a tennis bracelet she owned, but that was what made Myra so special. She loved wearing high-end goods, but she never allowed them to define her. I was floored when she asked if she could borrow a couple of my costume necklaces. They were truly statement pieces, and she wanted to make a statement. I had known her to lose a diamond earring that could probably pay for two of my car payments, but she was so pragmatic about things like that, she would never make a big fuss over it. She'd just go and buy another pair. That way, if she lost another one, she had an extra to spare. I was a lucky woman when it came to friends. I had to admit that I loved Pearl and Myra like sisters.

Myra was talking to Jenny Langston when we walked in. Pearl beelined to the necklace display. I wanted to see if Myra had had any luck.

"Hey Jenny," I said, coming up behind Myra. Jenny smiled that ten-thousand-dollar smile of hers because she had implants. She was so bucktoothed when we were in high school together that she could've eaten an apple through a picket fence. She had come a long way since high school. Like Myra, you could tell she shopped in some of the most luxurious boutiques. She had a beautiful short bob tucked behind one ear. Her white hair looked amazing.

"Thelma." She came out from behind the counter and hugged me and Myra. Like Myra, she also smelled expensive.

"I'm so happy y'all thought about us. We love seeing you three. It's just like high school all over. If you see one of y'all, you see all three. I envy that type of friendship. Most women can't do it. They're always trying to outdo one another when all they really need to do is love one another." I wanted to say amen and sing "Kumbaya," but I thought it would be tacky, so I didn't.

"I totally agree Jenny. It's been awhile since I've shopped at Langston's." I let the Langston part hang in the air to suck up to her. She loved that. They were the most prominent jewelry store we had, and I wanted her to know that I knew it, too.

"You are so sweet to say that," she said, placing her hands on the corner of the counter, making sure she didn't mess the glass up with fingerprints.

"It's the truth. You and Fred have always been the store I always talk to my ladies about." Yes, I was going a little overboard. I knew it and she probably did, too. But that didn't mean she didn't like it. She loved it. It would be like if you were in the presence of the Queen and didn't bow.

"What are you ladies looking for, Myra?" she asked nonchalantly.

"I've got a board meeting in a few nights, and I wanted to see if you have a necklace similar to one that I like." Myra showed her the picture she had sent to herself in the car.

"That's gorgeous," I said unsurprisingly.

"Isn't it," Jenny agreed, "and I hate to tell you, but that was custom made for one of our customers."

Jenny was making this easier than I thought.

"Custom?" Myra asked, as if it deflated her.

"Don't you worry, hon, let me get Fred out here, and see how long it would take him to make one for you just like it." Jenny smiled that ten-thousand-dollar smile. Who was she fooling?

"Jenny, you're a lifesaver," Myra exclaimed and beamed at her as Jenny walked to the back of the store and through a beautiful heavy golden curtain hung to hide the back from the front.

I'd love to see what they had back there.

"This is easier than I thought it would be," I whispered in Myra's ear.

"We still have to get them to tell us who they made it for," Myra whispered back. She was right. Hopefully, since they knew Myra had a deep pocketbook, we'd get the name. That was what we were here for, anyway.

Fred Langston came out of the back and was pushing his plaid tie tighter around his neck. He had on a light blue suit, perfect for the warm spring weather we were having.

"Good morning, ladies." Fred sounded like a funeral director when he spoke. "Lordy, Lordy, Lordy, it's been a long time since I've seen you three together. Hello Myra." He grabbed her hand and held it for effect. "Thelma. Pearl."

"Hey Fred," Pearl said from the necklace case across the U-shaped counter. I could tell she had more pep in her step after the talk we had in the car. I was also wondering if she was thinking about buying something for her date with Pick tonight. But she was careful not to even mention that word. The kids these days didn't *date*. They *talked* to each other. I suppose that meant FaceTiming them and talking into the wee hours of the night. I used to have to sneak out to meet Charlie after bedtime. My mama would have tanned my hide had she known. I would have tanned my hide had I wound up pregnant!

"So, Jenny mentioned that you have one of our pieces that you want me to re-create? Surely, you want something different from what someone else is wearing. Am I not right?" Fred said with very proper English and no southern accent at all. And believe me, before he met Jenny, he was trailer park trash. I had no idea what she saw in Fred Langston. Although I have to say just his name sounds expensive. Look at him now with the most prestigious jewelry store in Barnville County.

"Fred, you know me too well," Myra said, waving a hand at him playfully. "But I saw this necklace and thought maybe you could make me something similar." Myra showed him the picture. He raised his black Andy Rooney eyebrows as if he knew who had purchased the necklace. I hoped he wouldn't be reluctant to tell us.

"Myra. You know I run a very reputable business here. But for the life of me, we could make you something that has real stones. The person who bought this . . . well, let's just say that police officers aren't known for making a lot of money."

You could have bowled me over. A police officer? Then Myra went in for the kill.

"Police officer? Yes, I do agree. I would like something a little more, how should I say this—more substantial."

"I would definitely agree," Fred responded hopefully.

"But I have to say, Fred, this police officer has really good taste because for the life of me, when I saw this necklace, I thought it was the real thing. He must be a good police officer to have such good taste." It was like watching a dentist pull teeth with someone on laughing gas. He couldn't help but stumble all over himself.

"Why yes, I would say that's a perfectly accurate point. Detective Hansen has the most impeccable taste," Fred said discreetly, lowering his voice even though we were the only three people in the store.

"You mean Handsome Mulvaney bought this?" Myra was just as hush-mouthed as he was.

"That he did. And I had to pick the best stones I could to make it look impeccable, because his girlfriend knows quality when she sees it."

"Darn, he has a girlfriend." Myra had started to tug on that tooth.

"Oh yes, and from what I hear, she has wonderful taste. You probably know her, Myra. It's Katie Smith. She worked with Triston at his salon. I hope they can keep the salon open. Jenny goes there to have her hair done and she would be lost without her hairdresser, Bridgit Kearns."

"Is that right? I've been going to Triston since they opened and I'm happy to say that Arty is going to keep the salon open. Thank heavens. And Bridgit is a doll baby."

"I'm so happy to hear that. Jenny will be relieved. We both can't even imagine what you and Pearl went through, Thelma. And you too, Myra. I know you three were very close to Triston." He was looking straight at me, but all I was thinking about was Hansen buying that necklace for Katie Smith. Surely

Hansen didn't kill Triston. Or did he? 'Cause one thing is for sure, Katie Smith ain't strong enough to carry Triston's dead body into that Sunday school room. Myra elbowed me out of my trance.

"Oh yes, Fred, it was the worst thing I've ever seen. And poor Pearl was the one to find him. It gave us both a fright and still does," I said, thinking about Katie Smith. I kept thinking about what the M was for.

"Fred, since we all know now, what's the M mean on the back of the necklace?" I asked him in hushed tones. By this point, Pearl was beside me, listening intently.

"Oh, that's for her middle name: Katie Mae Smith," Fred replied like he was sharing the juiciest gossip in town. Katie Mae Smith. I couldn't believe what I just heard. Surely she couldn't have had anything to do with Triston's death. Or could she? She was his number two on the floor. Arty ran the salon, but other than Triston, Katie knew just as much about hair as he did. She was Triston's first assistant when he opened his first shop downtown on Flop Eye Street. Boy, did Triston and Katie Mae Smith come a long way from where they started. With the clientele she had and the prices she charged, she would definitely have a keen eye for expensive jewelry. But did she know the necklace was fake? It was beautiful. Fake or not.

"You learn something new every day," I distractingly said to Fred. I hoped he couldn't tell.

"Yes we do, don't we Thelma? And Pearl, it's so good to see you too. You still have the most gorgeous eyes." Fred was laying it on thick. Pearl did have pretty blue eyes for a sixty-year-old. But the way he said it was as if she looked like Elizabeth Taylor.

"Thank you Fred. My mother had blue eyes too." Pearl smiled back at Fred.

"Okay. Let's get down to business. So, Myra, are you sure you want me to make you something similar to what Katie Mae has? Or would you rather up the notch and have a Langston piece?" I have to give it to him. Fred knew how to sell jewelry and he also knew how to make it too, which put him miles above anyone else in Barnville. Who wouldn't want a Langston piece?

"And Fred, when you're finished with Myra, I would love to see a couple of your bracelets you have out," Pearl said quietly. It was like we were at a funeral home instead of buying jewelry. Of course, I wasn't buying anything. I didn't wear much jewelry to start with. And I surely didn't need a Langston piece.

"Of course, Pearl. Jenny." Fred raised his hushed voice a bit to get Jenny's attention. She must have been at that curtain listening because she came out immediately and led Pearl to the glass case where the bracelets were.

"Fred, you know me. I want a Langston. But can you have it done in two days? I know I'm asking a lot, but I have a board meeting with Sutherland and Sutherland, and I need something new to wrap around my neck. I wouldn't want them to think I wear the same ole necklaces all the time," Myra told him. Now who was laying it on thick? I didn't mean for her to come in here and buy an expensive necklace.

We just came to get info, and Lord have mercy, we did.

But how did Hansen and Katie Mae Smith play into this?

I couldn't see Hansen having anything to do with this. But something was off, because he did give her the necklace. I wonder if Pick ever got her prints off of it. If she did have something to do with Triston's death, that would make her the number one hairdresser at Triston's salon, and that could be lucrative. Especially if she was getting his clientele, and KDP used her to help sell the products!

"Let me go in the back. I just got in the most fabulous stones yesterday that I think you would love, Myra."

"That would be fantastic, Fred. There's nothing a woman loves more than beautiful gemstones and diamonds," she told him as he started walking backward with that light bright smile of his. What was it with people who had money? They always have the whitest teeth. I'd bet if he was outside in the dark, his teeth would shine. I suppose money could buy you a beautiful smile. But at what cost? We were about to find out. But I knew Fred too well. He wouldn't tell Myra the price of the stones or what the necklace would cost. We were dealing with people who, if you had to ask about the price, then you couldn't afford to have a Langston piece! They were known for quality and that meant money where we come from. Course, you could probably put a good down payment on a house for this Langston piece Myra was going to have made.

Myra turned to me, and she looked giddy. Like a child in a candy store.

"Myra, I didn't mean for you to buy an expensive necklace. I thought we were coming just for info alone," I whispered to her so Jenny couldn't hear from where she and Pearl were looking at necklaces.

"I know, but I do need a necklace for this formal I'm going to for the PAW Ball next week." Even though Myra didn't own a dog or cat, she was an avid animal lover. She attended the PAW Ball to help raise money for the premiere pet rescue in Barnville every year. The organization could find you almost any type of dog you wanted if you waited long enough. Plus, they spayed and neutered them before they would allow you to bring them home. You also had to have a fenced yard. They had strict rules regarding re-homing requirements.

But I'm sure they had seen the worst things a human could do to an animal. I give to the ASPCA. It's the organization that televises the most pitiful dogs left out in the heat or the frigid weather. I just hope the money goes to helping animals get a chance at a normal life in a forever home. Those commercials got so sad that I started changing the channel. With Sarah McLachlan singing the saddest song and showing those poor dogs being starved to death, trying to survive in the snow, or tied up with a chain around their neck and no doghouse in sight, it was so pitiful that sometimes I just cried. Now, I just turn the channel.

They were already getting twenty-five dollars a month from me. They didn't need my tears too.

Pearl came over with Jenny. She had three necklaces in her hands and one was already on her neck.

"What do y'all think? I love them all." Pearl pushed her neck up so that the light flickered on the necklace she had on her neck. It was gorgeous. But so were the other three she had in her hands.

"Pearl, honey, I love the one you have on," Myra said, smiling at her.

Pearl was smiling, too. It's amazing what diamonds will do to a woman. Just a few minutes ago, she was morose and now she was grinning like she just got away with stealing TVs out of Walmart. I just prayed she had her Amex with her. Even though Pearl had never married, she had always been frugal, and probably had more money than me and Charlie put together. I know they were paying her good money when she was a nurse at the medical center in Barnville. Because they had a nurse shortage, she could just about ask for any wage she wanted, and if it was within reason, she would get it. I know that she sometimes works there now and they pay her close to fifty bucks an hour!

"I agree with Myra, Pearl. The one you have on is gorgeous and I love the rose gold, too. It looks so good with your complexion."

"That's exactly what I told her, Thelma," Jenny piped up and smiled like she was about to win the lottery. Maybe Jenny was because it didn't have a price tag on it. I looked!

"I'll take it, Jenny," Pearl told her. Jenny smiled again, showing those expensive teeth of hers. It was like a shark in a pool filled with blood, looking for something to sink those teeth into. "Pearl, would you like it wrapped, honey?"

"Jenny, if you don't mind, can I wear it out of the store?"

"Of course you can, honey." That shark just got lunch and possibly dinner too!

"Thank you so much." Pearl was beaming from ear to ear. I prayed she and Pick had a wonderful time, even if it was just Applebee's. I've known Pick for a long time, and he treasured his wife. If anything came of this, I was sure he would treasure Pearl, too. She was always the one that got away.

Fred finally came back out and had all types of stones on a beautiful black velvet display that showed off the stones. You could tell he really did just get them in because they were all sizes and types. Now it was Myra's turn to smile. She still had her real teeth, which was something to really smile about.

I was still reeling from what we had learned about the necklace. I couldn't believe it belonged to Katie Mae Smith and that Hansen Mulvaney had given it to her. I never even knew they were a couple. How did I miss that? What other secrets did I not know? And the other thing that kept nagging at me was the fact that we still hadn't asked Arty where he was that night. I'm sure I could get Myra to ask him so that he wouldn't think a thing about it. But if Arty had something to do with it, which I still truly doubted, Myra could be in danger, and I didn't want to put anyone in danger. Hopefully, "Mission Hairdresser" would lead us to some more clues as well. Surely the girls at the salon were about to burst to spill the tea, and we needed our ladies to come prepared with a large tea set.

Chapter Ten

AFTER MYRA HAD BOUGHT the equivalent of a small town at Langston's jewelry store, the only thing we talked about on the way back to Sunnyside was the necklace belonging to Katie Mae Smith. I had never heard anyone call her Katie Mae before. Was it something that Hansen called her because he was sweet on her? Then the other question was even scarier. Was Hansen in on the murder? To say that all three of us were reeling from what we had just heard was an understatement.

Myra had also agreed to talk to Arty and find out what he had been doing on the night Triston was murdered. I also shared my reservations about her going to talk to him alone. I couldn't lose Myra. Not to someone who might be unhinged. I wasn't saying Arty was, but someone in this small town was a cold-blooded killer. With all the thoughts running through my head, I could hardly drive back to Sunnyside. I was so preoccupied with my thoughts running rampant in my head that I was afraid we wouldn't make it back home safely. I slowed down and became quiet, trying to center myself. I was also trying those deep breathing exercises I had seen on one of Oprah's shows.

It wasn't working worth a damn.

Then, I thought, *who am I kidding*? I turned into Jack's Gas It Up, which was the midway point between Barnville and Sunnyside. I had Myra hand me my bag, which I usually kept in the passenger seat, but since Pearl was there, I just put it in the back seat with Myra. They hadn't said a word. I think they were lost in their own scary thoughts as well. Had we found someone who was in on Triston's murder, or was there a simple explanation? We didn't know, and for me, that was debilitating. I was good at knowing the goings-on in Sunnyside. People told me things they wouldn't even tell Pastor Fairchild.

The mere fact that Hansen was dating Katie Mae Smith, and I didn't know about it, made me want to scream. I couldn't believe this. I needed more spies, and I would do whatever I needed to do to find out just what was going on with Hansen and Katie, and find out why her Langston necklace was found in the very spot someone used to bring Triston into the church after killing him. And why didn't the CSI team find it? They looked like they had slacked off on this murder investigation from the start. Almost as if knowing what Moon Pie Hubbard would do.

I grabbed my purse from Myra and rummaged around until I found my bottle of Xanax. Who was I kidding with all this deep-breathing mess?

I didn't do yoga and already knew how to breathe.

What I needed was a Xanax. I prided myself on not taking them often, but sometimes things call for something stronger than a cigarette, which I had before leaving Langston's. I got out of the car and went into Jacks to grab me and the girls something to drink. I got me and Pearl a coke in the glass bottles and Myra a huge Mountain Dew. After sharing small talk with Jack, I headed back to the car. I handed the girls their drinks and opened mine. I popped the Xanax into my mouth, cocked my head upward, and took a huge swig of the coke. The pill slid down my throat and the coke was cold and strong. Just how I liked it. I would only buy them in the glass bottles because they tasted better, and you got five cents back for taking each bottle to the recycling bin in Sunnyside. Charlie and I didn't drink many soft drinks, but I always had a six-pack of glassed cokes in the fridge, just in case somebody needed one.

I knew in about ten minutes my mind wouldn't be wandering all over the place like a wolf looking for food in the dead of winter. That's exactly what my brain felt like right about then. My psychiatrist would be proud of me for taking the pill in such circumstances. But I would never tell him about what was going on in my head. I might find myself locked up in a rubber room at some hospital, where they'd drug you up 'til you had drool running down the side of your mouth.

Once the Xanax had slowed me down to a pace where I could think, I looked into the rearview mirror and asked Myra, "When do you think you'll stop by Arty's place? I don't want you going by yourself. I no longer trust anyone who was in Triston's orbit on a daily basis. Not after we were blindsided with that information about Katie Mae's necklace." I emphasized the *Mae* part of her name since none of us had ever heard it before today.

"Thelma, you know Arty didn't have anything to do with Triston's death. Believe me, I was there for a week with him, and he was so depressed the whole time. The only person he really wanted to talk to was Chipper, and I think that was because Chipper had actually chosen Triston over him. And now Chipper was grieving as well." Myra took a huge gulp of her Mountain Dew.

"Let one of us go with you when you ask him about that night."

"Thelma, I promise you he's harmless."

I didn't believe Arty had anything to do with Triston's death, but I still didn't trust anyone. Not anymore. If Hansen and Katie Mae Smith were dating, it went straight under the radar, and if that had, what else had? What scared me the most was not knowing. We prided ourselves at the Ladies Auxiliary about knowing pretty much everything that went on in Sunnyside. I suppose we were slipping, and we couldn't do that. There was too much at stake.

"What are you going to say to him?" Pearl looked over her shoulder to look at Myra in the back seat.

"I'm just going in and acting like nothing is wrong. Then I'll ask how things are going at the salon and allow the conversation to come back to that night. I was with him for a whole week. I know he'll eventually bring up that night, or at least give me the chance to do it without him thinking I'm snooping."

"Whatever you do, please be careful," Pearl said.

"I left a few things in the room I stayed in downstairs, so that should give me enough cover to go over without raising any alarms. I also want to check in on him. Y'all don't have to worry about me, and once I find out what happened with him that night, I think it would be good for you two to come with me just to check on him."

I was thinking Myra was being too confident, but what could I say?

I would be the same way.

"You're right about that. We all three need to go over and make sure he's doing as best as he can. The ladies are still bringing food to him. I spoke with June Bug the night before last and asked her if she would make sure Arty was taken care of, at least when it comes to food. She told me she wouldn't let me down, and I know if she says she'll do it, it'll get done."

///////////////////////////////////////

Once I finally got back home, I took out a cigarette from my antique cigarette holder and lit one. I sat at the kitchen table. Our kitchen was small and our table, located over by the window, comfortably seated two people: me and Charlie. However, it could easily seat three if needed. After all, we weren't socialites who invited people over to the house that often. Myra and Pearl came over more than my daughter. Of course, she lived in Paris, which wasn't around the corner like Pearl's house was. Myra lived in a gated community off Shandon Street. It was a collection of what we referred to in town as McMansions. The only thing I couldn't wrap my brain around with the McMansions was that they were all built on top of one another. We had more yard space in the mill village, and we had postcard lawns. I supposed since they're so rich; they didn't want to have to worry about their yards, but I know Myra paid a small fortune to a landscaping company that kept her bushes cut like little Whoville shrubs and trees. The only time I had seen anything like it was the summer that Charlie and I went to Paris to visit our baby girl, Henri, and our grandbaby Lucie. They all skipped going to Versailles, because they had been more than three times. If I had known about all the walking, I would have skipped it, too, but seeing myself in the Hall of Mirrors was something else. Gold leafing everywhere you looked and there had to be over one hundred chandeliers dangling from the ceilings and statues that held them in the air. It was gorgeous. And the gardens were breathtaking, but they had over 1,900 acres of land! Do you know what all that walking does to your bunions?

I had gotten myself comfortable before calling Pick and telling him about what we had found out about the necklace. I wondered what he would say to Hansen. I know one thing: Pick never just played the fool. He'd say what needed to be said and if there was an answer he wanted to hear, he would hear it. He hadn't been sheriff of Barnville County for all these years because of his looks.

I picked up the phone and hit Pick's contact number. With these smart phones, you don't need to remember anyone's number anymore. The only numbers I knew by heart were Charlie's, Pearl's, Myra's, and my daughter Amber's. I didn't let my brain cells worry too much because if I needed to get ahold of anyone else, they were all on my contacts list.

The phone rang three times before Pick picked up. "Sheriff Lawson."

"Hey Pick. It's me."

He lowered his voice. "Hold on, let me close my door." I heard his door creak shut.

When he got back to the phone, I added, "Lord Pick, that door of yours needs some WD-40!"

"It's because the foundation ain't level." Pick seemed exasperated at something he couldn't fix.

"We've got bigger fish to fry, anyway."

"What happened?"

"Me, Pearl, and Myra thought it might be prudent to drive into Barnville and go to Langston Jewelers to see if they had sold that necklace that we found."

"What did they say?"

"Well, they sold it all right. Want to guess to whom?"

I could tell he was bracing himself. "Who?" he croaked, sounding like he needed some Pepto-Bismol.

"Hansen Mulvaney."

"No!"

"Yes. And he bought it for Katie Mae Smith."

"Katie Mae?"

"Exactly. We'd heard it's her middle name.

"Well, I can tell you this. The night Triston died, Hansen was with me all night from six o'clock until we showed up at the church the next morning. We were trailing some people that night."

"And you sure in all that commotion he couldn't have snuck away for twenty minutes or so around the time y'all think Triston's body was left in the Sunday school room?"

"Thelma, I'm positive. Hansen is my right hand in this office. Between you, me, and the wall, I'm thinking of retiring when my year's contract runs out. I told Hansen I wanted him to run for sheriff when that time came. There's no one better equipped to do this job than him. I told him I'd even campaign for him."

"Well, that sure makes me feel better. But it still doesn't answer why we found her necklace behind the church."

"You've got me on that one. Let me speak to Hansen and see if he knows of a logical explanation. They must have been dating for a good while now if he's buying her a Langston piece."

"Oh, good Lord Pick. The necklace was a fake."

"No!" He said, as if he had heard the juiciest gossip he'd heard in a long time, and then he laughed. "You bring the horse to water, but you can't make him drink. He should know better than to buy something fake from Langston's," Pick said, confounded.

"I agree, but I have to say that Fred Langston made it look real. I certainly thought it was real, and even Myra didn't notice that it was a fake."

"There is one reason it might have been lost out there. I don't know if you know this, but a lot of boys know about the woods behind the church and go back there for some . . . let's just say, alone time with their girlfriends, if you know what I mean?"

"At a church? Lord have mercy! What's this world coming to?" I was indignant. I couldn't believe kids were using our church's woods for some hanky-panky.

"I know Thelma. But Sunnyside is a small town and there aren't a lot of places for them to go, and you know, boys will be boys."

"Pick, I hope you're not condoning this."

"Oh no, not at all. I'm just telling you what I know about those woods."

"But Pick, they have places of their own. They don't need to be going behind the church to get their jollies."

"I agree with that. It does make you question why her necklace was back there. But why would she kill Triston? He was the one that took her under his wing, wasn't he?"

"He did. She was his right hand when it came to doing hair. If he was out of town, she would do some of his people for him. It had been that way as soon as he gave her a chair." I pulled another cigarette out and lit it with my pink BIC lighter. I took a draw and exhaled.

"Let me find Hansen and talk to him about Katie and see what he has to say. I'll call you back in about an hour if that time suits you."

"That works for me. I have to do some laundry, anyway. But don't keep me waiting too long or I'll have a mind to call you back."

"I won't forget. Not about this."

"Oh, and Pick . . . have fun with Pearl tonight." I smiled when I said it. I took another puff of my cigarette.

"Thelma, I have to say, I'm as nervous as a cat in a room full of rocking chairs."

I laughed. "Pick, it's like riding a bike. You'll know what to do."

"I sure hope so. I feel like I'm a little long in the tooth to be dating again."

"You ain't that old. 'Cause if you were, it would mean I was old, and I'm what I call 'at my prime,'" I said, laughing as smoke came out of my mouth with each laugh.

"Well, I truly like her. Pearl was the one who got away. I loved Sarah and still do. But it can get lonely when you come home each night to an empty house.

"Don't you tell Pearl this, but I think she feels the same way. Just go out and have some fun. That's what I told her. And if nothing happens more than you know you're better off being friends, you can still go out and have companionship. There ain't a thing wrong with that. And don't forget to call me back."

"I promise," he said and hung up the phone.

Chapter Eleven

I UNDERSTAND THAT HE HAS to be careful since he's not supposed to be investigating Triston's murder, but it had been two hours since I had spoken with Pick. I had done two loads of laundry and folded all my and Charlie's clothes and socks. What is it with socks? When I started washing his clothes, all his socks had their match, but once they were dried and fluffy, I couldn't find two socks that I knew were there when I washed them. It's one of life's little secrets that socks just disappear into thin air. I'm sure no one cares about me losing Charlie's socks. But I had to say something about them. Surely I'm not the only one who loses socks while washing.

Anyway, until I hear back from Pick, I feel like I'm going to go out of my mind. Maybe he's still talking about Katie Mae to Hansen. Even though Pick wants to crown Hansen as the next sheriff once he decides to retire, it doesn't mean that Hansen is going to open up completely to Pick about his private life. Maybe Hansen and Katie Mae Smith had been doing the nasty behind the church like some of the kids were doing.

I didn't want to think about that.

I wondered if the deacons knew about the kids going behind the church to play around. I surely hope not, because if they do and never thought it would be wise to tell me about this filth, we're going to have a problem. I've known most of the deacons all their lives and I'm almost positive if they had known something about this, they not only would have told me, but they would have also done something to stop it.

It's not only blasphemous, but it's also dangerous. What would happen if one of those kids went back there to make out, and they got bit by a snake? We would be liable and that could put the church in a very precarious position.

I decided to call "Pork Chop" Pierce. He would tell me if he knew this was happening, and he would've stood up to the other deacons. Surely they realized that this could put our church in a vulnerable position, subject even to being sued if something happened to someone on our property.

It was already 3:00 p.m. He would have eaten lunch already and taken his afternoon nap. I looked up his name in my contact list and hit the button to call him. He answered immediately. He must be like the rest of us, completely dependent on these phones that are listening to everything we have to say. I don't care what Siri hears me say. I don't say anything about anyone that I wouldn't say to their face. Plus, the last time I was with Amber and my beautiful granddaughter, Lucie, I had Amber change Siri's voice to an Englishman's voice. Now when I say anything to Siri, I hear a man with a beautiful English accent that just bowls me over every time I hear him. He sounds like Anthony Hopkins playing an Englishman. Sure, sounds better than hearing a female robot.

"Thelma Rue, to what do I owe this honor?" He sounded like he had just woken up from his afternoon nap. I'm glad I didn't call earlier. You don't want to interrupt Pork Chop's afternoon nap. You might get snapped at if you do. He was by far the oldest deacon we had, but even though his nickname was Pork Chop, he was still as sharp as a tack.

"Hey Pork Chop, I hope I didn't wake you from your afternoon nap?" I was fiddling with some fruit I had purchased at the grocery store. They had pears, black plums, and nectarines on sale, all favorites of Charlie's.

"Not at all. I got up about twenty minutes ago. What can I do you for?" Pork Chop always got to the point.

"I found out something that's been going on behind the church and want to bring it before the deacons to act on, before we get sued for negligence." I, too, could get to the point.

"You've definitely got my ear now." I could hear him sitting up straighter on the couch.

"The Ladies Auxiliary has found out that kids have been going back behind the church and possibly into those woods playing hanky-panky." I knew I'd have his ear now.

"Do what?" Pork Chop had obviously not heard anything about this. Apparently, the deacons *didn't* know about it either. Which was good, because had they known and not acted on it, I would have pitched a fit.

"Yup. I heard that from Pick himself. And then when we had one of our meetings, we went back there and found some things that shouldn't be back there, like a necklace for one." I wasn't about to blow our cover on the investigation. The deacons would find out once we had found the killer.

"Dear Lord. Thelma, do you know how long this has been going on?"

"I wish I did. All I know is that since Triston was found dead in that Sunday school room, there's been things I've found out about I'd never heard before." I sat down on the couch in our den/living room.

"Let me get ahold of Jimmy Pickles since he's the chairman of the deacons. I'll also call Skitter Smythe and Lester Gibs. I don't suppose Pastor Fairchild knows about any of this?" he asked, as if I'd call him before getting the pastor involved.

"Not that I know of. I thought to call you first before calling the pastor, since he has so much on his plate. He insists on handling all visitations for the sick and deceased members of the church and their families. I don't know how he does it all. Seems to me he should get some deacons to help. The Ladies Auxiliary could also help, but you know him. He's hardheaded and stubborn as an old farm mule."

I could hear Pork Chop give a phlegmy cough that rattled his chest. He'd smoked Marlboros without the filters all his life. Pork Chop had turned eighty-nine years old on his last birthday and to this day, smokes two packs a day. I know this because he comes out to smoke with me after Sunday School to get in a smoke before preaching starts. We had cigarette dispensers installed all around to keep people from throwing their butts on the church grounds. I had said something to him before about how he sounded. It worried me. He just laughed and said, "None of us are getting out of here alive." Which was true and at his age, he should be able to smoke as many cigarettes as he wants to. His wife, Magnolia, was only two years younger than him, but because she didn't have the stamina to get around anymore, which saddened my heart, she had to quit coming to the Ladies Auxiliary meetings. She could barely make it to the preaching services. Pork Chop and Magnolia lived across the street from the church, but still drove instead of walking.

"I'll make sure that all the deacons know what's going on and we'll put up No Trespassing signs in the back. We should've placed them back there after Pearl found that poor boy in the Sunday school room. Since someone was found dead in one of our Sunday school rooms, we've already contacted a security company to put cameras up all around the outside and the inside of the church. Between me and you, the cameras in the church will be hidden so people don't feel like they're being spied on. You know how some people can get, and the sad part is that it's for everyone's security." Pork Chop sounded very serious now, and I knew that what he told me would happen. I wouldn't even tell Pearl or Myra about the cameras being in the church. I don't know what they'd think about that, but I agreed it was for everyone's security.

"Thanks for listening to me, Pork Chop. I knew you would want to know what's going on."

"You know me well, Thelma. Rest assured this will all be taken care of."

"Please say hello to Magnolia from me and all the ladies. We sure do miss seeing her smiling face."

"You know I will. I need for you to do something for me if you would. Could ya put Magnolia on y'all's prayer list? She can hardly get around the house. Her legs done give out on her. She's got her rollator. I think it helps some, but we both know she ain't getting no better. It scares me, Thelma. I just had my six-month checkup with ole Doc' Williams and other than my smoking, he says I'm as healthy as a horse. If life were fair, it would be the other way 'round with all the smoking I do, and I have to admit to liking the taste of some good old-fashioned shine that Catfish makes. He still messes with that copper still of his. I have to give it to him. His shine has the smoothest taste I've ever had, so I suppose I like my alcohol to be illegal. I used to watch my grandpappy drank his shine every night on the front porch before going to bed. We'd be out on the porch shucking beans and watching lightning bugs blinking to one another like morse code before the sun went down. Then we'd take the beans into the kitchen if we hadn't shucked 'em all."

"My goodness, Pork Chop, that stuff will put hair on your chest. Charlie buys a pint every year from Catfish, too. I reckon he also likes to walk on the wild side. I tried it and thought my throat was on fire. It didn't seem smooth to me." Pork Chop laughed his phlegmy laugh. "Well, Pork Chop, I just wanted you to know. I know you'll do something about it. It's so nice talking to you. You're my smoking buddy. You know it's crazy how people are now about smokers. When we were knee-high to a grasshopper, everybody smoked. It looked so glamorous. I suppose when people started dying from lung cancer, it didn't look as glamourous as it had made us feel."

"You got that right. I wanted to be the Marlboro man. That's why I started smoking 'em and ain't never stopped."

"At your age, you ought a do what you want to do. You done outlived so many of these fitness nuts we knew that caught the cancer or got killed in a car wreck."

"Like I said, Thelma, we ain't getting out of here alive."

"You got that right. We ain't promised tomorrow. But I have to admit, I don't want it to come. I want to see my Lucie get married and have kids."

"I have a feeling we'll be like the 'cocka roaches' and outlive 'em all." He laughed again.

"I sure hope so, Pork Chop. Y'all have a good night. I'll see you soon."

"Yes, you will. Before I let you go, Thelma, I want to thank you on behalf of the deacons for being such a wonderful servant for the Ladies Auxiliary. No one can run it better'n you and I'm not just blowing smoke up your ass either, I truly mean it. You're always on top of anything that needs to be taken care of. You're a blessing to St. Johns and I hope you know that."

"That's so sweet of you to say." I was blushing on my end, but I wouldn't want him to see that. I also felt the need to be as strong as I could.

"It's the truth. So, tell Charlie we said hello. Y'all have a good one, hear?"

"We will Pork Chop. Thanks again."

"You bet. Bye, bye now." With that, Pork Chop hung up.

It was about four thirty when I saw the callback from the sheriff's department. I hadn't yet figured out how to exclude all the spam calls that come through to my cell phone on a daily basis, so I just let them go to voicemail. If you're not in my contact list, voicemail it is.

"Pick, it's 'bout time you called me back. I hope nothing happened at the police station that kept you away." I was pacing the kitchen floor again. If I kept this up, I was going to put tracks in our new parquet floors.

"Thelma, It's Hansen, not Pick. I'm sorry to bother you, but I need to ask you a few questions."

Hansen. I wondered why he called back instead of Pick.

"Hey Hansen. I suppose Pick told you what we found behind the church." I was biting on my top lip.

"Hey Thelma, I hope I'm not interrupting anything." He heard what I'd said when I answered the phone, so he knows I've been waiting to hear back from Pick. He just can't help it; he's always so well-mannered. That'll take him a long way when he takes Pick's place as sheriff. He would be a great replacement and a little easier on the eyes, too.

"No. Matter of fact, you can tell by the way I answered the phone I've been waiting to hear back from Pick about the necklace we found."

"Yes. The necklace." He sighed heavily.

"So, it is the one you purchased from Langston's for Katie?" I had to pretend I didn't know anything. I didn't want him to be angry at Jenny or Fred Langston for spilling the beans like they did.

"Yes ma'am, it is. I called Katie, but she's so busy at the salon, I haven't been able to talk with her yet."

"I'm sorry, Hansen. I don't know what to say. I was hoping that you could fill me in on what's going on. 'Cause when Triston left that night, Arty said he had a meeting. I always took it to be a business meeting. Maybe it was with Katie, but that doesn't explain why her necklace was found in the tall grass, next to the steps, at the back of the church." I was grasping at straws and I'm pretty sure he knew it.

"I'll be honest, there's been something going on with Katie Mae that I wish I could explain, but I can't."

"Can't or won't?" If he was going to play poker, I wanted to see his cards.

"It's neither. I wish I knew why you found the necklace behind the church. I think I know why, but until I speak to Katie, I won't know the truth and it's driving me crazy, Thelma. We've had some relationship issues, and it's like we get close, and then she starts pulling away. I don't understand what's going on, but I do try to be there for her. I feel like we're two ships sailing in the night, but on different voyages."

Not only good-looking and debonair, but a poet, too. *Dear Lord, have mercy!* I needed to sit down before my knees gave out on me. I tell you one thing, it's those eyes of his and that chiseled jawline. His eyes look like the bluest water in the Caribbean or some romantic place in Greece.

"I didn't even know that you and Katie were dating," I said and hoped he would continue talking about their relationship. "Surely it can't be someone else," I said, as an incentive to keep him talking. I hoped it wouldn't scare him away.

"I don't even know anymore. I think she may be seeing someone else, and it's not like my job allows a lot of downtime. When I do get time off, something happens, and I'm called to a crime scene since we only have four people in our division. I think she's growing weary of it."

"Hansen, let me tell you a secret about women, in general. We all want what we don't have. I suppose that's more of a human situation than just a woman's issue."

"I'm not following." He was the most handsome man for miles around, but he was still young and didn't have a clue about what a woman needs from a man.

"Let me just be blunt, if you don't mind."

"No, please do. It's driving me crazy, the not knowing how to handle it."

"Well, for one thing, women need to know that you're going to be there for them. I know you have a demanding job, but sometimes you just have to leave work at work. Hire some more people. Pick has already told me that once his term is up, he's going to retire, and he wants you to take over as sheriff, which I think is a wonderful thing."

"He told you?"

"Yes. Pick and I go back a long way. When I saw Pick on the day of Triston's death, I was floored by how he looked. Yes, he's still the good-looking man he has always been, but something about him was different. I could tell the job was working him instead of him working the job. Does that make any sense?" Here I was, acting like Dr. Phil again. I could hope that Oprah would call me up for a Super Soul Sunday show to talk about relationships.

"Sort of."

"What I'm saying is this. You may become sheriff, and if you do, that job can consume your whole life if you let it. Now I know when Pick's wife, Sarah, was alive, she wouldn't put up with Pick working all day long. There has to be a balance between your work life and your home life. If you're going to be sheriff, I would tell you to hire more deputies, especially for the Major Crimes Division y'all work in. You can't possibly do that job and have a normal life with the minimal number of people you have working the unit. There are just not enough hours in the day, or enough people to spread around. The people you have are top-notch, but it wouldn't hurt to start looking for some more people." I had told him what he needed to do if he wanted a real life and a good wife by his side.

"I know when Pick's wife died, a part of him died with her. That's why he's up at all hours of the night, going here and there, when he could have someone that he trusts in his division to keep the scene clean until he can show up."

"I'm afraid I've messed things up with Katie. I look up to Pick like a father. I've been talking to him about my relationship with Katie a good bit. My real dad passed away from drinking when I was in my early teens."

"Oh sweetheart, I'm so sorry to hear that about your father. But one thing's for sure, you can't get advice about relationships from Pick Lawson. When was the last time he went out on a date?"

"He has one with Pearl tonight. I thought you knew."

"I know that. But before Pearl, did Pick ever show any interest in any other women?"

"Ok, so what you're telling me is that if I become sheriff, I need to delegate more, so that I'll have time for my both my job and my family? I hope to marry Katie one day and would love to have a house full of kids. I guess I need to focus more on what needs to be done to make this happen."

"Exactly. I don't know what's going to happen there. I don't know if Katie's dug herself into a hole, or how far. I hope I'm not jumping to conclusions that aren't there."

"Well, you've been right on the money as far as the relationship thing. I'm going to talk to Pick and explain to him that I need more time off. The last thing I want is to be sheriff of Barnville County, and have no one to celebrate that with. And the night that Triston was killed, Pick and I were out following Katie around. I wanted to see if she was messing around on me."

"Well, I hope she never finds out about that. You need to come clean to her.

"I know. So far, it seems that she's just been with her girlfriends. But I also know that she could have hooked up with someone in one of the bars we saw her and her girlfriends go in." Hansen was a mess.

"Hansen, the first thing you do today is come clean with her. Show her the necklace first. Then ask her if she's been stepping out on you. If she has, I think she'll let you know, and then, if she's feeling slighted with your time, she'll probably let you know."

"I hope you're right Thelma. I love her and I want to make this work. She could have met a guy behind the church and lost the necklace then. I just don't know. But I'm going to ask her to tell me the truth."

"See how easy that is, Hansen? You already have a game plan. Stick to it and let her know how much she means to you. And let the chips fall where they fall. It's all you can do. And Hansen, you'll be a fine sheriff. Just learn to listen and learn how to allow others to help you. That's what a real man does. He gets out of his own way so that life can be his to live. Not the other way around." I needed a cigarette, but I couldn't find my antique cigarette holder.

"Thelma, thank you for sharing some of your wisdom with me. No wonder they all go on about you running the Ladies Auxiliary."

"Now who's blowing smoke?"

"No. I'm serious. Even Katie talks about you and how you and those women have done so much for Triston and his salon."

"Well, when you find a good hairdresser, you tell your friends about them. That's a woman's golden rule. You can divorce your husband, but it's harder to divorce your hairdresser. Hansen, I could be your grandmother. We all have a lot to learn. Just when you think you have everything figured out, you learn something new."

"I hate to have to go, but I am at work. Thelma, thank you so much. I don't know if your advice will save me and Katie Mae, but the next relationship I find myself in, I'll definitely know my priorities."

"That's how relationships work. You have to put the time into them. I hate that it's gotten so bad you feel you have to keep up with her. But that's not fair to you or to her. If you trust her, you won't be surveilling her. I have to admit you have a lot to sort out. Does she know that you want to run for the sheriff's position?

"Yes ma'am, she knows. I told her months ago when Pick told me he was retiring, but she didn't congratulate me. She got really quiet."

"Well, just do what I told you and follow it up with real actions by hiring more people. And let them do the grunt work for you. If Pick has a problem, you tell him to call me. Because if I knew he wasn't retiring, but started dating my best friend, he and I would have a talk. 'Cause I cannot allow him to break Pearl's heart."

"Thelma, thank you for telling me what I needed to hear. I love Pick like a father, but I want Katie to be my wife. I'll talk to her tonight. And if there's anything I need to tell you, I'll call you back if that's okay."

"Honey, you know it is. And I have to admit, you two would have some pretty babies!" I had to say it!

"Then they'd definitely look like their mother, but we're jumping the gun here. I have to make sure we're still dating first since I've turned our relationship into a crazy fiasco."

"Just remember that word—relationship—it takes two. She has to do her part and you have to do yours. Then you'll both be fine."

"Tonight, she and I are going to have a long talk." I could sense Hansen had been putting this talk off for a while. Good Lord, if you're tailing your girlfriend all over town, you're past talking. But I hope not. Katie was a good girl, and I know if he is truly sorry, she'll forgive him, especially when he gives her necklace back.

"One other thing, Hansen. If Katie loves you, she'll pick you. I wouldn't try to make her explain the necklace. If you know she went back behind the church with someone else, that may be something you'll have to live with. You've been cheating on her, too, with your job, and if that had never started, I doubt she would've looked at someone else for attention."

"You've been helpful and kind. Thank you so much. I feel so much better now that I got that off my chest. I hope you and Charlie have a good night."

"Good luck with your conversation with Katie. But if it doesn't work out, believe me, you'll find the perfect girl for you. Have a good one." With that, we ended the call.

Chapter Twelve

A GOOD NIGHT'S SLEEP was what I had needed, and a cigarette. I went through the house searching for my antique cigarette holder, and finally found it on top of the dryer in our pantry, which was really just a small closet off the kitchen that doubled as our laundry room. I felt so much more glamorous taking cigarettes out of the antique cigarette container than from a pack.

I had fixed myself a cup of steaming coffee, and I was in heaven. Nothing goes better with a cigarette than hot coffee. I know they're not good for me. Do you have any idea how many times I've read the surgeon general's warning on the pack before putting them into the cigarette holder? Myra had given me the vintage cigarette holder for Christmas last year with a tag on it that read, "If you can't stop them . . ." I loved it, although I wondered if the cigarette companies put out more cigarettes in the packs now than they used to. Myra told me she had seen it on eBay and instantly knew I would love it. For the life of me, I can't remember what I bought *her* last Christmas. All I remember was that it was a wonderful Christmas. Henri had gotten a chance to work remotely, so Amber thought it was the perfect time to come home for Christmas. Lucie was about to have her first birthday. She was born on January 9, 2022. It was wonderful having them home for Christmas. We combined a small family impromptu birthday party that Pearl and Myra both attended. Of course, Myra had to outdo us all by starting a college fund as her birthday present to the tune of $10,000.

Yes, you heard me. $10,000!

At the time I was furious with her! However, after she explained that even though she had married three times, she never had the chance of having a child (much less a daughter), and that she had always thought of Amber and Lucie like her own family, she made me cry for being such a jackass about the whole thing.

After talking with Hansen last night, I wanted to talk to Pearl. I also wanted to find out more about her date with Pick. I called her and asked if she'd like to come over. I sat at the kitchen table and took a long draw on my cigarette, exhaled, and took another sip of my coffee. I'll never be able to quit smoking at this rate. I also took my Xanax's.

I kept thinking about the investigation. I felt like my feet were in quicksand. Every time I thought we had a lead, it fizzled out.

There was something in the back of my mind that I had overlooked, but it wouldn't crystalize yet and I couldn't force it. I wasn't Miss Marple. I suppose I didn't have enough information yet for whatever was in the back of my mind to come forward, but I felt like I was getting close. I could feel it. I just hoped the killer didn't feel it or know what was going on. At least that's what I kept telling myself. I started to doubt if I knew what I was doing trying to carry on a murder investigation.

This wasn't the game Clue, and I knew I couldn't allow a butler to kill anybody!

I heard the storm door open and then a knock. I looked up and saw Pearl heading toward the kitchen. The sun was coming in through the side window shining on the kitchen table; it felt good on my joints. I think I might be getting arthritis. I have a doctor's appointment in a couple of months. That was a mighty long time for an appointment. If my joints didn't hurt now, they surely would by then. Arthritis must be a lucrative business if it takes that long to get an appointment.

Pearl waltzed into the kitchen wearing a cute pale-blue jumpsuit she had bought at Belk when they had their red-tag sale a couple of months ago. When it was all said and done, she paid six dollars for the jumpsuit. She looked like a million bucks in it.

I got up and we hugged each other. She went to the fridge and got a coke.

"Don't you look pretty!" I said to her, thinking that she might have another date tonight.

"Thank you. But I can't take the credit for it. After all, you picked it out."

That part was true. I had seen it on the rack and was looking at it for myself, but it didn't fit me even though it was a size twelve. I am taller than most women I know at five feet nine inches tall.

"You look good too."

"I called Pick when I got home yesterday and talked to him about Katie Mae's necklace." I blew the smoke up in the air so I wouldn't blow it on Pearl or in her face. That would be tacky and rude, and in this case, it didn't call for that. I wanted to know if Pick was a good kisser. I know in high school he looked like he would be a good kisser, but looks can fool you. Who knows what Myra would have asked her!

"What did Pick say about the necklace?" Pearl sat in her regular seat next to mine on the left.

"Well, I told him what we'd learned at Langston's and he was supposed to call me back. But guess who ended up calling me back?"

"It wasn't Pick?" Pearl was getting forehead wrinkles when she scrunched her face like she just did. I don't think mentioning this to her would be being a good friend. We weren't like Myra; we would age and do it like our mothers did, gracefully.

"No, it was Hansen. Apparently, he and Katie are having relationship problems because he puts that job before her." I sipped my coffee and took another drag of my cigarette, letting that gossip hang in the air like the smoke from my cigarette.

"Did he know why the necklace was behind the church?"

"He thinks that she may have been back there with another guy, but I told him he couldn't get angry at her for cheating because he was doing the same to her with that job of his."

"You have a point, Thelma." She sipped on her cold coke.

"So, he was supposed to have a talk with her. He told me that on the night of the murder, he and Pick followed her all over town to see if she hooked up with another guy. He said she went into bars, but he couldn't go in, or she would know what he was doing."

Pearl put her hands to her mouth and giggled like she did when we were twelve years old.

"I know. I told him that he had to hire more people for their department. Four people couldn't handle the Major Crimes Division for two towns. It is too much."

I looked at Pearl to see if she would say something about Pick accompanying Hansen.

"I can't believe that Pick would think that was okay." Pearl seemed dumbfounded. Bless her heart.

Changing subjects, I said, "So, we'll know tomorrow why that necklace was found behind the church."

"I suppose I'm going to have to have my own talk with my own boyfriend."

"Boyfriend? That was fast!" I couldn't believe what I was hearing. But Pick was the one that got away. I prayed they would make it work this time. But couldn't they take it a little slower? Of course, at our age, time is of the essence, so I suppose hurrying's not a bad thing as long as Pearl's happy.

"I know, but we stayed on the phone talking to each other until our chargers were about to run out. It all comes so easy with Pick. Thelma, I feel like we're back in high school until I wash my face before bedtime and see all these wrinkles. When did I start getting wrinkles?"

I wasn't going to touch that with a ten-foot pole. "Pearl, I'm so happy for you and Pick. Now we can go on double dates like we used to before I married Charlie." I hadn't added before Pick got away. She had learned her lesson.

"I was thinking the same thing on the way over here this morning!" She beamed at me while sipping on that coke like it was the last one in the world. I had more in the pantry that I hadn't put in the fridge because it was too full when I got groceries the other day.

"How was your date last night?

"Me and Pick went to the Applebee's in Barnville last night." She had a mischievous grin on her face.

"From the look on your face, you must've had a good time. But couldn't he find another place to take you?" I took another sip of my coffee. My cigarette was in the ashtray, but I snubbed it out. I wanted to enjoy my coffee and any gossip Pearl was about to spill.

"It was my idea. We had a wonderful time. I had forgotten how smart Pick was." Pearl took another tiny swig of her coke.

"Tell me more." I reached out and clasped her hand in mine. I was so happy for her. But her nursing that coke was getting on my nerves.

"Well, I didn't order anything that would make my hands dirty. I know they give you those cloths with the baby back ribs to clean up afterward, but no matter how bad I wanted them, I ordered a Caesar's salad with grilled chicken." Her face radiated. She had been alone for years. Every now and then, she'd go out on a date with someone, but it never led to anything.

"I felt like I was back in high school dating the boy I had a crush on all these years later. And to be honest, I still do

Thelma. I can't explain it. I had butterflies all night long. It was as if time had stood still." She smiled at me, and it was the best smile I had seen on her face in a long time.

"What happened after Applebee's?" I wanted to know if he could kiss.

"Well, we went riding around like we did when we were in eleventh grade. Thelma, he drove all the way to Barnville where we got milkshakes afterward from the Cook In and Out, and you know how high gas is now." Penny-pinching Pearl had struck again.

"They do have the best milkshakes," I agreed. "I always get their peach and pineapple. It sounds like they wouldn't go together, but the pineapple makes the peach even sweeter."

"I got the watermelon milkshake. They only have it during spring and summer. It was so refreshing with chunks of watermelon. I had to eat most of it with a spoon, it was so thick. We sat in the parking lot just talking up a storm, and before we knew it, it was going on ten thirty, which was why I am a bit tired this morning. I haven't stayed up that late since I watched Barack Obama become President."

I loved Pearl, but I wasn't going to talk about no Barack Obama. We didn't agree on politics. Not that I'm a MAGA woman. I'm more of a Ronald Reagan Republican, but from the looks of it, there weren't that many of us left. So I voted for Trump. I don't know anyone else that uses a gold toilet. Could you use bleach to clean it?

"I'm so happy for you, Pearl. I really am." I grinned at her like she had won the lottery and the wonderful thing was that maybe she had.

"Thelma, he talked about his wife for a bit, about her death, but then he told me that after she died, he had lost himself in that job of being the sheriff. He even told me he was going to retire when the next election comes around and that he's been grooming Hansen to take over. He is tired, and all he wants to do is leave and retire in peace. He told me that he didn't care if he ever saw another dead body." Couldn't blame him for that! I didn't want to see another one either.

"Pearl, I can't wait! He'll be asking to marry you soon. You watch and see."

"What?" I knew that would wake her up a little more.

"Pearl, you were the one that got away. I think if y'all keep dating, you never know where this could lead and y'all ain't getting any younger."

"You think so?" She had a weird look on her face. I couldn't tell if she was questioning my opinion or if she was constipated from that watermelon milkshake.

"I do. What would you do if he did?"

"Oh . . . I've never thought about it! I thought that part of my life had gone and went. I never dreamed that I would be dating someone in my sixties."

"Stranger things have happened," I said, elated for her. I was always worried that she would die alone and never fall in love with anyone. But from the look on her face and that jumpsuit, I was wrong all along. God works in mysterious ways.

The phone rang. It must be Charlie calling me from his part-time job at the Ace Hardware.

"Hello," I said absent-mindedly, still thinking about Pearl's date.

"Thelma, it's me." It was June Bug. Maybe she'd had her hair done and had some gossip for us.

"Hey, June Bug. How you doing, sweetheart?"

"I'm fair to middlin'. Listen, I don't know if this is anything, but when I went over to Triston's, I mean, Arty's condo, earlier this morning to bring over some more food some of the ladies had made, that woman from the KDP shopping network channel was there. And when I walked into the condo from the elevator, they didn't even hear me, because they were fussing up a storm at each other. I couldn't tell what they were fussing about, but whatever it was, she was hot under the collar."

"What happened when she and Arty finally saw you?"

"I was standing there with a cardboard box filled to the brim with food. I kept thinking if they didn't soon come and help me, I was going to drop the cardboard box on the floor. I should have gotten Tony to help me with it. He told me he would be glad to take it up there himself, but I thought it was more fitting for me to bring it, so they knew that the ladies were still doing our jobs."

"June Bug, was the woman's name Twilight? She would have been the one on the air with Triston when they had that soft launch for his product line?" I looked at Pearl and mouthed that it was June Bug. Pearl came close to me and I put the phone close to her ear and mine so she could hear what June Bug was saying as well.

"That was her, but she's not a blonde anymore. Now she's got dark brown hair with copper-colored highlights. I have to say she looks even prettier in person." I could tell this had shaken June Bug. She was always the quiet type, and I've never even heard her raise her voice.

"Did you hear them say anything? Think hard about it, June Bug. This could be important."

"Well, let me think a minute. I was so shaken up by it all. You know I don't like raised voices."

"I know you don't, honey."

Jesus wept!

"I could hear them fussing when I got close to the condo. They were making a mighty racket. When the elevator doors opened, they didn't see me at first. I remember her saying something about a contract or contact. I was so jilted by the whole thing that I was helpless." I'd never heard June Bug so upset.

"Don't you worry about it anymore. I want to personally thank you for taking that food over to Arty for me and the rest of the ladies. You're doing God's work and that's really all you can do. I'm sure whatever it was they were fussing about, Arty got it straightened out." Contracts? Had Arty not signed the contracts yet? They would probably allow KDP to take over the making of the products and the sales of them on their channel, too. What was so wrong about that? Unless they had changed the terms about how much Arty would get paid.

"I hope so, Thelma. I couldn't believe how that woman was yelling at Arty. It was like she wanted him to do something he didn't want to do. At least, that was the first thing that came to mind when those elevator doors opened up." I could see poor June Bug standing there with a cardboard box filled with food and them fussing so badly they didn't even hear the elevator ding.

"Don't you worry about it, June Bug. You hear?" I wanted to help her calm her down, but for the life of me, something she heard that might not register right now had scared her. I don't like it when my ladies worry about something like this.

"Thelma, I'll try and put this out of my worries, but I'll tell you one thing. She means business. She's going to get what she wants."

Dang!

"Listen June Bug, you probably walked in on them talking about what they were going to do with Triston's product line and if they were going to sell it on the KDP shopping network. That's probably all it was. Now you go about the rest of the day and don't you worry about a thing. Okay, sweetheart?" Pearl and I looked at each other conspiratorially. What had they been fussing about? What contract? Was Triston supposed to sign a contract? Was he murdered beforehand? These were all good questions that I didn't have answers to.

"Okay. If you think Arty is going to be okay," she said gloomily.

"Arty's a big boy and he can take care of big boy problems. So, go on about your day and just let it go." For a few seconds, she didn't say anything, and I felt a cold chill run up my arms. "You still there, June Bug?" I said, looking down at the chill bumps that had raised on my arms. When you turn sixty years old, the doctors don't tell you about all the hormone changes you go through. You think once menopause is over, it's the end of night sweats, hot flashes, and weight gain. But no. The more you age, the more different you look 'til one day you look in the mirror and don't recognize the woman staring back at you. Course, I've seen some women with mustaches. Thank the Lord that didn't happen to me! I'd die.

"I'm here, Thelma. Thank you for listening to an old woman complain."

"First of all, you ain't old. If you were, it would mean I would be that old too, and you know how I feel about that." She just laughed at me. Pearl, holding her coke, had had enough of craning her neck to hear June Bug and went to sit back down at the kitchen table.

When we disconnected, I looked at Pearl. "Were you able to hear?"

"I was, but do you think it means anything? I'm sure that Twilight Woods woman has a lot of things on her plate, and you know how Arty can be." Pearl was probably right, but something about it set my teeth on edge. I clamped down on my dentures and was thinking about what they could have been fighting about.

"Yeah, you're probably right, but it burns me up to hear that she was yelling at poor Arty. He's been through enough." I said, holding my warm cup of coffee in both hands.

Pearl and I talked more about her date and how he had asked her if she'd like to go to the drive-in theater off Carlyle Street. Charlie and I used to go, but they started playing the same movies each weekend, so we stopped going. The fun of it was putting the speakers in your car window. Of course, now you can hook it up to Bluetooth in your car. I had no idea what a Bluetooth was. Fortunately, Charlie's good with things like that since Amber's not around to help bring her poor mom into the next century.

Myra finally stopped by a couple of hours later. We were wrapping things up. I had to make dinner and had no idea what I was going to throw together, although I had been thinking of a bowl of hot tomato soup with a grilled cheese sandwich. Charlie and I both loved grilled cheese sandwiches with Campbell's Tomato Soup.

Myra stopped by to tell us that Arty didn't have an alibi, other than he had called the police that night to report Triston missing since he didn't come home.

"Thelma, he said that he and Chipper didn't get a bit of sleep that night. Chipper kept asking for Triston and Arty kept telling him he'd be home soon. To be honest, I think we all three know he didn't do a thing to Triston. It's just not in him." Myra looked like she had just run the Copper River Bridge marathon. She was sweating with all that cashmere she had on. Today had gotten hotter than the weatherman had predicted.

"I agree Thelma," Pearl said. "I don't think Arty had anything to do with Triston's death, either. You don't either, do you?" Pearl and Myra both looked at me quizzically.

"No. I don't, but it would be nice to be able to scratch him off the list. It's not looking good. Every person I had on my list is getting scratched off for one reason or another." I didn't know what to think. There was something I couldn't put my finger on.

"Did you ask him about Triston's meeting that night?" I asked Myra, who had gotten some paper towels off the counter and was busy dabbing at her hairline and patting lightly at her face.

I knew Myra would rather die than be seen without makeup. She told us once about making friends with some drag queens she had met at the Piggly Wiggly late one night in Barnville. They had hit it off, and she had gone to The Metro, where they were performing, and she got to go backstage. One of the drag queens sat her down and showed her how to put her makeup on correctly. I had always thought her makeup looked great until I saw her the day after she had learned from the best. Now she could contour her cheeks, make her nose look smaller, and even make her lips look bigger with the illusion of makeup. I asked her to show me some tips, but it was way too much makeup for me to wear. However, I have to say they know makeup better than any woman I have ever seen, except for Twilight Woods.

Her name was just popping up everywhere.

I looked at Myra after she had gotten the sweat off her brow without taking half of her makeup off. "He told me Triston said he would be back within the hour. He said Triston said he had a meeting, and he walked out. You should have seen Arty's face when he told me 'he walked out.' He almost started to cry but somehow stopped himself."

"So, he didn't know what the meeting was about? Doesn't that seem odd to you?" I asked Myra, but knew Pearl would weigh in too.

"No, not if he was in a hurry to go to the meeting and get back home. It may have been a meeting with someone at the salon. I don't know, and apparently Arty doesn't either." Myra started patting at her face again and went and got a bottle of water out of the fridge. We love Sunnyside, but living so close to the mill, we never drank water from the spigot.

"I agree, Thelma. If Triston was in a hurry and had some things on his mind, I could see him saying that because he thought he would be back home after the meeting. But either he didn't make it to the meeting or whoever he met could have been the killer." Pearl's eyes locked on to mine, her expression grave.

All I know is he left, and never came back.

Someone had killed him, and whoever it was wanted to see him suffer.

Chapter Thirteen

RIGHT BEFORE PEARL AND MYRA LEFT, Myra told us she had gotten tickets for the PAW Ball for all the ladies. She thought we should all go to the PAW Ball this year. I had never gone to the PAW Ball before, because I was afraid if I did, I'd wind up coming home with a dog or a cat that needed a home. I asked Myra why she wanted all the ladies to go this year. Surely there would be socialites all over, and Myra would be in her element.

I am a homebody if I am telling the truth, and I know there is no way Charlie would go with me. He'd rather sit in his recliner and watch *Gunsmoke*. But I also knew it was for a good cause, so I called Mitzi and asked her if she could help call the girls for me. I told her about Myra getting tickets for the ladies who were helping with the investigation. Mitzi had told me that she was already going, and she thought it would be good to have the ladies get our own table. It was a thousand dollars a table, but it would be plenty big enough for us all. I thought a thousand dollars was steep for a designated table, but she informed me that if we didn't have one, all the ladies would be spread out at other tables all over the Bi-Lo Center. I didn't want that. We were safer in numbers.

I asked Myra about the table, and she told me it was taken care of. So, I told Mitzi not to worry about getting us a table because Myra had taken care of it. Myra might have gotten it free with all the money she gave to the PAW Patrol.

We might even hear about Triston's death with all the socialites that go. I'm sure that would be a topic of discussion, since almost all the women from Barnville County and Sunnyside had been going to Triston or his salon for years.

I wondered if the salon still made Triston's Cherry Cokes, since it was used to kill him. Whoever he met that night knew him well enough to make one of his Cherry Cokes. I had never had one, and don't know if I would since the killer disguised the poison in his drink. I wonder if they put extra cherry juice and cherries to tap down on the taste of bitter almond oil. I had no idea if it tasted bitter or not, and wasn't about to find out if I could help it. But I could see Triston drinking it anyway, since the killer had gone through the trouble of making him his favorite drink. I'll bet he ain't drinking them in heaven. Speaking of Triston, I needed to find out about my hair appointment. I could tell the last few days my hair wouldn't do a thing, so I looked at my appointment card I kept on the fridge, and thankfully, it was tomorrow at ten thirty. I wondered who would do my hair. I called the salon and spoke to one of the front desk girls. I can't remember their names to save my life. She told me that they'd placed me with Sherry Haster since I had gotten pedicures with her in the past. She asked if I'd be comfortable with her doing my hair. I told her I would give Sherry a try, but that I couldn't promise anything. Sherry was nice and all and gave wonderful pedicures, but she had never touched my hair. But I would give her a try and see if I liked what she did. I may as well try to find someone else at Triston's because there really wasn't anywhere else to go in Sunnyside that was on the same par as Triston's salon. I'd get my cut done tomorrow, then have enough time to go to Belk to look for a new dress. I still hadn't worn my Easter dress since the church was still cordoned off because there was still an ongoing investigation. I called Myra and Pearl to see if they'd want to run to Belk with me tomorrow after I had my hair done. They both hopped at the notion, saying they also needed to find something to wear to the ball.

I got to the salon just after ten twenty. I was always a little early. You never knew what was going on at the salon. I could see Sherry's station toward the back of the salon, which seemed to give more privacy than most of the stations near the front of the salon. Most were side-by-side in a line that went six chairs down, and you could probably hear every conversation on both sides of you. Your ears would think they were at a tennis match trying to hear both conversations. Course I'd never heard of an ear lash but each time I tried to watch tennis I always felt like I got whiplash from watching the ball go from one side to the other. It just wasn't a sport I could get into.

The salon was hopping. All the stations were filled, but I didn't see any of my ladies here. I thought I'd see at least a few since the PAW Ball was tomorrow. Maybe they had appointments later in the day. I still hadn't heard from anyone about any gossip that was bound to be spreading around this place like wildfire. If you get all these women in a room this size, someone is bound to bring up some juicy gossip you could sink your teeth into. I was hoping I would hear some myself. The day was still young. I was sitting up near the front desk looking at all the pretty colors of the product bottles and the new 'do's being done.

Then Arty saw me and came over. He had that blasted bird on his shoulder! *Lord help*!

I'm surprised he didn't have bird poop all over his shirt. Maybe Chipper used a litter box. I know they could teach rabbits, opossums, and racoons to use a litter box, but I didn't know about birds. I knew I didn't like them. Chipper surely hadn't done anything to make me want to go out and buy a parrot Not with that potty mouth of his.

That bird had called me a bitch!

I hadn't been called that since high school. Most women who knew me knew better than to call me that. I'm a lady of the church, and I tolerated words like that from no one. Especially not from a bird that loved *Jerry Springer*. Tacky, tacky, tacky is what it is! I can't believe Arty let him talk like that. But I'd bet twenty bucks that Chipper didn't say things like that to Arty or Triston. God bless his soul.

Just pure tacky!

Arty came over to me in the waiting area.

"Thelma." I got out of my chair to give him a hug, but thought better of it since Chipper was on his shoulder.

"Well, I was going to give you a big ole hug, but I see you have Chipper with you today."

"He's been a godsend for me, Thelma. I wanted to personally thank you and all the ladies for being so kind to me. It just fills my heart every time I see all that food. I bought a food vacuum so I could freeze what I couldn't eat. I also gave some of my neighbors some of the food, too. It was a huge hit in the building. Is there nothing the ladies can't do? It seems like every day, someone stops by and brings some more food. If I keep this up, I'm going to have to buy all new clothes." He laughed, and I could see the laugh wrinkles on his face as he rubbed his stomach as if he was getting fat. He must have laughed a lot when Triston was alive. I know they loved each other. It was nice to see him laugh, especially with what he was going through.

"Well, we don't want you to have to worry about anything, especially food."

"I can't tell you how good your ladies have made me feel with their generosity and the pure joy they bring to me when they stop by to check on me."

"Yeah, I talked to June Bug." He looked weird when I brought her name up.

"She was the lady that came in when me and Twilight were having a difference of opinions, right?"

"That's her. To tell you the truth, she was worried because

she said y'all were fussing so much you didn't even hear the elevator ding when she stepped into your apartment." I smiled up at Arty and cooed at Chipper like Myra did.

"Here, hold him, Thelma, he loves to be loved on."

Dear Lord, have mercy!

The next thing I know Arty had placed Chipper on my shoulder. I kept looking out the side of my eye looking at him. I was too scared to move my head. I didn't want that beak of his to take a chunk off my nose.

"Hey Chipper," I said to the bird. I didn't know how to talk to no bird. "How's the pretty boy today?" I tried baby talk and, he seemed to relax a little. I think he liked the sing-song way you sound when you're using baby talk.

"Hello," Chipper called to me.

"Hello to you, Chipper. Are you having a good day?" I kept looking at him without trying to move my neck too much.

"He likes you, Thelma," Arty said. "He normally wants to come back to me when I've put him on other people's shoulders, but with you, he seems calm."

He might be calm, but I sure wasn't. I was scared he might start nibbling at my ear and take a chuck out of my earlobe. But he just bobbed up and down like he was break-dancing on my shoulder.

"I have to be honest, I don't know diddly squat about birds."

"All you need to know is that they need to be loved on, too. Ain't that right, Chipper?"

"Chipper loves. Chipper loves." Oh my, loves what? I couldn't for the life of me tell what Chipper loved. Hopefully,

Arty knew. One thing was for sure, he better not poop on my blouse before I get my hair done. I kept talking baby talk to him, "Chipper's so sweet."

Yes, I was sucking up to a bird! You would, too, if he was sitting on your shoulder with a beak that could take half your nose off!

"Chipper is a sweet boy." Arty took him back and placed him back on his shoulder. I hoped he couldn't tell how uncomfortable I was with that bird riding shotgun on my shoulder.

"He really likes you. He likes you a lot. I've never seen him sit on someone else's shoulder like that. You're a bird whisperer, Thelma." Arty laughed while he rubbed the feathers on the top of Chipper's head. I wouldn't have tried that. I was afraid if I put my hand to close, I'd end up with a nub.

"Pretty girl. Chipper likes pretty girl," Chipper said, looking at Arty and back at me.

"He thinks you're a pretty girl," Arty informed me.

"You sure Chipper has good eyesight? I'm far from being a girl. I have to say that when I was younger, I had men turning their heads. Now, I'm just an old fogey. The only way for me to get men to turn their heads is by running into them at the grocery store with my buggy. You'd think they thought it was on purpose, but you can't hardly turn the buggy's no more because one or two of the wheels don't work right."

"No, Chipper calls all women girls. I don't think he understands age. But he really likes you," Arty said that like I was going to take him home.

"Well, I think Chipper is a pretty boy." Two can play at that game.

"Chipper pretty. Chipper pretty," he said, then turned his head and was preening some feathers on the back of his neck. Just looking at it made my neck hurt.

"Thelma, I've got to do my rounds and make sure everyone is doing okay. We tried our best to place certain people with hairdressers we thought they would like. I hope you enjoy Sherry. I know she's done your pedicures before, so at least you know her. Can I get you something to drink?" This was what Arty was so good at, being attentive to his customers.

"Whatcha got?"

"Well, we've been making people Triston's favorite Cherry Coke. You have to try one. I know you'll love it." Chipper was bobbing up and down, calling me a pretty girl again. I hadn't heard that in a long time and I didn't even care if it came from a bird. At least he thinks I'm a pretty girl.

"That sounds good, Arty. I've never had one of Triston's Cherry Cokes before," I said, cooing at Chipper. I was beginning to act like Myra, the way she was oohing and aahing at that bird.

"I'll be right back. If they take you back, I'll have it brought to you at Sherry's station. Okay?"

"Sounds perfect."

He went toward the break room where I'm sure they had tons of cherries and cherry juice to make Triston's famous Cherry Coke.

I sat back down in the waiting room chair and was looking at a woman who had just had her color and cut done and was paying the receptionist at the front desk. I adored her cut. It looked like a stacked bob and the stacking in the back made her hair look thicker than it really was. She had very fine hair and I doubted she'd be able to make it look as good as her hairdresser. We all try to do our hair just like our hairdresser styles it, but we're so used to doing it our way, we normally go home and fix it the way we're comfortable wearing it. Triston always made my hair look gorgeous. I just couldn't get used to it. Charlie loved the way Triston had done my hair. I suppose since he's a man, he could pretend to be with another woman because every time I had my hair done, he would get that twinkle in his eye. The one that got me pregnant with Amber. I'd pretend I had a headache. Anything to get him off me. I love my husband, but he can be some kind of kinky when the mood hits. The only problem was it never hit me. I don't do kinky!

A skinny girl with pink highlights and a dragon tattoo on her right arm came up to me and introduced herself. "Hello, Mrs. Rue. My name is Ashley Gant; I'm Sherry's assistant today. She asked me to see if you were ready to come back to her station." She was a cute little girl, but with that tattoo and those pink highlights, it felt like she was trying to make up for something she didn't have. But of course, that's what the young kids do nowadays. They got tattoos to make their parents mad and put pink highlights in their hair to stand out or fit in. I really didn't know which. She took me to Sherry's station, where Sherry was just finishing sweeping up the hair around her chair.

"Hey Thelma, how are you doing today?" Sherry had a calming demeanor about her that automatically put you at ease.

"I'm doing good. I hope you are," I said, as she ushered me into her styling chair. She threw a cape around me and sat on a stool that was the perfect height for talking to her clients.

She started by putting her hands into my hair and checking out what Triston had done on the last cut. At least that's what it looked like to me.

"So, it looks like Triston was putting rounded layers in your hair to give you maximum volume." She was pulling my layers out, checking each side.

"Yes, well, we never really talked about it. He just did it. But it sounds about right. I have thicker hair, so he would sometimes take those weird-looking shears and take some weight out of it." She grabbed a pair of shears that looked like they had teeth in them.

"This type of shear?"

"That's it."

"We call these texturizing shears. What they do is cut some hair shorter while leaving some hair longer. The shorter hair helps to push up the longer hair, giving you more volume."

"You learn something new every day. Thank you for explaining that to me. I've always wondered about those shears. They look like you could carve a good jack-o'-lantern with them." Sherry laughed at that.

"I never thought of that, but you're right, they do look that way. So, today, I'm just going to follow what Triston did for you on your last cut, unless you'd like to change some things up today?" She lifted her eyebrows like she was going to talk me into something I would regret.

"Let's just stick to what Triston was doing with the cut. The last one he gave me, I didn't have any trouble at all styling. It was great."

"I'm not Triston, but I'll try my best," Sherry replied. I felt like I had insulted her at first until I saw the smile.

"I hope I didn't insult you, sweetheart," I said and hoped I hadn't hurt her feelings. She wasn't Triston and all she could do was her best, and I believed she would.

"Not at all, honey. Listen, I know how gifted Triston was. He cut my hair for me since I started working here." She patted me on my shoulders. "I'm going to have Ashley wash and condition your hair. Then she'll bring you back to my chair, honey."

"That sounds wonderful. Thank you."

"You're so welcome." She got up from the stool and as I got out of the styling chair, she came over and gave me a brief hug. Sherry was born in Sunnyside and went to cosmetology school while she was in high school. They had vocational classes, and she got her license to do cosmetology and nails for free by doing it at the vocational school during her high school years. I think every high school should have vocational schools so our kids can learn a trade and get a very good-paying job out of high school. Not everyone was meant to go to college. With vocational schools, you can learn your trade for free! It's a win for the students and the schools.

Ashley came over, right on cue, and washed and conditioned my hair. I felt like a wet noddle after her scalp massage. She had also used Triston's Japanese Cherry Deep Conditioning

Treatment on my wiry gray hair at the end, and it made my hair feel like pure silk. Now I know that no matter how much of the product I use at home, I don't have to worry about the bitter almond oil since it had been replaced with a safe alternative. I had to get a bottle before leaving. My hair has never felt like this before, even though I would assume that Triston would have used it on my hair. Maybe his assistant didn't use the conditioner because she knew what it had in it. Who knows?

My Cherry Coke was sitting on the cutest little drink table they had placed beside Sherry's station.

"Thelma, you have to try your Cherry Coke. They are so wonderful. I thought Triston had lost his mind until he made one for me. All it takes is one and you're hooked."

"I've got to try this then." I grabbed the glass and took a swig with the metal straw they had in the cup. The only other person I had seen drink out of a metal straw was Oprah! "Get out! That's so good it makes you want to slap somebody!" I exclaimed. I had never tasted anything like it. They had even topped it off with two cherries. "Sherry, I have never tasted a drink that good in my life, and it's not as sweet as I thought it would be."

"It's the coke they use. Triston ordered pallets of coke from some dealer in Mexico, because there, they use real sugar in their cokes, and they taste amazing."

"They certainly do." I was just sucking away on that straw like a baby suckling its mother's tit. I had to slow down. I wanted to savor this drink. "How's it been since Triston's gone?" Sherry stopped cutting my hair, and I could have sworn she was sizing me up.

And then she said, "It's not like it was when he was here. And that woman from KDP has been here almost every day since Triston was killed."

Every day? How did we miss that? With all the girls I have that are socialites, I was sure we would have things covered. Seems like I was wrong.

"What is she doing here?" I asked, sucking down more of my Cherry Coke.

"It's supposed to be hush-hush, but I don't know why. She and Arty are in talks to franchise the salon by offering some of us the opportunity to buy into the business, and then they would set us up in a place of our choosing." Sherry was good at gossiping, making it look like we were just talking.

"You mean to tell me that with a certain amount of money, you could open your own Triston Stylz Apothecary Salon?"

"Yes. And the first five would be in South Carolina. They want to open one in Charleston, Columbia, Hilton Head, Greenville, and Myrtle Beach. We would get Triston's products to sell and all the right furniture so that the salons looked similar. They would even come to wherever we wanted to open, and help us put the salon together to look like a Triston Stylz Apothecary Salon." Sherry was deftly cutting my hair while she explained everything that's been going on.

"Anybody going to take them up on their offer?" I asked, finishing off my Cherry Coke. I would've asked for another one, but I didn't want to look greedy. Gluttony is one of the seven deadliest sins.

"I talked to someone at the bank about getting a line of credit to do it myself. I figure I'm young. I know how Triston ran the place, and I would love to move to somewhere like Charleston or Myrtle Beach. I just love the ocean." I wondered if this was what June Bug had heard Twilight Woods and Arty fussing about the night she took over the food.

"You the only one so far thinking about doing it?"

"No! I heard that Katie wanted to open the first one since she'd been with Triston from day one." Katie's name sure did keep popping up. I wondered how Hansen's talk went with her.

"Well, whatever you do, be careful. I don't know about that Twilight Woods."

"Oh, believe me, I know what you mean. I asked to see some of the contracts for the franchising so I could have my lawyer look over them to make sure I'm not getting screwed. To open one store, it starts at $200K!" She talked in hushed tones.

"Good Lord!" I couldn't believe what she was telling me. Two hundred thousand dollars to open a salon? That was a pretty penny. And I wondered how many people could even afford to do it. But if Twilight Woods was in the middle of it, then she would have other people not just confined to Triston's salon, to open stores all over the country, not just in South Carolina.

"Tell me about it. We had a meeting the same week that Triston passed, which I thought was tacky. But I know business is business and if that was what Triston was going to do with KDP, then I thought it would be even better because you have a company like KDP backing you up."

"KDP? I didn't know they opened salons or anything else they sold. I thought they just sold products on their television network."

"Thelma, that's what I thought too, but with Twilight being their biggest star, I'm sure she could twist some arms with management because I heard that GCV wanted to hire her away from KDP, so she's got a bargaining chip if she needs one."

Boy, does she. With KDP footing the bills, I wondered just how much they got in return. Surely the $200K wouldn't be all they wanted from you. I'm sure they wanted you to sell a certain number of products too, which wouldn't be hard if they started selling them full time on KDP. You'd have every woman's magazine talking about Triston's products. They'd be in *Vogue, Cosmopolitan,* and *Woman's Weekly,* to name just a few.

"Did you ever get those contracts you asked for?" Sherry and I had talked the whole time in hushed tones.

"Not yet. Twilight said that KDP was working on them, and we would get them as soon as their lawyers had okayed everything."

"Sherry, that's a lot to chew on."

"You don't have to tell me. I'd have to move from Sunnyside, which would be fine with me. Like I said, I love the ocean, and being right near the beach would be amazing."

"You're young enough to do it, and I know you would be a great manager of a salon like Triston's."

"Thank you, Thelma. But this is between me, you, and this wall. They told us they didn't want this getting out to others until at least one of the franchises was opened."

"So, is Arty gung ho about all this, too?" She had finished my cut. I could tell she was stalling on the blow-dry because we wouldn't be able to talk.

"Yep. He wants it as bad as she does."

"And you said Twilight's been here since Triston passed away?"

"Yep. She got a room at the Hyatt Regency in Barnville. Nothing but the best for her. I'm sure KDP is footing the bill since she's here for business trying to close a deal with Arty to sell Triston's products exclusively on KDP, and to open franchises for Triston's Apothecary Salon. Of course, we'd be able to sell his products at our own Triston Apothecary Salon if we opened a franchise."

"I wish you all the luck. You'd be great at it." She would. She was young, smart, and knew how to make customers feel at ease. She's always been that way. Much like Triston made you feel, except he was a little older, which meant he understood from experience how things should be run.

"Thank you Thelma. You're so sweet. You going to the PAW Ball?"

"I am! I can't wait. I've never been. Me and my girlfriends are running over to Belk to see what they have. I'm hoping to find a dress there, preferably one with a red-tag sticker on it."

"I love their red-tag sales. It almost feels like you're stealing it from them."

"I know and that's exactly how I feel about it, too." Then she started blow-drying my hair, and we didn't get to talk anymore about the franchises.

What else does Twilight Woods have up her sleeve? I wondered.

Chapter Fourteen

WE WERE ON OUR WAY to Belk in Barnville in hopes of finding a dress for me and Pearl for the PAW Ball tomorrow night. They would have to fit perfectly because we wouldn't have time to have it altered before the ball. Needless to say, we crossed our fingers that we would find dresses that would be perfect for such an event as the PAW Ball.

Pearl and I had never attended one of these PAW Balls before. Myra was on the PAW Patrol board and had told Pearl and me that helping animals, especially those about to be put down because the city couldn't afford to feed and house them, was one of her callings in life. She told us that each year, more than thirty thousand dogs and cats are euthanized in SC due to lack of funding, even though most are healthy animals that could bring joy and unconditional love into someone's home and change their lives forever. The PAW Patrol was adamant that your animal was spayed or neutered before you were allowed to take them home.

I had already told them about my conversation with Sherry Haster. They were both shocked and wondered if Twilight

Woods was a snake in the grass trying to get Arty to do things he may not want to do.

"I think that Twilight is holding the selling of the products over Arty's head to make sure all these franchises work out. That's what *I* think. Do you know how much money is in franchising? Especially with a proven salon system and salon-ready products that they could make at a moment's notice?" Believe it or not, Myra was staying all the way in the back seat of the car today. Normally, she sits up so far in the middle of the Cadillac's back seat that she's almost sitting on the console between me and Pearl.

"I can't believe she's been here since the day after Triston's death. How did we not know she was here then?" Pearl pondered. I could tell Pearl was in deep thought about all of this by the way she was furrowing her brows together. This was an automatic thing Pearl did when worried or concentrating on something.

"Maybe that's why she dyed her hair brown. I've never seen her with brown hair. I wonder if she's wearing one of those wigs she sells on KDP?" Myra piped up from the back seat.

"That makes sense to me," I said. I was still processing everything Sherry had told me. "I wonder just how much money Arty was getting out of this deal."

"Thelma, with franchises, if they could make them happen, Arty and Twilight could rake in millions of dollars." Myra looked at me as I was watching her in the rearview mirror.

The day had started with a chill in the air, blue skies with rolling clouds, but now it seemed to have warmed up close to seventy degrees. I liked the heat myself and thought it was so comfortable for the low country. We were really on the dividing line between the low country and the upstate, which many call the fall line between the two. I had on a pair of slacks and some slides, and for some reason I couldn't get my feet to warm up. I wished I had worn my new tennis shoes because socks would have surely been perfect for my cold feet. I'm sure walking around Belk would warm them up.

"That's a lot of money. My question is, do you think that Triston would have wanted all this?" I was still looking at Myra. She looked out the window in thought and looked back. "I think he would, Thelma."

"I agree with Myra. Triston was the one who pushed to get his products on KDP to start with." Pearl turned her head to look at me. I turned a little so I could see her, but was careful not to run us in a ditch. I'd never live that down.

"But y'all don't think Arty had anything to do with Triston's death, do you?" I needed to know if they had changed their minds.

"No, I don't think so. Why do you keep asking?" Myra and Pearl inquired almost simultaneously.

"What would Arty gain from all this?" Pearl asked.

"Nothing he couldn't get if Triston were alive. Matter of fact, if Triston were alive, it would have made things a lot easier." Myra had on big, black eighties sunglasses. They were huge and helped shield most of her face from the sun. Who needed SPF with those glasses? But I knew Myra still wore sunscreen religiously because of her pale skin. Yes, she gets her hair dyed red, but when she was younger, she was a towhead with the same pale skin. I wondered if they called her Casper when she was a kid. It's funny how if you live long enough, you see every decade of your life return in some way. Yes, there would be some differences. But I know people who were starting to get body waves trying for that easy beachy look you saw all the celebrities wearing. Personally, I couldn't handle the smell. I definitely didn't want my hair smelling like rotten boiled eggs for weeks on end. Not to mention how long it took before you could wash your hair afterward. Thank the Lord I have thick, gray hair that holds curl and whatever I choose to do with it.

"I agree. I think if Triston were alive, all this would be easier. He would be able to go into these franchises and teach the hairdressers his way of doing business. Triston made sure they had marvelous systems in place." And they did. You could even schedule your own hair appointments online, which I would never do. Some things need to be done in person or over the phone, talking to a real human. Not another Siri! He also had his Assistant Program, where new hairdressers assisted for a year while learning the building blocks of hair cutting and coloring. They also attended classes on Tuesday nights after the salon closed. This was wonderful for someone starting out, as they were able to get their own station after having received on-the-job training for a year.

"I don't think Arty had anything to do with Triston's death, but things are moving mighty fast," Pearl confessed. "I'm more confused than I was when we found his body in that Sunday school room."

I had to admit when we thought we were getting closer to the truth, the farther away it seemed to be. My prayer was that Arty, or any of my ladies, weren't sitting ducks for the killer. If we didn't figure something out soon, I was afraid that another murder might happen, and we still didn't have any conclusive evidence of anyone being involved. There were people we thought had something to gain from this, but they would have gained from this even if Triston was alive. I still kept wondering why Triston was murdered. Did he borrow money from some unsavory people to keep things afloat until they had the deal with KDP? I can't even imagine what the overhead at the salon is, never mind the products.

We had decided that I would pick Pearl up, and we would meet Myra at the party since she had to be there earlier in case the PAW Patrol needed help to get things prepared for the evening. The drinks they had decided to serve were Triston's Cherry Coke with a splash of bourbon in it, and, of course, champagne. Rich people love champagne.

Myra said they had found some bourbon that had a sweeter taste and that it went perfectly with Triston's recipe for his Cherry Coke. Course I'm sure if they knew that drinking Cherry Coke had caused Triston's death, they would have changed the drink of the night. Guests who were not Cherry Coke or bourbon drinkers had other drink options. I decided I would be drinking the Cherry Cokes myself with the sweet bourbon. I hadn't had bourbon in a while.

I didn't think I would like the famous Cherry Cokes until the girl at the salon made one for me. It was delicious, and I'm sure with a splash of sweet bourbon, it would be over-the-top amazing. I know what you're thinking and yes, a lot of Baptists drink wine and other spirits from time to time. I often wondered why they called them spirits. I suppose if you drink enough, you'll start seeing spirits. That was as far as I could figure that out.

Thankfully, I had found the most perfect dress at Belk. It was an A-line chiffon dress with lace sleeves and a modest V-neck in a rich emerald green. It would go perfectly with my bib necklace with emerald-colored crystals and gold detailing. I couldn't believe I got so lucky, and because I'm a bit taller, the tea-length dress was the perfect length. They finally started making dresses for taller women. Myra already had picked out a dress at a small boutique in Barnville called One of a Kind.

Pearl said she already had a dress, but then found one that eclipsed the one she had at home. She found a gorgeous burgundy velvet dress with long sleeves, the lace overlay making it appear as if grape vines were growing down your arms. It had a boat neckline with an empire waist that perfectly showed her figure. I had no idea that Pearl still had that gorgeous hourglass figure. She always wore clothes that detracted from her beauty, mostly going for comfort over glamour.

When I arrived to pick Pearl up, and she walked out that front door, she took my breath away. She looked beautiful! She had curled her hair and took pieces and placed them on the top of her hair and pinned them up with bobby pins, almost as if she had a ponytail on top, but not quite. I had seen her wear her hair like this years ago when she was being courted by some lowlife I couldn't even remember. I knew how she had fixed her hair that night because I helped her take the curls down. She had secured them with bobby pins, so that the ends curled every which way, giving it a lot of movement. The burgundy was the perfect color for her skin tone, and she wore her mother's pearls. If things worked out with her and Pick, he would be a lucky man.

She opened the car door, and I could tell she felt beautiful by the way she walked, as straight as a rod making her neck look longer than it was, and the empire waistline of her dress showing how small her waist was. She was going to be the envy of the ball. I was so happy for my best friend, and I prayed each night that things would work out between her and Pick. I already had a feeling they would. But I needed to see them together before deciding. I knew Pick had always been nothing but a Southern gentleman, but since the death of his wife, I have no idea how he acts.

"Pearl, you look like a dream doll. Your hair is gorgeous, and that dress makes your waist look even smaller. You've been holding out on me. Why don't you wear clothes that accentuate your beautiful figure all the time?" She smiled like a opossum eating cantaloupe.

"Do you really like it, Thelma? My heart's about to beat out of my chest." Her face was beaming with pride. I could already tell she had fallen for Pick and Pearl is no dummy, so if that was the case, he had fallen for her as well.

"Pearl, you look gorgeous! I can't even put into words how beautiful you look." I really couldn't. I put on a lot, but not usually with Pearl. She was my ride-or-die girlfriend, and even though we loved Myra, Pearl and I had been this close all our lives. It was as if we were the sisters we never had. Being the only child in our family, during an era when most families had at least five children, could be rough. But we had found each other, and we lived just a block apart. Growing up, she was always at my house, or I was always at hers. Her parents were wonderful and would take me on beach trips with them in the summers. My parents never went anywhere. My father loved being at home and Mama would take off to the beach with some of her friends from the church each year, but she knew that I would be able to go with Pearl, so it worked out for all is us, including Dad (and I'm sure he had more shine during the weeks we were gone).

"You don't look so bad yourself and that necklace with all those crystals sets off the emerald of your dress. Oh, Thelma, we look like we did when we were in school and going to the prom. At least that's how I feel. I have butterflies in my stomach."

I couldn't wait to see what the ladies were wearing tonight.

I wondered why she wanted me to pick her up, then she told me that Pick would meet us at the venue since he had some work to do beforehand. With a murderer on the loose, I am sure they had really beefed up the security at the PAW Ball. The last thing they needed was something to happen to anyone or any of those pets; that would be awful. They have been holding this ball for six years running, and have never had issues with anyone drinking too much and making a scene. I hope that Pick had enough sense to make sure nothing happened. There was a murderer in our midst, and I felt like the murderer was close. It was the strangest thing. I didn't believe in any of this, but it didn't stop the way I felt. We still hadn't figured out how they found the key to the church.

I had spoken with June Bug earlier, and she indicated that Mitzi told her that all the ladies we had chosen for the investigation would be there. She said that she would pull out a gown that she hadn't had a chance to wear. She said it had sequins and fringe all over, and that it flowed to the floor, covering her shoes, so she could wear flats. With the bunions she had, she just couldn't wear high heels anymore. She'd bought it for her niece's wedding, but since the couple broke up and canceled the wedding, she had never worn it. I told her to wear whatever she wanted to. If the dress was that long, no one would even notice what type of shoes she was wearing anyway.

"I can't wait to see what the other girls are wearing." Pearl was giddy. She reminded me of the Pearl I knew in high school right before our first prom. She had snagged Beryl Foster from the football team. I knew she was a virgin then, but didn't figure she would be after that night. They looked so beautiful together. But unfortunately, Beryl died in the Vietnam War (which neither of us believed in), causing much heartache. I think this is one reason that Pearl shields herself from men. She and I had actually marched against our parents' wishes on the capital in Columbia to show our dissension.

"Me too. You know they're all going to look amazing. They wouldn't go if they didn't have something head-turning to wear." I had known most of these women my whole life and knew that as Southern women, things were done just so, or they would happily stay home and allow others to shine. That was the way it had always been done in the South. I have no idea how Yankees bring up their girls, but to be honest, I would have to think they teach them in much the same way, but I could be wrong. I was praying that I wasn't wrong, because we had some Yankees in our group. But they were always adorable and had always fit in so perfectly with the rest of the ladies. So they can't be as bad as some Southerners think, which, if I'm being honest, isn't fair. I have always looked at everyone as an equal until they show me differently. This included Yankees and/or rednecks.

We got to the PAW Ball, and to say that it was packed would be an understatement. We had an assigned parking space thanks to Myra, and after driving around the arena, I finally saw where Myra parked her car. I took out the parking ticket and placed it around my rearview mirror, making sure anyone could see that we were a part of the Paw Patrol, even though we weren't. It's always good to know people in high places.

I took out a cigarette and lit it before we went into the ballroom. The PAW Patrol building had been turned into an area filled with oversized tents. The tents were massive and stretched from the outside parking lot of the animal shelter into the venue, where dancing, drinking, and hopefully raising a lot of money were to happen.

I could see people walking around the massive tents, with their pets on leashes. I saw the cutest dogs and cats, with bows and ribbons around their necks. I haven't ever seen tents this big before and wondered where they got them. You could fit whole buildings into the four huge tents they had erected.

I looked at Pearl and noticed her mouth was opened in awe, just as mine must have been because when she saw me, she gave me that grin of hers that was filled with mischievous thoughts and pure joy.

I wished Charlie could have been here. I was lucky I was here. As we got closer, we saw where to check in. We both had handheld clutches that didn't hold much more than our driver's license, a few credit cards, maybe a compact, and some lipstick. The check-in tablecloths had the most whimsical black paws all over them in differing sizes. The girls who were checking people in also had on masks that were either cats or dogs. There must be a number of masks they have to choose from, because the girls all had different masks of various dog and cat breeds.

For some reason the masks put me on edge. You couldn't clearly see who you were dealing with if they didn't want you to. I didn't like this. I didn't want to be blindsided; I wanted to know who was coming up to me in case it was someone with whom I didn't want to socialize. After I finished checking in, the young lady asked if I'd like a mask and showed me a sheet of paper with ten different dog masks and ten different cat masks. I chose a dachshund mask because of Brownie, our last dog, who was a dachshund mix, although he looked like a purebred. She went behind the desk and found the dachshund masks and handed me one. They had sticks to hold them up to your face.

The official PAW Patrol personnel must have been asked to actually wear the masks they had chosen. I was so happy to not have to wear a mask with a rubber band that would mess up my hair. The poor girl behind the desk could barely see out of hers, because the rubber band was so tight around her face. They will be very uncomfortable tonight while trying to raise money for the PAW Patrol to continue their mission of saving dogs and cats everywhere.

I looked over at Pearl and found her holding the cutest poodle mask to her face. With the color of her hair, the mask seemed to match her perfectly. I have never known Pearl to have a dog. She always thought it would be cruel to keep a dog in the house while she worked twelve-hour shifts at the hospital. So, all her life, she had cats. Cats tend to live their lives the way they want—with or without you.

We both started into the ballroom, where balloons and flowers were everywhere, along with the cutest dogs and cats I had ever seen. I couldn't believe they were behaving. At least for now. Most were puppies and baby kittens that wanted to play and you could see some of them looking at the balloons for some good old-fashioned fun.

"Thelma, this is magical," Pearl said, taking everything in. The wait staff carried around trays of fluted champagne and platters with various types of hors d'oeuvres. I picked up a glass of champagne and it was dry to the taste. Just how I liked champagne. It should be a little dry. All these companies that seemingly popped up overnight with different flavors of vodka and other spirits were not doing much for my taste buds. If I wanted a drink, I went for the classics like a dirty martini or a pina colada, depending if I wanted something sweet.

Myra had told us that they were serving Cherry Cokes in honor of Triston, because he was a huge philanthropist, giving thousands of dollars to PAW Patrol every year. He had been an avid animal lover and once had a beautiful pit bull named Grace who came to the salon with him every day. When Grace was ten years old, they woke up one morning and noticed something badly wrong with her. They immediately took her to the vet and were told she had a huge tumor in her belly that had burst, and she was bleeding internally. The veterinarian told Triston and Arty that the tumor had grown so large that it had moved her intestines from one side of her belly to the other. They indicated they could operate, but due to the size of the tumor, there was no way to remove the whole thing. She had been Triston's heart, but he knew it was time to say goodbye to his baby Grace. Thinking about it brought a tear to my eye, thinking they were together again. I knew she was running around catching the ball that she carried with her everywhere she went. I put my mask up so no one could see my tears. I got a napkin and patted my eyes carefully like I saw Myra do the other day. I didn't want to mess up my makeup.

Pearl and I continued making our way into the crowd, looking for any of the ladies in the Ladies Auxiliary. We were supposed to have our own table, but we couldn't find it. Finally, Myra came out in a dress that looked as if she had come from the set of *Dynasty*, definitely giving Crystal and Alexis a run for their money. She wore a bright pink fake stole around her neck.

"Don't you look gorgeous," I said to her. Pearl came up with her poodle mask and took it off as if to surprise Myra. Maybe she had, or Myra was playing along, but she went on and on about how beautiful we were. It wasn't every night you got to dress up like this and pretend to live the lives of the rich, even if it was in your mind.

"Pearl, honey, you look fabulous. Who did your hair?" Myra had taken her mask off so she could see Pearl without any hindrances.

"I did." Pearl radiated with pride.

"What?" Myra was truly amazed. "Well, the next time I have a party, I'm going to have you do my hair. You look astonishing! Let me see the whole dress."

Pearl turned around slowly, allowing the dress to flow in the air as she turned. "Pearl, I have never in my life seen you look as beautiful as you do tonight."

"That's what I told her," I said loudly to Myra hoping she could hear me over the orchestral music.

"Thelma, oh my Lord, look at you."

I have to admit, when we wanted to, Pearl and I could clean up well.

"Oh Myra, are you talking about this ole thing?" I put my hand on my hip and looked coy. My tea-length dress showed my long legs, which I have always thought were one of my best features. Men seemed to think so. I still had construction workers howling at me when I happened to stroll by a construction site.

Myra looked amazing in her dress, which flowed like soft taffeta. Her breasts were very prominent tonight. But like I always say, if you've got them, flaunt them. They could help move mountains in the right circumstances. Myras could move huge mountains and even some molehills if needed.

"Look at you. You look like someone right out of *Vogue* magazine with that beautiful dress. And I absolutely love your pink stole. Where did you get that?" I looked at Myra, confused, because she was always bringing new items of clothing to the house to show me what she had bought from this or that boutique. I had never seen this pink stole.

"I decided at the last minute to try this on and see if it would fit. And when it fit me perfectly, I knew I had to wear it. I got the stole last summer in Paris, in a beautiful shop in the Marais district." Myra was moving to the music playing in the background. They had hired the Barnville orchestra to play all night. As she moved, her breasts moved like Jell-O. "Watch it Wiggle, See it Jiggle," I sang the tune to Myra, looking down at her moving breasts.

"Thelma!" She laughed and grabbed a glass of champagne. We all stood there, taking in the room. I wasn't hungry. I always ate before shindigs like this because you never knew when the food would stop coming around. From the looks of it, all the socialites were in attendance.

I leaned over and said in Myra's ear, "Do you know where our table is at?" They had round tables all around the room and some had people at them already, but most people were taking in all the sites and listening to the orchestra play Frank Sinatra's hit, "Fly Me to the Moon." Some people had taken to the dance floor they had created in the middle of the tent. One couple was doing a waltz to Frank's hit.

"Myra, who are those people on the dance floor? Watch 'em doing the waltz. It's so beautiful. I would've done broke my neck or Charlie would have." I laughed at the thought of me and Charlie doing a waltz. We would be good to do a walk, much less a waltz.

"That's Frank and Shirly Pointer," Myra answered, after turning to look at them and turning back to us so we could hear her. You could tell she was in her element. She had removed the mask from around your head. She had a Pomeranian mask in her hand, but she hadn't held it up to her face so far. I doubted very seriously she would. Myra knew how to work a room and a mask like that could get in the way.

Then, out of nowhere, Pick showed up holding a mask of a hound dog to his face. He dropped the mask, and to our astonishment, had on tails. He also cleaned up well.

Good for Pearl.

"Pearl, you look breathtaking." He took her hand and kissed it. Myra and I looked at each other and smiled. I had to say that Pick didn't look like he did when he walked into our church that Sunday before Easter. You could tell he had a little more pep in his step tonight.

"I would be honored if you would dance with me, Pearl." Pick looked into her eyes, and she beamed. If it was any darker in the tents, she would have glowed in the dark.

Pearl lightly slapped his shoulder with her poodle mask and said, "I would love to." With that, Pick and Pearl took to the dance floor. They were doing the waltz to a song I couldn't recall, or maybe it was so new I had never heard it.

"Look at them, Thelma. You think they'll make it this time?" Myra smiled as she watched Pearl and Pick acting like high schoolers. They were having fun and whatever he was saying to her, she was laughing, which was always a good start.

"From the looks of it, I'd say they were made for each other." I wasn't lying. They had liked each other since high school. But you know how that goes in high school. You get out and scatter like the wind. Pearl went off to nursing school, which took all her time. And she seemed to like being by herself, although I know at times she had to be lonely, but she never showed it.

"I think it's so sweet. He doesn't even have his toothpick in his mouth," Myra said. Once Pearl took off for the dance floor, Myra and I stood next to each other sipping on our champagne and looking at the Barnville's upper crust as they entered the room, all holding various types of masks.

"Oh! You're right Myra! I can't believe that he doesn't have a toothpick in his mouth! Yeah, I would say they had a good chance if she could get him to take that toothpick out of his mouth, even if it's for the night."

"That's exactly what I was thinking," Myra yelled back. The decibel level had gone up in the room and it would soon be hard to hear anyone.

"I don't like these masks, Myra. You can't tell who's who. And with a killer on the loose, you'd never be able to find him or her."

"Her? I thought that Pick was certain it was a man because someone would've had to bring Triston into the church. And to be honest, I wasn't fond of the masks either. I like to know who's coming my way, but it's hard to do with masks."

"The whole team wanted to do something different. Last year we had cat ears and dog ears we put on our heads, but most of the women wouldn't wear them for fear of messing up their hair, so they thought of the masks so that you could hold them up to your face when you wanted to."

"I do love the different types of dog and cat faces you can choose from, but I wished I could tell who was here and who wasn't, and these masks are making it hard to do."

"By the end of the night, those masks will be on the tables. People will get tired of holding them," Myra countered, taking another drink of her champagne.

"Is that June Bug, Skitter, and Mitzi?" I was looking at the door when all three walked in at the same time. I hated leaving Pearl, but she was in good hands. The ladies looked amazing.

"Come on, let's get them and find our table." Myra put her arm into mine and we started walking toward the girls. Mitzi had spotted us and was waving her mask in the air. You could tell she was telling the others, as they all pinpointed us at the same time. All three were waving their masks to get our attention.

"I'm going to go up front and look at the table placements. I'll be right back and take y'all to your tables. Then I'm going to have to go through the room and turn on the moneymaking charm, since this is our biggest fundraiser of the year." Trying to keep my eyes focused in front of me to avoid running into a table or a person, I cautiously looked in Myra's direction.

"You do what you need to do, but don't forget us lowlifes over here." I smiled at Myra. She was almost skipping through the room. You could tell she was having fun in a room filled with people with money. It used to be tacky to talk about money and how much so-and-so made in a year, but times have changed. You hear someone tell you they own such-and-such's law firm and they bill so much every quarter that it almost seems expected these days.

"Mitzi, Skitter, and June Bug, don't you ladies look fabulous tonight! I have to say we all clean up well." Skitter and Mitzi had smartly worn clothes they would wear to church, so they could wear their dresses again. I had no idea when I'd be able to wear my dress again. I suppose I could take it with me when we go to Paris this Christmas. Henri and Amber loved taking us to nice restaurants all over Paris.

Skitter even looked good, and her thin white hair looked a little more tamed than it normally did. I wondered what she did to make it lie down like it was doing because in all the years I've known her, her hair always looked like she had stuck her fingers into an electrical outlet.

June Bug had on a long sequined dress with beaded frills wrapped all over it, and each time she moved, those beaded frills did a shimmy, catching the light so that they glistened like glitter, but without the mess.

"Thelma, you look gorgeous," June Bug said rather loudly in my left ear. Bless her heart; she couldn't hear in one ear and the other was losing ground each day. But she would not buy hearing aids, because she heard perfectly fine to hear her tell it. We all knew she was hard of hearing, and I imagine that would make you lonely in a room like this, with the orchestra playing and people talking in the background.

"Thank you, June Bug. I *love* your dress. Those sequins and beaded frills look like something Cher would wear." Of course, if Cher wore it, the dress wouldn't be at her feet. It would be above her knee and the collar would have been a lot lower, too.

"Mitzi and Skitter, y'all look beautiful in your dresses," I said to them.

"Thank you, Thelma," Skitter said. She had grabbed a glass of champagne when she arrived and was sipping it.

"Thelma, now that's a dress. I love the color of emeralds. And that necklace you have on is just GORGEOUS!" Mitzi said.

"Thank you Mitzi. Amber gave this to me two Christmases ago when they still lived in New York City. I saw it on KDP, and I immediately called Amber and told her what I wanted. She turned her TV channel to KDP and ordered it right then and there over the phone."

"It's something else!" I could tell Mitzi was going to tear off into a rant, probably about her garden, so before she could, I politely said, "Excuse me a minute, Mitzi. I'll be right back." I was looking for Myra to see if she'd found out where our table was, because I had two-minute shoes on and had had them on for the past three minutes, and they were beginning to bite into my feet.

I went back up to the front where we had checked in and saw Myra looking over a chart with a diagram of the tables on it.

"Thelma, I can't find your table. I know it was on here before we left last night." She looked at one of the other girls at the table. "Angie, could you be a doll and tell me which table we had the Ladies Auxiliary of St. John's Baptist Church seated?"

"Oh, someone called last night right after you left. I think her name was Thelma . . . Rue that's it," Angie recalled and went on, "She told me she was the president of the Ladies Auxiliary at St. John's Baptist Church, and that they would no longer need their table. I tried telling her that once the table is paid for, we don't offer refunds, but she just said she understood. Then she ended the call."

"Look here, Angie. I'm Thelma Rue and I did *not* call you last night, or the night before, telling you no such nonsense. I am the president of the Ladies Auxiliary, and we need a table. I never called you and told you that. Are you sure you didn't misunderstand?" And then I wondered if it was the killer playing with us. Whoever it was knew we were investigating. What else did they have up their sleeve?

"Myra, it was the killer who called and did this. Something is going to happen. I think we need to get the girls and get out of here."

"Thelma, I know someone called in and lied about the table, but what could they possibly do in front of all these people?" Myra was trying to calm me down, but it wasn't working.

Then the poor girl feebly tried to explain, but I was thinking to myself, drowning her out. "No ma'am, I didn't misunderstand. I heard exactly what you said to me over the phone yesterday evening." This Angie chick was about to get her neck wrung if she kept calling me a liar.

"Angie, something is wrong. Thelma is one of my best friends, and she would have never called you to give away their table. So, if you've already given it away, we have to find them another table." Myra looked at Angie and took control of the situation. Angie could tell by the way Myra was talking to her that she had made a huge mistake, and it needed to be rectified.

The more I thought about it, the more nervous I became. The killer knew who we were and what we were doing. But what could he do in front of all these people? I needed a Xanax, and thankfully, had put them in the small Tylenol bottle so it would fit into my clutch. I got out the small bottle and popped a pill, downing it with my champagne.

Myra had gone over and was huddling with Angie and another girl. Hopefully, they could get us a table. We couldn't stand up all night. We were all senior citizens, but some in our group were older than others and would have to sit down, and soon.

Now I was on edge. I clenched down on my dentures. If I kept that up, I was going to need more teeth.

The killer is taunting us. Why would anyone call up here and do that? It made no sense, and I could tell when talking to Angie that she really thought I had called her last night. I didn't call her, but I was now pretty sure I knew who had. And I knew I could prove it, too! I asked Myra to borrow Angie's phone to find out what time the person had called her last night.

Myra wrote down the number and the exact time of the call on a napkin and returned Angie's phone to her. The girl looked dumbfounded. The call came in at 7:39 pm last night from a phone number with a Barnville area code.

I grabbed the napkin and went outside. I opened my clutch, got my iPhone out, and called the number. No one answered, but I immediately knew who it was when the answering machine came on. I hung up abruptly. Things started slowing down now. And I could think in the cool night air. I then dialed Pork Chop's number. I hated calling this late, but I remembered something about the key to the church and needed to make sure I was correct. Pork Chop answered on the first ring.

"Pork Chop, it's Thelma. I'm so sorry for calling this late, but I have a question about when the Sunday school wing was being built. When the work was almost complete and the guys needed to Sheetrock the walls and paint, did y'all leave them a key under a rock or something like that out back? I know it sounds crazy, but it's very important, Pork Chop."

"Oh Thelma, please don't tell me that's how the killer drug that poor boy's body into the church."

"So, it *was* hidden under one of those fake rocks like you see on TV?" I was biting at my cuticles; I was so nervous.

"Thelma, you're right. The guys needed to get back in the church and no one was available; I had bought a couple of those fake rocks to hide the keys in and I don't remember ever going out there to get it back." I could tell this took a toll on poor Pork Chop. That was the last thing he needed to worry about.

"Listen to me, Pork Chop. You had nothing to do with Triston's death. They placed his body in the church to make us wonder why and throw us off. They wanted us chasing our tails, trying to figure out why he wound up in one of our Sunday school rooms. Now don't you worry about this. You hear me, Pork Chop?"

"Oh, Thelma. What have I done?" He was crying now, thinking it was his fault they had placed him in the church.

But they would have done it with or without a key. The killer would have broken the Sunday school window to get Triston in there if need be. There was no rhyme or reason, other than for us to try and figure out why Triston was in the church. It kept us busy wondering what the significance was when there never was one to start with.

"Pork Chop. Listen to me, sweetheart. They would have broken the window to put him in there. They did it to make us wonder why they put him in the church and for no other reason. So, go to bed and don't worry about this. Allow the Lord to take it off your mind. And if that doesn't work, take a nip of that shine. It'll put things in perspective. You hear?"

"I hear you, Thelma. I'm going to get the shine and a glass. That'll take my mind off it and help me sleep."

"That's right, Pork Chop. I have to go, but I'll call you in the morning with all the details if I'm right."

"I'll be waiting for your call, Thelma. Have a good night if you can."

"You too, hon. I love you, Pork Chop."

"I love you too, Thelma." With that, he hung up.

Damn it!

That was what was in the back of my mind this whole time, but it took this long to figure it out.

The killer made a huge mistake by calling to cancel our table. It's one they will pay for. I went back into the tent. It had gotten hotter with all the people milling about. I looked to the front check-in desk, and Myra was still looking for a table for us. I needed to find the girls. I had questions for them, too.

"Okay Thelma, we always put three extra tables up for any extra people who might show up at the last minute. A lot of high society people don't think they need to RSVP. So, we always leave the worst tables open for them. We have a table that's near the kitchen." Myra looked at me with dread. "It's not the best table on the floor, but at least y'all can sit down." Myra scrunched her face up as an apology. I had seen that face many times before, and it wasn't her best look. But she was trying to remedy the situation, so I needed to cut her some slack. She took my hand, and I followed her into the ballroom again. I could see the table close to the doors of the big tent. I could see people going in and out of the kitchen, which was nothing more than a tent next to the big tent we were in. I honestly didn't think it was that bad, but I wasn't high society, so it didn't matter to me or our group. But I still had the feeling someone was watching us and everything that happened around us.

"Myra, hold on, let me get Skitter, Mitzi, and June Bug. I'm sure June Bug needs to sit down. She's got problems with her feet, and I'm sure she would love to sit down." I took my hand out of Myra's. She stayed where she was as I gathered the girls up, and they followed us to our new table near the kitchen door. We were opposite the orchestra, which was better for us to hear one another. I took Myra to the side and filled her in about everything. She just stood there with her mouth wide open.

"Myra, it was the killer that called that poor girl last night. And I also know how the killer got into the church. The killer put Triston there as pure subterfuge. There really was no reason other than for us to try and figure out why the church when it didn't mean a thing. There was no reason other than the fact that the killer knew where the key was. That was what was in the back of my mind all this time, and I just called Pork Chop to make sure I was right. I also called the number of the person who canceled our table. The killer made a mistake doing that. I'm pretty sure I know who did it. I need to talk to Pick when I get a chance." I turned to Mitzi. "Mitzi, did you, Babs, and Bunny get ahold of those bank account statements like we talked about?"

"Lord Thelma, I have a copy right here in my purse." Mitzi pulled the statements out of her purse and handed them to me. I looked them over and saw what I needed to see. This was more confirmation that I was on the right track all along.

Putting Triston in the church was ingenious on the killer's part. That's what kept us guessing because it didn't fit, but it was never meant to. It was to throw us off the scent.

"I couldn't make heads nor tails out of them. I don't think Babs or Bunny did either, or they would have called you earlier." Mitzi looked at me to see if I could figure anything out. "Thelma, why don't you sit and think a bit? Then take it to Pick and tell him everything you know." Mitzi was right. I had to do something quick. I felt safe knowing that the killer wouldn't show his face at the PAW Ball. I could be wrong, but maybe not. I started looking for Pick and Pearl on the dance floor but didn't see them. Then, out of the blue, they came from behind me.

"Where have y'all been?" I looked at the two lovebirds. At least something nice had come out of this nightmare. I asked Pick to sit down, and I told him everything, showing him the bank statements that he had gotten for Mitzi, Babs, and Bunny. He told me he had looked at them and questioned a few deposits, and when I told him what they were for, he understood. I also told him about the killer impersonating me and calling Angie last night to cancel our table.

"Pick, it all fell in place when I saw the number that called Angie last night. It's a Barnville area code. I called it and now the killer knows that I know. That's the scary part. But I doubt he'll show his face here tonight."

"Surely he wouldn't be so stupid as to try something here in a room filled with all these people. I would hope that my presence would scare the killer away, but if the killer knows you know, then all bets are off because sometimes it puts them over the edge," Pick said to me, pulling Pearl closer to him. At least I didn't have to worry about Pearl.

"You and Pearl go dance if you want. I'm just going to sit here and watch while I think about our next move, unless you want to take over from here." My shoes were biting into my feet even more and once seated under the tablecloth, I took them off. My feet felt better once I slid off my slides. It was times like this that I wished I vaped. I tried it once, but it was so strong, I understood why kids get addicted to them so fast.

"Thelma, you're doing a great job. I think you've figured just about everything out. But I have to say it's an odd case. I would have never thought of that." I couldn't tell if Pick was just blowing smoke up my butt or not. However, if he didn't mean what he said, I think he would've just kept quiet. Maybe I was on to something.

"Thelma, I need to take my shoes off. Do you think anyone will notice?" June Bug asked. She was sitting beside me and I hadn't noticed. I was so entangled with this killer to pay any attention. That's what scared me. They could be here, and I would never notice them with those stupid masks.

"You go right ahead! Look down, June Bug." She looked down toward the bottom of the table and I showed her my naked feet, dangling them near the tablecloth. She smiled and I could tell she was taking hers off under the table as well. Thankfully, the tablecloths were floor-length.

By this time, the place was hopping. I had a bad feeling in the pit of my stomach.

I looked around the room. I didn't notice anything out of the ordinary, except people holding those masks over their faces. It seemed as if I were in a house of mirrors and those masks were playing tricks with my head. Something wasn't right. I could feel it. I started to panic and then looked at every one of my ladies and they were all doing fine.

Maybe I was just panicking because someone called using my name, telling them we wouldn't need our table. That was so odd and I couldn't help but worry. Why would the killer do that? All it did was help me put everything together. Or at least I thought it had. I wouldn't be counting my chickens until the killer was in handcuffs.

I knew then and there whoever killed Triston was watching us, and I wondered if he would try something tonight with one or more of the ladies. But I couldn't see how. The other girls took to the dance floor, and I sat beside June Bug and told her what had happened, explaining why we were at this table rather than the premium table we had purchased. Myra wasn't in sight. I'm sure she was blessing Angie out for the mix-up, but it really wasn't her fault. She didn't know me from Adam's house cat.

Pearl and Pick were slow dancing on the dance floor. That brought a huge smile to my face and my heart. They both deserved to be happy and if things continued as they had been, I believed Pick would make an honest woman out of Pearl.

I scanned the room and didn't see Babs or Bunny anywhere. That gave me pause, then Mitzi came to the table and told me that Babs and Bunny were up front having their pictures taken in one of those old-fashioned photo booths. Thank the Lord they're okay. Now all the ladies were here except for Fifi.

"June Bug, have you heard from Fifi?" June Bug shook her head like she had forgotten something.

"Thelma, she called me right before I left. She wasn't feeling that good, so she told me she was going to sit this one out. I don't think she had a dress either, Thelma. She only draws her social security. And you ought to know there ain't no security in those measly checks. I didn't say anything, because I didn't want to hurt her feelings. But I would've given her the money for a dress. But you know Fifi. She would die if she knew we were talking about her and her money situation."

"That's pitiful, June Bug. I wished she wasn't so proud. We all could've chipped in and got her a dress."

"I know. But you know Fifi. I don't think she was able to get her manicure done either."

"That reminds me, did you find out any gossip at the salon?"

"Not really. Katie did my hair and she's one serious lady. She's a wonderful hairdresser, don't get me wrong, but she has a way to do everything. It's like if she would have to deviate, she'd get all thrown off."

"That sounds like Katie. Triston was the same way, but you could tell that he was learning to roll with the punches. Katie needs to work on that if she's going to take over the salon." I thought about Katie and how much she was like Triston, mostly due to him teaching her everything. But you would think your own personality would take over at some point. Katie was very regimented; she would've made a good drill sergeant.

"She is?" June Bug asked. Apparently, Katie didn't gossip either.

"That's what I heard when I went for my cut. They put me with Sherry Haster, because I've used her to do pedicures for me. I have to say she did a great cut on me." I was pushing at my hair playfully and June Bug laughed.

I still couldn't shake the feeling that we were being set up in some perverse way that would harm one or more of us.

I looked around the room and it was filled with high rollers. And the man of the hour had just walked in with his wife, Eleanor. George Moon Pie Hubbard.

"Look who just showed up and is fashionably late, I might add." June Bug followed my eyes and could see Moon Pie making his rounds, shaking hands with all the high rollers and people who probably greased his palms to get around having permits for jobs and anything else he could do for you at the right price.

"Excuse me, June Bug, I'll be right back." We were on the opposite side of the room from the orchestra, making it easier to talk to everyone. I left June Bug at the table and went over to Moon Pie to give him a piece of my mind!

"Well, look what the cat dragged in." I looked over at Moon Pie and Eleanor. I could tell, at first, he was running through the Rolodex in his mind trying to figure out who was who in the room. Some people were so predictable and dull. I could see on his chubby face right when he realized who I was.

"Thelma Rue. Don't you look lovely tonight." As he said this to me, his chins wobbled back and forth on his neck like loose turkey skin. Eleanor was just as big as he was. Weren't they two tons of fun? Eleanor wasn't even paying me any attention. She had also picked a Pomeranian Mask and held it up to her face so she wouldn't have to deal with Mill Village trash.

"You are one low-down snake, I'll tell you one thing. What you did to Triston Stylz was unbelievable!" I could feel my face getting hot. I'm sure my blood pressure was through the roof.

"Thelma, Thelma, Thelma, you must understand, we have to make calls we don't like every day for the good of the police department. There was no good reason to start an investigation when it was nothing more than an accidental death."

"Accidental my foot. How did he get into the church? He was dead before someone dropped him off there."

"Thelma, I'm sorry, but I have a strict policy. I don't talk business when I'm out with my beautiful wife, Eleanor," He said, as his neck wobbled like Jell-O. The old Jell-O tune popped into my head, "Watch it Wiggle, See it Jiggle." His jowls were doing both. I'm sure that's why he wears bolo ties instead of real ones. They would probably choke him to death if we were only that lucky.

"Well, I have a policy to get people out of office that ain't doing their jobs, and I promise to the Lord above that you'll wish you had never met me."

"I'm beginning to feel that way now," he said with a grimace on his face. Eleanor was looking bored out of her mind, and I wanted to slap him across his face. If I knew I could get away with it, without going to jail, I would have. I leaned in close to his ear so I knew he would hear what I had to say. "I promise you that I'll get you out of office if it's the last thing I do. Do you hear me, Moon Pie?"

A flash of disgust came across his face. He knew what people called him behind his back, but I don't think anyone had the balls to do it to his fat face.

"Well, I never!" He yelled at me, and his chins started dancing on their own. Eleanor whipped her head my way and dialed in on me.

"I could have you arrested this minute," she said with indignation.

"You do it and I promise you, I'll make your life a living hell." We were staring at each other as if were dueling. Eye-to-eye contact was an Olympic sport in the South. Whoever moves their eyes first loses. I'd be damned if I move mine. Moon Pie knew he didn't want to be in the middle of me kicking his wife's butt, so he intervened before things got out of hand.

"Let's go sugar plums; the air is getting stale." He looked at Eleanor to divert her from our stare-off. She placed the Pomeranian mask up to her face, but it only covered a small portion since her face was just as big as Moon Pie's. I watched as they waddled off in his white tux that made him look just like Boss Hog of *The Dukes of Hazard*.

He was Humpty Dumpty who hadn't had his fall yet. I had made a promise to myself that night, then and there, I would push Humpty Dumpty off his wall and all the kings' horses, and all the king's men, wouldn't be able to put him back together again.

When I turned, I could tell everyone had seen our exchange and heard every word I had said. I thought I was being fairly quiet, but by this time the place was almost elbow-to-elbow with people milling about with champagne and petit fours. Eyes were boring a hole into me.

I started to walk off and ran slapdab into Myra. I was so flustered, and mad, from my encounter with Moon Pie that I could barely speak.

"Myra, I'm so sorry. I didn't spill champagne on you, did I?" I was so mad, I was seeing red, and it didn't register right away that she didn't even have a glass of champagne.

"No, but you sure told old Moon Pie Hubbard. Thelma, you better be careful. I don't know anyone that's called him that to his face. He can be a dangerous person to mess around with, sweetheart." Myra looked worried for me. Had I just started a war with one of the most powerful men in Barnville County? "Please tell me everyone couldn't hear what I was saying."

"I wish I could. But with the place being this packed, you just made yourself an enemy. C'est la vie," Myra said, throwing her hands in the air and laughing until she was bent over with the giggles.

Then I started laughing with her. It sure made me feel better.

Thanks be to Jesus!

Myra laughed some more, doubling over. She finally stopped laughing and her face was as red as a beet. Her brow looked wet. She grabbed some napkins from the table beside us and started blotting her face. Myra was using her mask as a fan to cool herself off.

It had suddenly gotten hot in here. With the rush of people in the tent, we had to be at full capacity. It would sure be a hit for the PAW Patrol. They would rake in the money tonight.

"Let's go over to the table. I need something to drink." Myra followed me to our pedestrian table.

"They're about to start serving the Cherry Cokes Triston loved so much."

"Good Lord, where did they get all that maraschino cherry juice from?"

"They had it ordered in from some commercial restaurant outfit." Talk about having a budget for a party. The PAW Ball was looking like a smashing success. All the tables were full, not counting all the people leaving checks up front that could have paid for Amber's college tuition. I wasn't used to seeing all this money in one room, even though one of my best friends had gobs of it.

We arrived at our table and saw Fifi Jones sitting with June Bug. I was shocked to see her. She looked gorgeous and I know June Bug was happy that she decided to come. She got up, and we hugged while complimenting each other on how nice the other looked. She still had the fairy hair, but in the ballroom, it looked more fitting. She looked like a Chinese crested dog that had been shaved everywhere, except for the hair on the dog's head.

Thank you, Jesus, for my ladies.

I wouldn't know what to do without them.

Then Babs and Bunny, holding one of Triston's Cherry Cokes, came over to the table. They had them in deep beer mugs with cherries floating on top.

I'd hate to pay the bill for this party.

I knew then that something was about to happen. I braced myself and waited. I looked down around the table to see if anyone had left a box with a bomb in it. I know I was going off the deep end. I had just insulted the mayor of Barnville County in front of God and everybody. Myra was right. He wasn't one to mess with. He could make my life a living hell if he wanted to. I hoped he would have a wonderful evening and forget about what I had said. But I had decided then and there that I would find someone to run against him and I would make sure they won, too. I also had some pull in this town.

Myra was still beside me, and I told her as I grabbed a Cherry Coke from a waiter who was bringing them to our

table, "I've got to start making these for Charlie. He'd love 'em."
The kicker was the cokes from Mexico had real sugar in them.
Then you just put as much maraschino cherry juice in it as you
want and top it off with cherries marinated in the maraschino
cherry juice. And voilà, you had Triston's Cherry Coke.

I took another gulp of the drink. It was getting hot in
here and I could see the PAW Patrol going around, opening
the edges of the tent to let in some night air. It immediately
dropped the temperature in the room. The iced cold Cherry
Cokes helped. It had to be one of my favorite drinks of all time.
I liked it better than Pina Colada's, and I loved them.

I spotted Pick and Pearl standing at the bar in deep
conversation, sipping on Cherry Cokes. They looked like
teenagers again.

Love was in the air.

Then I turned to look at the girls at the table and something
was wrong with June Bug. She was pulling at her collar and
gasping for breath. I was praying it was just the heat, but
somewhere deep down, I knew better. I immediately yelled
for help. The orchestra stopped playing and a young gentleman
ran to our table, saying he was a doctor.

He immediately saw June Bug in distress and went to her
side. He ripped her dress in the front because she was having
respiratory distress. The doctor was looking into her eyes, and
her pupils were like tiny pinpricks. Then June Bug fell face-
first onto the table. The young doctor pulled her away from
the table as we all watched. All eyes were on June Bug as the
doctor placed her on the floor and quickly felt for her pulse.

I bent down. "What can we do to help?" I asked the doctor. June Bug was on the floor looking much like I had seen Triston look the Sunday before Easter. She also had a grimace on her face, but was at least still alive, although barely.

"Call 911." He kept checking her pulse and said it was ragged. He didn't think it was a heart attack. You could tell she was sweating something fierce. "We have to get her to the hospital immediately. Grab her legs. We don't have time to wait for an ambulance." But just as he said it, two paramedics ran into the room carrying a gurney and other medical apparatus. Myra told me later that the PAW Patrol always had an ambulance on standby, just in case something like this happened.

They took her out of the tent as fast as they could move.

"Mitzi, which drink was hers?" I asked. Pick came up behind me with Moon Pie Hubbard in his wake. He looked serious now. If she died because of this man's inability to do what was right to begin with, I'd have his head on a platter!

Pick grabbed her drink with an untouched table napkin in his hands, making sure to keep any fingerprints, if there were any, intact. I doubted this murderer would be that foolish. He placed it in a ziplock bag he had in his pants pocket. Did he think something was going to happen at this party or was he always prepared after being the sheriff for the past twenty years or so?

I looked around the room and didn't see anyone that stuck out to me at all. Was the murderer still here? Most people at this point had forgotten about their masks, and from where

I was standing, I had a clear view of everyone in the room. I noticed people that I had known for years, but I didn't see anyone I thought was the culprit.

All the ladies were around the table holding on to one another like someone was going to jump out of the crowd and take their friends away. They already had, though.

I told them all that I was going to the hospital in Barnville and wanted to see what the prognosis would be for June Bug. I couldn't believe that the same murderer had poisoned another one of my friends and her life was hanging in the balance. I instinctively knew it was poison, delivered in Triston's favorite drink. This killer was playing with us. But what could we do? I didn't have a smoking gun on the person I thought was culpable and Pick's hands were tied unless . . . It was a long shot, but it might work. First things first, I had to go find out what had happened and make sure June Bug was going to make it.

It was all too much. I wanted to scream at the top of my lungs. How could I have been so stupid? The murderer was taunting us. He or she knew what we were doing and was showing us if we didn't back off, more people could potentially die. But the murderer had made a mistake by calling and acting like me. That clarified more; I was beginning to piece things together. At least I hoped I was. I couldn't allow the murderer to kill another one of my friends. They'd do it over my dead body.

So much for a party!

Chapter Fifteen

WE WERE ALL IN THE WAITING ROOM at the hospital. Pick had told the attending doctor to check June Bug for poisoning. She was in the ICU, hanging on to life by a string. She was hooked up to a ventilator that breathed for her and a cardiac monitor that was tracking her heart's electrical activity, and its rate and rhythm. The IVs in her arm were delivering fluids and nutrients directly into her bloodstream. I knew all this because Pearl explained everything they were doing to keep her alive. Once the tox screen was back, they could give her an antidote, if there was one, to the poison used to try to kill her. For all intents and purposes, she was in an induced coma to allow her body to rest and try to heal. I couldn't stand seeing her with all those tubes everywhere, but also thankful for the ventilator that was keeping her alive. But if the tox screen didn't come back soon, we could lose her. How could I have been so stupid not to know that right after someone had messed with our table, they could get to one of us without anyone even knowing what happened? How had they gotten the poison into her drink and was it meant for me or Pearl or Myra? Or just any random person at our table?

It could have been for anyone.

Knowing that if they poisoned one of us, they could poison us all.

I wondered if the ladies in the waiting room would start backing away from this investigation. That's what the killer wanted. That much was evident. I was holding Pearl's hand when I heard Charlie's deep voice in the waiting room talking to Pick. Pearl looked up at me and said, "Go." She slowly followed me out of June Bug's room until I was running into Charlie's arms. Myra had called and told him about the poisoning. He got to the hospital as fast as he could.

I was crying into his shirt. I knew I would have makeup and mascara all over his shirt. He liked starched white shirts, and I had them monogrammed with his initials on the top of his shirt pocket. Last year for Christmas, Amber bought him different colored button-up shirts, but he always went back to his white shirts. They were a part of him like Chanel No. 5 was to Myra. He held me and I knew all the women from the Auxiliary were looking on. If you can't be vulnerable in front of your friends, then they aren't friends.

"You're going to be okay," he whispered over and over in my ear.

I looked into his eyes. "I can't believe someone poisoned her right in front of all of us." He pulled me back to him. I could see the makeup all over his white shirt and I knew in a time like this it didn't matter. Then I heard a ping from the elevator, and Barry Ashford stepped out and came over to Bunny and held onto her for dear life as well. I felt like I had failed as the leader of all these wonderful ladies. Had it all been a fool's errand? I couldn't think like that. If I did, I knew the murderer would get away with all that had been done. What else could happen? I couldn't think that way either because if I did, I would stop myself and it would have all been in vain.

The other women held on to one another. Some of their husbands were not with us anymore, which made me even sadder. They didn't have someone like Charlie they could count on.

I needed to know what the poison was that had been used tonight. I don't think the killer cared *who* drank the toxic tonic, as long as one of us did. I pulled away from Charlie. I needed to be alone and think for just a few minutes. If what I was thinking was right, then everything had changed. There was one piece of the puzzle still missing. I walked away from Charlie, and he came after me.

"Thelma, are you okay, honey?" His voice was soft, and it was almost as if I had hurt him by leaving his arms. But I needed to think and couldn't do that cuddled up with Charlie, no matter how much I wanted to.

"Charlie, honey, I'm sorry. It's not you. I just need some time to think, that's all. I'm okay. I promise." I looked at him lovingly and knew from the look on his face that he understood.

I grabbed Pick and told him everything I was thinking. I know how it all sounded crazy and far-fetched. It sounded that way when I was piecing it together at the party. Then June Bug was poisoned. Did she know something that scared the killer? I didn't know.

The culprit was trying to send me into a spiral. And they would have, had it not been for Charlie being here, telling me everything would be okay. I had to believe that. I had to believe that June Bug would survive this.

I would know for sure once I heard what the poison was. At least I thought I would. It would tell me if what I was thinking was accurate or if I was way out in left field.

Pick had agreed it was far-fetched, but not impossible. That gave me hope that this might all possibly end tonight or tomorrow morning. The killer had been very deceptive. More so than I ever imagined. I could tell Pick was trying to put it all together in his mind. But if I was right, it would rock this whole town.

Pick went into another room on the floor and took out his flip phone. I knew he was calling Hansen to tell him to be on standby. But knowing Hansen, he would come straight to the hospital. There were a lot of things still up in the air. But I knew in my bones I was close; so close I could taste it. This had to end tonight or tomorrow at the latest. We couldn't have any more carnage.

Pick was still on the phone, but it didn't look like he was talking to Hansen now. Maybe he had called Alma, his secretary, or Susie Bright, requesting that they be on the ready if needed. I wouldn't know until he finished his phone calls.

I went back over to Charlie after looking in on June Bug. I kept running things over and over in my head. I took Charlie's hand in mine. He held my hand, which seemed to ground me a little. The waiting chairs were so uncomfortable that my tailbone was hurting, and we had only been here thirty minutes. I looked over at Bunny and Barry sitting in the same concrete chairs. Bunny's back was as straight as a two-by-four and never touched the back of the chair. These little idiosyncrasies made us all different and yet many the same. I looked at my ladies. They were standing with one another or sitting in groups, talking among themselves. All of us had seen June Bug and kissed her hand to let her know we were here for her, and that she couldn't leave. Not like this.

I think they made these chairs impossible to sit in on purpose, so people would get tired and leave. It had to be old, white men making these stupid decisions. You'd think the chairs would be comfortable. The pews at St. John's were more comfortable than these and that was saying something. They were made of pure cherrywood and were as hard as a brick. But from people sitting in them so much over the years, it had softened the pews so you could at least get through the Sunday's sermon.

I looked again at Pick, and he was walking to an empty room, dialing another number. He was talking in whispers too low for me to hear. Pearl was at the door waiting for him. Who in the world was he calling? Was he checking to see if the glass June Bug drank from had fingerprints on it other than hers? I doubted it. Or was he calling in the calvary? There weren't that many people he needed to call. But if I were the sheriff and had just heard what I had told him, I'd probably be on the phone to make sure I wasn't going to get in trouble, because if I was right, all hell was going to break loose.

I heard the elevator ping again and looked up, expecting the doctor to give us an update on June Bug, but it was Hansen Mulvaney, in a crisp starched white shirt just like Charlie's, except his wasn't monogrammed. He was wearing his cowboy boots and looked good. Katie Mae was one lucky woman.

I couldn't believe myself. One of my ladies was fighting for her life, and I was googling over Hansen Mulvaney!

Of course, if you could see his butt in the Levi's he wore, you'd be distracted, too. You just couldn't help it.

Charlie noticed me looking at Hansen's butt, and whispered in my ear, "Would you like to trade me in for a younger model?" as if he were talking about trading in cars. I playfully slapped at his chest and he laughed. It sounded good to hear that laugh. I needed it so badly. I hadn't told anyone but Pick what I was thinking. I didn't want them to think I was crazy. Because as soon as I told one of the ladies, they would tell me to really think about what I was saying. I know it might not make sense to them just yet, so I held it close and allowed Pick to decipher the details. After all, he is the sheriff.

Myra told me before the ball that they would also bring all the animals on stage to see if anyone wanted to give them a forever home. But with what happened to June Bug, they called the party off because it immediately became a crime scene. I also noticed, as we were leaving, that people were placing their drinks on the tables just in case the killer tried to poison anyone else.

I felt terrible for the poor animals. This was their night—their night to find perfect families to take them home and enrich their lives. I rescued every dog I ever had, only to find that they rescued you, too. When all this is over, we would have to do something through the Ladies Auxiliary and try to find homes for these dogs and cats. They deserved it. Bless their hearts.

I told Charlie I had to stand up; the chairs were killing my behind. He continued sitting. I stood for a few minutes, then sat back down. I was so fidgety; I couldn't help it.

I pulled my shoes off and began massaging my feet. They felt like they were about to fall off. Charlie looked at me and smiled. I said softly, ensuring no one else could hear me. "You are not going to massage my feet. Get that out of your dirty mind." In a hospital waiting room to see if one of my dear friends would live or die, and he's thinking about doing the nasty. I raised my eyebrows at him in disgust and he laughed again. But massaging my feet felt too good to stop and bicker, so I let it go. Plus, he had, for a few seconds, taken my mind to another place, no matter how raunchy it was.

Men!

"I'll be right back," he told me and went to the elevator, pressing the down button. It automatically opened and closed. At least I supposed he was pressing the down button. Maybe he needed some air. Who knows? I was too tired to care as long as he came back. He would have told me if he was leaving.

I looked around the room and Babs was sitting with Bunny and Barry. Mitzi, Skitter, and Fifi were sitting together, all lost in their thoughts.

I looked for Pearl and she was in the corner talking with Pick and Hansen. Myra wasn't here yet, but I'm sure she had so much to do with shutting down the PAW Ball. She'd probably be busy most of the night. I called her on her cell.

"Thelma, how's it going at the hospital?" I could hear a good bit of commotion in the background. It sounded as if they were taking down tables and loading chairs to go back to the rental company.

"They put her in an induced coma until the tox screen comes back. Pick told Doctor Zabar to check her tox panels along with whatever else they would be checking to find out what happened." Myra sounded defeated that this had happened at her event. But there was nothing she could do. The murderer had this planned way ahead of time. The killer knew we were going to the PAW Ball.

Who had I told? Who had I not told?

"I can't believe this happened at the PAW Ball. We've never had any troubles before. Ever." I could tell Myra felt completely exasperated.

"I know, Myra, but we've never had a killer on the loose, either. It's not your or anyone else's fault? But I think I know who the killer is. It's hard to swallow, but if I'm right, all of Sunnyside will be reeling from it." I heard her suck in some air.

"I'm about to leave here, Thelma. I'll be at the hospital in about fifteen minutes, and you can tell me then." I hadn't told her that I hadn't even told Pearl. I didn't want to look stupid if I was wrong. And there was a chance I could be. But every time I thought about everything that had happened, I knew I wasn't.

"Sounds good. Oh, and Myra, please be careful. Have one of those strapping waiters walk you to your car."

"Well, in that case, I'll be about thirty minutes late. But the sad part is that these young boys couldn't hang with me for too long, anyway. As young as they are, I'm sure about ninety-five percent of them are *minute men*." Then Myra cackled, which made me cackle too. Everyone in the room looked at me like I had smallpox. I couldn't believe she had thought about sex at a time like this. But I was happy for the intrusion.

Good Lord, can't a woman laugh in distressing times?

She was as bad as Charlie was, but I suppose that was one reason she had been married three times. She put herself out there.

We hung up and I couldn't wait until she got here. Pearl was so used to hospitals. When she'd explained to me why they put June Bug in an induced coma and what fluids they were administering in her IV drip, I felt like I was talking to a doctor.

I don't speak "doctor"!

But she just kept blabbering on until I finally told her I understood, even though I really didn't. But I had the gist of what she was going on about, and that would have to do until the doctor came out and told us what was going on.

The elevator dinged again and the doors opened. It was Charlie, walking in and holding a canvas bag. He sat down beside me and handed me the bag. I looked into it and wanted to kiss him. He was an angel sent by God. He brought my good slippers that looked like real shoes. I put them on, and they made my feet feel so much better. If only I had a robe that looked like a normal wrap, I would be in heaven, even though my butt cheeks were in hell from sitting on these concrete chairs. I looked down at the chair legs and could see that they were bolted to the floor.

Dear Jesus!

Who went around stealing hospital chairs? They wouldn't have stolen them if they had sat in them first, unless they were going to torture someone with them!

The room was dead silent and when Pick's phone rang, I almost jumped out of my skin. He still had one of those cheap flip phones, and they had one ring to them and it was always loud. He went into the empty room again to talk privately. I didn't know what he was up to, but I prayed he would at least give me a chance to test my hypothesis. Of course, when I told him what I thought had happened, he looked at me like I had three heads. I don't blame him because it sounded crazy. And the most ironic part was that I had figured it out on my own. That may be why I continued to question it. The ladies had done everything I asked them to. But thinking back on it, I thought we were being safe when actually, we were playing right into the killer's hands, if I were right.

The elevator dinged again and everyone turned to see Dr. Zabar walk in.

Thank You Jesus!

He went straight to Pick, and I got out of my chair and went to see what he had to say.

"Pick, I'm glad you told us to check for poisoning. If we hadn't, she wouldn't be alive now. She's tough. She's still in a coma, but I think it's going to take time for her body to heal itself. We'll know more in the morning if she pulls through, but my hopes are high. Once we checked her tox screen, we knew what we needed to do. We stabilized her, and she should wake up sometime tomorrow if things go the way I think they will."

"What was the poison?" Pick twirled his toothpick around his thin lips. Dr. Zabar must see a lot of Pick, because he didn't look like he thought Pick was a good ole redneck from Sunnyside, which he was.

"It looks like it was tetrazine, which is commonly found in ClearSight eye drops."

"ClearSight eye drops?" I asked Dr. Zabar. I looked at Pick and everything I told him was falling into place. I bobbed my head up and down, letting him know I thought I was right all along.

I looked at Pick and he gave me a quick nod, letting me know he understood what I had told him. He looked at Hansen, and Hansen went to the elevator to get things set up.

I turned to Dr. Zabar and asked if I could see June Bug again. He told me not to stay too long as she still wasn't out of the woods. But instinctively, I knew everything was going to be okay. I just wanted to let her know she was going to be okay, and that she had helped me figure this whole thing out. I went to her door and there stood a deputy outside her room. I could tell I was going to have to wring his neck to let me in, but Pick came around the corner and told him it was okay for me to go in.

Police presence?

Thank the Lord that Pick was on the ball. This way no one else could get to June Bug without making a huge fuss. Pick had to work fast. I'm glad because if he hadn't been on the ball, I was afraid the murderer could disappear into the night.

I went in and held June Bug's hand and told her she was going to be okay. I told her I would check on her again in the morning. I also told her she had helped me figure out this whole masquerade. I knew she was in a coma, but I just felt that telling her would do some good. Maybe it would, maybe it wouldn't, but I had to tell her. I kissed her hand and left the room, the cop still standing beside her doorway as I walked back to the waiting area.

Chapter Sixteen

I TOLD CHARLIE WHAT I HAD TO DO to wrap this up before the killer got away. He didn't want me to leave his side. But when Hansen returned to the hospital with our informant in tow, Charlie knew I would be in good hands. I didn't think once cornered that the murderer would do anything except possibly try to lie their way out of jail, but that wasn't happening. First, it was Triston who was murdered. Then the murderer tried to kill one of my ladies and I wouldn't stand for that.

I rode with Pick and had never been in a police car before. Normally he drives his old Ford truck around, but when Hansen got back to the hospital with our cargo, they had to use a police car to be on the safe side.

We had already spoken to the person in the back seat, her hands cuffed behind her back. Hansen sat on the driver's side in the back with her. At first, she was denying everything until I told her how I had found out what was planned, and how the murderer was going to dump it all in her lap. I told her I knew she had called Angie at the PAW Ball and told her we wouldn't need our table after all. I took my phone out and showed her the number I had gotten from Angie. She looked at my phone and saw her number. I could tell she knew she was between a rock and a hard place. Hansen told her that if she got out in front of it, they would personally talk with the DA to have her sentence reduced to manslaughter since she didn't outright kill Triston, but she did try to poison June Bug. Because she hadn't succeeded, the DA might reduce her sentence, which would at least keep her off death row.

In South Carolina, we still believe in frying 'em!

I'm sure that was the straw that broke the camel's back, because she told us things I hadn't even thought of.

We got to The Mills just in time. Tony was loading two Mercedes' with Louis Vuitton luggage. Bless his heart, he was sweating up a storm. He had sweat running down his brow and kept wiping it with the sleeve of his shirt. At that rate, his entire shirt would be soaking wet before he finished packing them up.

Hansen and Susie Bright had been on the phone with the banks going over bank accounts since June Bug had been poisoned. If they had left our table at the PAW ball alone, I would have never figured all this out. But most sociopaths think they're smarter than the rest of us.

We all three went to the elevator, and Tony told us that Arty had asked to be left alone.

I bet he did.

I looked at Tony like he had four heads. He had seen us get out of a police car with other police cars behind us. Was he trying to help someone escape?

Lord, please don't tell me he was involved too!

"You can see we're here on police business, Tony. Surely you don't want to get on the wrong side of this, do you?" Hansen asked in his deep, authoritative voice. I watched as Tony got a handkerchief from his desk and wiped his sweaty forehead.

"I was told he didn't want any disturbances." Tony pulled out five crisp one-hundred-dollar bills he had been given to keep people from going up to the penthouse. They had to know that it wouldn't be long before everything fell into place. Sadly for them, it had.

"Tony, we need your key, now!" Hansen was tired of playing around. It was now close to 2:00 a.m. and getting later by the minute.

"Did you ever stop and think why someone would want to pack in the middle of the night?" I asked Tony, and watched as he pulled the chain of keys from behind his desk.

"I'm so sorry! I was told they wanted to pack tonight because they had an early flight tomorrow." Tony was looking like a little child who had been caught with his hands in the cookie jar. "Do I have to give the money back?" Tony whined.

"No," Hansen said, on the verge of losing his temper.

Tony rushed to the elevator and put the key in the lock for the penthouse.

Pick, Hansen, and I rode the elevator up in silence. We had left our informant in the police car. Pick told me to get behind Hansen. They both had their guns drawn when the doors opened, but no one was there to greet us.

We looked around the apartment and didn't see anyone or hear anything. Hansen went to the apartment below, looked in all the rooms, came back to the stairs, and yelled up at Pick, "All clear, boss."

That's when I remembered the stairs. "They took the stairs down. They must have seen us when we pulled up," I said.

Immediately, Hansen found the exit sign on the far right wall and started running down the stairs like he was in the Olympics.

I headed to the elevator, followed by Pick. We were too old for the Olympics. I still had on my slippers Charlie had brought to the hospital for me. "Do they seriously think they're going to outrun us?" Pick said to me with a grin. He pulled his pants higher, making me nervous that his swaying gun might go off.

I was thinking they just might get away if they hadn't already. But Susie Bright pulled into the parking lot right after us and was told in great detail by Pick who we were after and why, and if they evaded us, she was to stop them, guns a blazing, if needed.

I had never been in a shoot-out and wasn't fond of the chances we might have when those elevator doors opened. We could be under heavy fire. The bell rang and the doors opened. I closed my eyes, scared that we'd be shot. But it was all quiet.

Sitting on a bench, in front of the gorgeous flowers they always had in the waiting room, was Arty. He had on dark blue jeans with tears in them, his Gucci slippers, and a linen shirt. Chipper was in his cage next to him. Beside Chipper sat KDP's own Twilight Woods, but now she was a blonde. I thought she must have been wearing a wig on the night June Bug saw her and Arty fussing. She must have worn it as a disguise when she arrived in town the day Triston was murdered.

Pick had spoken to one of her producers on his way to The Mills, who had been more than happy to explain that Twilight had been on vacation for the past two weeks, and anything we saw her sell on KDP had been taped in advance.

She had her arms crossed and her lips pursed. I noticed she had lip injections. They must have been fresh, as her lips were poking out pretty far from her face. She almost looked as if she had a duck's bill.

"Going somewhere?" Pick asked Arty and Twilight.

"We were packing to leave tomorrow. We're heading to the KDP Headquarters so I can oversee the start of producing Triston's products for sale on KDP exclusively."

"Then why do you have red-eye tickets for Vietnam?" Pick said flatly. I had to give it to Pick. They had called banks, airlines, and other pertinent places to make sure they didn't leave town before we got to them.

"They don't have an extradition policy with the United States. Did you honestly think you could kill Triston and poison someone else and get away with it?" Hansen asked.

I could tell Pick was hanging back. "You might as well tell us because the first one who talks, well, we'll let the DA know you cooperated. That alone could keep you from getting the death penalty. You know in South Carolina we still have the death penalty?" I could see Arty looking at Twilight, who was acting like a statue. She hadn't moved the whole time. Neither had her big lips. I couldn't get over just how big they were.

She acted as if she was above all this.

"Are you arresting us?" Twilight finally asked, looking at Hansen. "If so, I would like to call my attorney. This is a sham. I came to help Arty figure out what he's going to do with Triston's legacy, and *Magnum PI* is talking to me like I'm a common criminal," she huffed, looking toward Hansen.

I surely didn't see the *Magnum PI* part at all. Hansen looked better than Magnum ever did, even with that mustache he had worn.

"So, you're trying to get me to believe that you didn't have anything to do with Triston's death?" Hansen looked at the Ice Queen.

Could I see her melting? She had started to perspire.

"Of course I didn't have anything to do with Triston's death. I was on the air selling products when he was murdered," she said somewhat defiantly.

"That's not what your producer, Susan Wentworth, told us. She said you were on a two-week vacation, and anything we saw you sell on KDP had been taped earlier," Hansen said.

"I was not at *this place* at the time of Triston's murder." She said it like Sunnyside was some dump of a town. It was a shame she was so nasty in person.

She had pressured Arty and Sherry to do what needed to be done to get the contracts to sell Triston's products and franchise the salon.

Pick seemed satisfied, but I wasn't.

"Arty, what do you have to say for yourself?" I looked at Arty, my voice filled with shame at what he had done to Triston.

"I'd like to speak with my attorney." Arty looked out the dark mullioned windows in the lobby. You could see the pulsing lights from the police cars flashing blue all over the parking lot and into the streets. I could hear a commotion from upstairs and the phones began to ring. Tony had his hands full trying to explain that nothing was wrong in Sunnyside's premiere condos when everyone in Sunnyside knew better.

"Look, Arty, we already know what you did." Hansen looked at Susie Bright and tilted his head. Susie left the building's annex for a few seconds and returned with Sherry Haster, her hands cuffed behind her back. Sherry looked at Arty as if to say she was sorry, but nothing they did could be explained away.

"Listen, son, tell us what happened and that may go a long way in helping you with the DA." Pick applied more pressure, even though I doubted he had any say in what the DA would or wouldn't do in a homicide this vile. And, not to mention what they found out about how Sherry had tried to poison June Bug because Arty told her it was the only way. I had seen the ClearSight eye drops in Arty and Triston's bathroom downstairs where Myra had stayed, but I had no idea the drops were poisonous. Why would they allow those on pharmacy shelves?

Sherry Haster stood there beside Susie Bright in her USC sweatshirt and yoga pants, hair tousled from sleeping. I don't suppose she thought her night would end like this. I still couldn't believe they had done it.

"You might as well tell them because I've already told them everything." Sherry looked at Arty, trying to get him to talk. I knew they had worked something out with the DA for Sherry, as I'd heard them talking in the car on the way here. But she would be in prison for the rest of her life, especially after confessing to poisoning June Bug with ClearSight eye drops. She had placed them in a glass of Cherry Coke at the PAW Ball in the kitchen area and told a waiter that someone at our table was asking for another Cherry Coke. She had pointed to June Bug from the tent curtain inside the kitchen. Apparently Arty thought June Bug had heard too much when she stopped by to drop the food off just days before. They assumed she had heard them fussing up a storm when the elevator doors had opened. They had no idea she couldn't hear well enough to understand what they had been fighting about.

I went over and stood over Arty. I didn't want to look at Twilight Woods. She could go to hell as far as I was concerned. They all would in the end, but I was not leaving without an explanation, even though I'm pretty sure why Arty and Twilight were fussing that night.

Arty knew what needed to be done when Triston had changed his mind. He was fine with having just one salon and didn't care if KDP made his products or not. In the end, he killed Triston for pure greed. Money was the root of all evil.

Twilight had killed Triston, just as much as Arty had. The only difference was she was smart enough to keep from getting her hands dirty.

"Arty, I can't believe what you did to Triston. He loved you more than money, and the way you had killed him." I froze for a second, remembering the grimace on Triston's dead face.

"Nobody deserves to die that way, Arty. I knew Triston, and I knew he loved making his own products, putting them into their bottles, and labeling them for sale. That meant something to him, far greater than any money he could have gained. I can't believe you tortured him like that for pure greed. You must have made a very sweet Cherry Coke to mask the taste of that bitter almond oil." I didn't know what else to say. I was mentally, physically, and spiritually exhausted.

Arty looked up at me and started crying, then I could see the murderous fire behind his eyes. "*He* was tortured? Please don't kid yourself, Thelma. Do you know how hard it was to love someone like Triston? Everything had to be perfect, or he would yell at me, call me lazy, say I didn't care about his precious products. Shampoos and styling products were his babies. I remember when *I* was his baby. How he used to love on me. I remember the days when we had talked about having our own children." Arty started crying. Anger and rage had welled up from deep inside him.

He wanted to tell us what had happened. Pick had told us earlier that he thought Arty would be on the verge of confessing to everything. He was right. I didn't know how much more I could handle hearing all this.

Arty started again, anger tearing him into pieces. He wiped his face with his shirt and continued. "The past three years, I would have been lucky to get a real kiss from him. It was always about the salon or the product line. Then when Twilight gave us the chance to get out from under the product line and have them created in a real lab where they would be perfect, he wouldn't go through with it. So, don't you *dare* lecture me about torture! The last three years of my life were torture, consumed with the salon and that stupid product line. He was working himself to the bone, and for what? He wanted the world to know about his line of products, but he wouldn't let go. He sat there and told me that if I didn't like it, then I knew where the door was. He was going to leave me because we didn't share the same dreams anymore. It would have been so easy to allow Twilight and her team to take care of everything. But no, he wanted to be present when the labs created his products to make sure they didn't skimp on any ingredients. It was so stupid! He was a complete control freak. But when he told me if I didn't like it, then I could 'hit the door,' I had had enough." Tears were streaming down Arty's face. His fury was palpable.

"I pulled Sherry aside and told her about the franchise deal, and asked if she thought she could get the money to start a salon at the beach. She told me she would have to figure out a way, but she was totally interested. When she finally told me she wanted to go ahead with it, I told her that Triston had changed his mind about everything!" Arty was almost yelled at this point to get it all out.

"I told her we had to get Triston out of the way to do what needed to be done or everything would stay the same. I couldn't take it anymore. We would be in our sixties making shampoo, and for what? So, I called Twilight and told her everything. I needed her help. She had dealt with prima donnas like Triston before and knew how to put them in their place." He stopped talking long enough to wipe tears from his eyes and face. His eyes were red and puffy and filled with indignation. His face and shirt were wet from tears.

Twilight started shaking him, telling him to shut up, but Arty looked at her with daggers in his eyes. She finally stopped and crossed her arms over her chest.

Arty continued, "I told Twilight what I was going to do. At first, I didn't think she'd go for it, but she saw the opportunity and jumped at the chance. She could finally stop peddling other people's products and create franchises that would bring in *big* money. More money than I ever dreamed of making. She came into town the night before I ended it all with Triston. Once he was dead, Twilight told me about another hairdresser who had sold products on her show. That hairdresser had franchised her salon. First, all over Texas, then California, and then the whole Midwest, and in a few years with the franchise stable, she sold her business for over $40 million dollars! I was not going to allow Triston to just let all of this go!" Arty yelled. He had become defiant.

"I had nothing to do with Triston's death," Twilight kept saying, trying to get out in front of it. But the damage had been done. She knew what Arty was going to do to Triston, but didn't do one thing to try to stop him. She wasn't going to wiggle her way out of this one. Lord knows what all she's done through the years to advance her career. For people like her, no amount of money would ever be enough, and even if she didn't pour the poison into Triston's drink, she had colluded with Arty after knowing what he was going to do, and then once it was done, she just went along with him like nothing had ever happened. Plus, she also knew what Sherry was going to do to June Bug and didn't try to stop her either.

Arty wasn't finished though. He continued explaining and making excuses for why he took his lover's life. In his twisted way, it was as if he felt everyone would agree with him.

"It had been a very long week at the salon and Triston was cooking dinner for us. He asked if I would make him a Cherry Coke with a little bourbon in it to help him wind down. It was the perfect time to act. So I went downstairs and got the bottle of bitter almond oil. I knew it wouldn't take much to get Triston out of the way. But I had no idea he would suffer the way he did. I thought it would just kill him. At first, he got a really bad headache and then became dizzy. I thought I hadn't put enough in the drink, but then he started acting confused and anxious. He had difficulty breathing and was gasping for air. He asked me to call 911, but I told him to go lie down because he probably had gotten Covid from someone at the salon. Then his breathing got really bad and before he got to the couch, he fell. He started throwing up all over the place. Curling into a ball, holding his stomach. I thought it would never end." Arty started wailing this time. Hansen brought him some Kleenex.

I almost felt sorry for him, but I couldn't, not after what he had done. I didn't want to hear the rest, but I felt obligated because of Triston. I wanted to walk away, but I feared if I did, Arty would stop talking. I couldn't let that happen, so I stood there as stoic as I could, but inside it was killing me, hearing how Triston had suffered. The pain and agony he went through. At first, I thought all this was about money, but hearing all this, I realized that it was more than just the money. It was also about their relationship, and how they had allowed it to die. I was so thankful for Charlie, Pearl, and Myra. I didn't know what I'd do without them.

Arty started talking again, trying to gulp in air from all the crying. "It was horrible to watch. Once Triston stopped vomiting, I was praying he would be okay. I didn't want him to suffer, but then he started having bad seizures. I didn't know what to do. I couldn't call 911. I didn't think it would matter if I did, so I just held him as tight as I could, as he had seizure after seizure. I took my belt off and placed it in his mouth to keep him from biting his tongue in half. That's how bad it was. Then his skin started turning red, and I thought it was from the cherry juice, but afterward, I looked it up, and it was because of the bitter almond oil. He lost consciousness and his breathing started slowing down. I knew he was having a heart attack, and then he died, and everything went quiet. So quiet." He was holding onto the edge of the wooden bench, his knuckles turning white from gripping the bench so hard.

Arty just moaned, remembering how badly Triston had suffered. "Then the food on the stove started burning and the fire alarm went off. I jumped up and threw the pot in the sink and poured water over it. Then I went back to Triston, and he had this look on his face. He was gone. I couldn't believe I had killed the only person I had ever loved. I sat there holding him in my lap, vomit on the floor all around us."

Arty got quiet and I prayed he was finished. Then he whispered while looking down at his lap, "We were living a façade. He hadn't touched me in months, and every time I tried to cuddle with him on the couch or in the bed, he always pushed me away, saying he was too hot, or his arms or back hurt too much. I was tired of him pushing me away. But as long as I played his perfect boyfriend, and everything looked perfect in front of everyone else, he was happy. He loved for me to manage the salon and take care of his business, but when I needed taken care of, he couldn't do it. He would kiss me, but it was always just a peck on the mouth. Nothing sensual. He was sadistic. We hadn't had sex in over a year. What was I supposed to think when the person I loved more than anyone else didn't want to have sex with me anymore? It was like we were roommates sharing a bed. He had his side; I had mine. I was pretty sure he was seeing one of his assistants at the salon on the side."

Twilight sat there with her arms crossed around her chest. "He's crazy. I hope you don't believe what he's telling you. You can tell he's crazy. And I'm not going to sit here and allow him to drag me down with him." She looked at Pick, and he didn't say a word. Everything was being taped. So, when the DA heard Arty's confession, she'd go down with him. I'm sure she'll hire some Perry Mason-type to try to get her out of this, but I had a feeling that KDP just lost their best anchor.

Arty looked into my eyes. What a poor, lost soul. I looked back at him because I needed to know why he wanted Sherry to hurt June Bug.

"Arty, what I don't understand is why Sherry had to hurt June Bug? She's never done a thing to you, except make sure you had enough food to eat, to make sure your life was a little bit easier after Triston's death. We all did. She called me when she left your penthouse and told me she had heard you and Missy here fussing up a storm, and it had scared her. But she had no idea why you were fussing. Why did you have to do that to her? She didn't have anything to do with any of this. When the doctor at the hospital told us that she had been poisoned by ClearSight eye drops, I knew it was from the stash you had in the medicine cabinet downstairs." He was still crying. His face and eyes were red and bloodshot. He had begun to sweat.

When he spoke again, his voice was raspy. "I didn't know what June Bug heard and when I told Twilight everything I had done, she went ballistic. But she didn't turn me in because she wanted this as much as I did. She knew how much money she would make bringing Triston's products to market on KDP, and she had talked to one seller about franchising, and they told her who she could contact. We only needed two people to franchise a Triston Apothecary Salon, and Twilight would come in and help with all the lawyers' fees and create contracts to ensure everyone was making money. Like I said, Sherry had told me she wanted in after she knew she could get the money. In the scheme of things, it wasn't a lot of money for a franchise. At least that's what Twilight told me. I also spoke with Katie Smith, but she declined, saying that she was happy here and didn't want to leave Sunnyside. So, I thought if no one else would open one, I would do it. I could go back and forth from Barnville to Columbia, and keep up with both salons. That was another reason we were fussing. She had started acting like Triston. Everything had to be done her way. But I was the one holding all the cards. I knew I could franchise the salon with or without her. Once Twilight had spoken to me about franchising, she had no idea what she had placed in my hands: a way to expand everything and run it the way it was supposed to be run. Do you think Triston could do what I did, day in and day out, at that salon? Please! He would have been lost doing payroll, let alone paying quarterly taxes and keeping up with the day-to-day minutiae that had nothing to do with cutting or coloring hair. He was always the creative one in our relationship. Until it started souring. I gave him thirty years of my life, and I was going to get what I had worked so hard for all these years. Not to have it snatched away because he was a control freak. I was supposed to be his baby. Not his products! He treated them with more love than he did me." Arty stopped, his face blood-red and splotchy. Pick had told us that he thought Arty was at the end of his rope, and he was going to allow him to hang himself with it.

And boy did he.

Arty seemed to have come back to himself after a few minutes of silence. Then he looked at me, tears running down his face. "I've lost so much. I miss Triston more than I ever want to admit. Why couldn't he just let things go and we could ride off into the sunset and retire in the mountains or at the beach? Hell, we would have had enough money to have a place at both. But he couldn't let go. And I am sorry about June Bug, but I thought she had been standing there when I told Twilight that I had killed Triston."

He continued, "I also didn't know what to do with his body. Then I remembered that a lot of kids went behind the church to smoke pot and whatever, and I thought I would put him in the woods. He was so small, I used one of my garment travel bags to put him in. I pulled the car up close to the elevator that led out the back way of our penthouse, put him in, and left. But when I got to the back of the church, I tripped over something. It was one of those fake rocks you put keys in. I looked inside it with the flashlight on my phone and it had a key inside. I tried it on the back door of the church and the door opened. When no alarms went off, I dragged Triston up the steps and into that back Sunday school room. I knew people would wonder how he got there, and it would divert suspicion away from me. When I left, the sun was almost coming up. I wiped my fingerprints off the doorknob and was planning to put the key back inside the fake rock, but I couldn't find it. I looked everywhere. I never found it and I had to leave. I was careful when I used it, so I didn't think my fingerprints would be found on it, anyway. I threw the empty fake rock and the garment bag away in some woods on the way back to The Mills." He sat there. I could tell he was exhausted. He had literally spilled more than the beans. I still thought about June Bug in the hospital holding on for dear life.

"I'm sorry Arty. I *don't* feel sorry for you. A dear friend of mine is in the hospital, holding on between life and death. She had no idea why you and Twilight were fussing. She just told me she had walked in with a box full of food and heard you yelling at each other. I'll never forgive y'all for trying to kill her.

I can't believe you killed Triston. All this time, me, Pearl, and Myra said there was no way Arty could have killed Triston the way he was murdered. He suffered so much. I don't believe you know what love is. If you think you loved him, it's the most twisted kind of love I've ever seen." He was looking at me, still crying. He placed his hands in front of his face and cried into them. I looked at Twilight then. "I can't believe you didn't say a word to anybody after he told you he had killed Triston. You came down here knowing what he was going to do. That makes you just as guilty."

Arty looked at her with streaked tears falling down his cheeks. "She knew everything. She didn't care as long as she made her money. She was the one who told me to use the ClearSight. She told me it had some type of chemical in it, that if ingested, was poisonous."

"Don't you dare try bringing me into this mess you made for yourself. I didn't have anything to do with any of this." She scowled and looked at Pick. Her blonde hair was perfectly styled. She was in a black jumpsuit that fit her body perfectly. You could tell she took great care of her looks. "I did tell him about the franchises, but I had no idea about him murdering Triston or that June Bug person." She said June Bug like she was superior to her and all of us.

"Twilight knew about everything. She stayed in the room downstairs and found ClearSight in the medicine cabinet. She told Arty how to get rid of June Bug." Sherry Haster had been so quiet that I'd forgotten she was in the room. I couldn't take my eyes off Arty. He was a pure sociopath. He could charm you to death, then kill you to death, and the worst part was, he would always have a good enough excuse for doing it.

"Arty, I pray one day you will feel what true love is. You're sitting here telling us all this because you feel lonely. You don't care at all about the lives you have destroyed, and that includes your own. Did you ever stop to think that relationships change over the years and become so much more than just sex? Yes, you need affection, but I've seen the way Triston looked at you, and he loved you, Arty, whether you knew it or not." I didn't know what else to say. I just shook my head at him and his cohorts.

Then, in the middle of all this mess, I wondered, the most trivial thing: who was going to cut my hair now?

Sherry screwed her life up by following Arty. Now I was left without a hairdresser. Again!

First Triston and then Sherry. You might not be able to divorce your hairdresser, but they could surely divorce you.

Of course, I'm not talking about Triston. Bless his heart. I will never forget him and all he did for Sunnyside. He brought true love to Sunnyside and showed it to everyone who graced his salon. Even to us old women. I just pray that once the air clears, someone will take over the salon and keep it up and running. Triston would have wanted that.

"Okay, we've heard enough. Thanks, Thelma." Pick had had enough.

I couldn't believe it was over. But in my heart, it would never be over, knowing how Triston had suffered so much before he passed.

"You're welcome, Pick, but I didn't do anything." I winked at him. Now who was being modest?

Hansen and Susie Bright were cuffing Arty and Twilight. I just hoped that when Moon Pie Hubbard heard that I was the one who cracked the case, that he would not come after me. He was a dangerous man, not unlike Arty, but he'd never get caught. Moon Pie had been doing this for far too long, and personally, I think it's high time he retires. That's next on my list.

"Wait . . . please," Arty begged, as they were taking him and Twilight to the police vehicles waiting outside. "What's going to happen to Chipper? He can't be left alone. He needs someone to love him." I was surprised how Arty could care so much about a bird, but not think twice about killing a human. Maybe there's hope for him after all.

Yeah right. A psycho is a psycho.

"Thelma, please take him and find him a home," Arty pleaded. Pick was trying to move Arty forward, but he resisted until I finally gave in.

"Okay. But you have to tell me what he eats and how often." I looked at Pick, who was trying hard to keep from smiling. Lord, what have I got myself into? Charlie's going to have a fit. I would look for Chipper a new home, and I'd get to wash his mouth out with soap when he cursed, too. There was a silver lining. Now who's sounding like a psycho?

"Can I write everything down for her? Please." He begged Pick, who looked like he was about to fall in the floor. It certainly had been one of the longest days of my life.

Pick uncuffed Arty's right hand and cuffed his left hand to his own. If Arty thought he would get away on Pick's watch, he was mighty wrong. Hansen was walking Twilight toward the police car, with her repeatedly telling him that she'd have his badge over this, and once her lawyer came to this dump of a town, he would get her out.

I didn't think there was a chance in hell that any lawyer could get her out of serving a lot of time. One thing was certain: she had surely lost her job as Queen B at the KDP Shopping Network. I doubt they'll send one of their attorneys to help her. I'm sure with Arty's consent, they could and probably would bring Triston's products to the channel to sell. They were wonderful products, products that had cost Triston his life. They still sold Tammy Faye Bakker's makeup long after she passed from cancer. You'd need to purchase a lot of makeup if you were going for her look. That is for sure.

Speaking of Tammy Faye, you could look at Jim Bakker and tell he had sugar in his tank. I was a straight woman and could see that. Triston had told me once while cutting my hair that if you ever had to question if someone was gay, you already had your answer. I wasn't sure it was that cut and dry, but there are times when it's as plain as the day is long. Not that there's anything wrong with being gay. I'm sure Pastor Fairchild and I would differ in our opinion. I never chose to be straight, so I suppose gays don't choose to be gay.

Arty came to me and handed me a sheet of stationery that read 'The Mills,' in gold script, at the top. He had written down the treats Chipper liked, the type of food and where I could get it, and how often to feed and water him. What Arty had written looked like the same instructions you would need to feed a dog, but obviously with different food. I looked it over to make sure I didn't have questions. I wondered if I could get the food and treats left in their penthouse.

"Pick, I need to make sure I have everything before you take him away." It could be a while before I spoke to Arty again, if I ever did. I still can't forgive him for June Bug. That might make me a bad Christian, and if it does, I will live with that.

Good Lord, I can't believe I'm taking this bird!

It suddenly hit me. Chipper was really Triston's. Chipper loved Triston more than he loved Arty, even though Arty's aunt left Chipper to him. Animals sense a lot about people, and I think that Chipper knew what had happened to Triston. Maybe he even watched it. I'm pretty sure he heard everything that happened that night. Thinking about it, I'm surprised Chipper allowed Arty to hold him. But I supposed he was grieving and needed love, too. We're all God's creatures and we all need love.

Chapter Seventeen

AFTER EVERYTHING WAS SAID and done last night, Arty, Sherry, and Twilight were taken to the slammer. The following morning, the news stations were reporting how Twilight Woods was involved in the killing of Triston Stylz, who was supposed to be her best-selling product maker of all time, and about the poisoning of June Bug Akins. They showed all three of their mugshots. They didn't look happy at all.

Even though Twilight had not actually killed either one of them, she had put into motion all the parts to make for their murder. She wasn't anyone's fool. She knew what she had done, and she had allowed everyone else to get their hands dirty, while she sat back and watched with a huge bowl of buttered popcorn in her lap as they did her bidding.

Pearl and Myra came over to the house after lunch the next day, allowing me time to get some sleep and ponder everything. I was so frazzled that sleep didn't find me last night. I tossed and turned, finally getting out of bed around 4:00 a.m. I walked into the living room, where I reflexively turned on the TV. This was a mistake, because I couldn't get away from the murder there either. It was on every news channel. The one time Sunnyside was featured on national news, and the coverage was all about a bunch of psychos and sociopaths!

It was crazy how many news channels showed up in Sunnyside early the next morning, making it impossible to get in or out of The Mills. Their trucks and vans were everywhere. And the news anchors were like roaches, looking for any crumbs they could find. I had to take our house phone off the hook. At least Amber, the last time she was home, had done something to our iPhone that would send any calls that weren't in our contact lists straight to voice mail. The news that a handful of the ladies from the St. John's Baptist Church Ladies Auxiliary were the ones to crack the case had gotten out. Hallelujah, they didn't get any of our names, except for June Bug's, or they'd be all up in our yards trying to see when one of us leaves. I wasn't Angelina Jolie, so I didn't want to be on TV. I ain't one for fame. Even Myra didn't want them at her house messing up her hydrangeas, azaleas, and magnolia trees.

It didn't take KDP very long to throw their star seller under the bus. The producers told anyone who would listen that KDP had no idea why Twilight Woods had gone to Sunnyside, nor what she had intended to do. After all, they had an entire division that dealt with getting contracts to people like Triston Stylz. They reported that Twilight had gone to Sunnyside on her own, without KDP's direction, knowledge, or consent. She had told KDP that she was taking a two-week vacation. I turned the TV off. I was sick of hearing about it all. I had lived it once, and that was enough.

Tony got plenty of airtime, though, explaining everything he had heard that night. I'd bet he was even taking notes, as we were all listening to Arty spill the beans on the whole sordid affair.

Pick didn't really care. He was finished with it all, had already put in his retirement papers, and given his two weeks' notice. He was focused on Pearl now. He finally got the one that got away.

"I'm still shocked that they all were involved. I would have never thought that," Pearl said, sipping her coffee at my kitchen table. Myra was across from her, and I was in my usual place at the top of the table.

"Did we ever find out how they got into the church to start with?" Myra turned to me for answers.

"One of the deacons, and I won't say which, had the bright idea of keeping a key hidden inside one of those fake rocks when they were building the new Sunday school wing. When the deacons called the locksmith after this fiasco, he was able to tell by the shape of the key that kids had been coming and going in and out of the church all along, and lest we forget a murderer as well. Apparently, it wasn't a secret where the key was hidden. Arty had heard, at the salon, about the kids going behind the church and thought he'd stash Triston in the woods, but when he got there, he almost tripped over that fake rock with the key in it. That's how he was able to open the door to put Triston's body in the Sunday school room. Arty knew it would throw the scent off of him and the others. It was Arty that placed his body in the Sunday school room all along."

Myra just shook her head. "What I can't get over is the gall of that two-bit hussy, Twilight Woods. If she hadn't come into their lives, Triston would be alive today. And what a mess Sherry Haster has made of her life simply for a chance to own a salon. I know it would have been a Triston Apothecary Salon, with his products, and they would set her up to make a good bit of money, but what they didn't tell her is that it was a huge gamble, because they needed to make sure that the first few franchises made a really good profit. If they didn't, they wouldn't have a leg to stand on. Getting more money to open other salons would be hard. I learned all that from my dear Fairfax when he was opening all the Citizen's First Federal Credit Unions all across South Carolina."

The sun was shining through the kitchen window, and it felt good on my face. I was thankful that we still had family, wonderful friends, and a beautiful town that was so special to all of us.

It isn't every day someone is murdered. We rarely hear of any crime, other than petty stuff like kids smoking pot or fighting over a girl or a boy.

It's surely a new and more colorful world.

Praise be to Jesus.

June Bug woke up the next morning confused about what had happened. She'd been in a coma for two days. Mitzi was there when she woke up and told her everything that had happened. Mitzi called me right after June Bug woke up and handed the phone to June Bug. I told her how much I loved her, and I knew she was going to be okay. I also told her that we'd be up to see her that afternoon if she felt up to some company. She was happy to be alive after all Mitzi had told her. I told her we were so relieved that she came back to us. I had a good feeling about June Bug after all the dust settled. As I drove home in the wee hours of that morning, I just knew June Bug was going to be okay. I thanked the Lord and left it in His hands.

"Have y'all seen the new detective yet?" Pearl asked us. She had on her favorite cardigan, but she wasn't trying to stretch it into a straitjacket. I took that as a good sign. I wondered how Pick had hired another detective so soon. Pearl told us Pick had been working on it for a few weeks after he had a talk with Hansen, who told him that he wouldn't be working as many hours as he had been. He was smitten with Katie Mae Smith, and he wasn't going to let her get away from him again.

Pick knew he had to do something since he was retiring after this case was closed. All the paperwork had been completed. The only thing he said he regretted was listening to Moon Pie Hubbard and getting us to investigate the case. But all in all, I have to say it was a challenge and not something I would want to do every day, but I told Pick and Hansen we were always there if they needed us.

"No, who is he?" Myra said, pulling herself closer to Pearl. Myra goes crazy over new men in town.

"His name is Antonio McClain, and I have never seen anyone as beautiful as that man. I'm as old as Methuselah, but when I saw him, I felt things I ain't felt in years." We all roared with laughter. I couldn't believe Pearl said that; she never talks like that. That was usually Myra's area.

"I'm going to have to get myself locked up," Myra said. I could tell she was thinking about his handcuffs by the way her eyes were glazing over.

"Oh my Lord, Myra. Look at you. You haven't even seen the man yet, and you're thinking nasty thoughts already," I said playfully and smiled at her.

"I know! But I can't help what a good-looking man does to me," Myra said in agreement and shimmied her breasts in front of us. If she wasn't careful, she was going to knock herself out or give one of us a black eye! Me and Pearl were shaking our heads. Myra was a trip without the luggage.

"He's that good-looking; his dance card will stay full," Pearl added, trying not to spit her coffee all over the table. It felt so good to laugh after all we'd been through.

"Pick wasn't playing around," I said to Pearl and Myra. I didn't tell them about the conversation I had had with Hansen. He told me that everything I had told him had been the truth, and that he and Katie Mae were starting over. He would make sure that he was there when she needed him, instead of working all hours of the day and night. In the end, Pick had not only hired a new detective, but had also given Fred Becker a promotion from deputy to a detective in the Major Crimes Division. That should give Hansen some breathing room when he takes over as sheriff of Barnville County. He would be able to delegate work to his detectives in the Major Crimes Division.

Thank the Lord we didn't have much crime to start with, but at least if something did happen, Hansen would be ready to do what needed to be done and delegate to others as needed.

He had earned that. We were all sure that he would be voted in as our next sheriff because no one was even running against him, which said volumes. Pick had also sung his praises and gave him a full-throated endorsement.

"I know someone else's dance card that's going to stay full." Myra sipped on her coffee and looked at Pearl sheepishly. We all laughed again and looked at Pearl, her face turning bright red with embarrassment.

Myra said to her, "Pearl, you don't have a thing to be bashful about. We're all so happy that you and Pick are finally together."

"And I've got the ring to prove it, too," Pearl told us. We looked at each other and didn't know what to say. Pearl wasn't wearing a ring when she arrived, and we still hadn't seen one.

Pearl opened her pocketbook, put the ring on under the table, and flashed it like Beyonce did with her hit song.

Myra and I were both quiet at first. We couldn't believe that Pick had put a ring on it. It was gorgeous. It had been his mother's ring and had small but dignified diamonds on the band. He had Langston Jewelers add a rose-cut diamond, with a dome-shape top, covered in triangular facets. It even looked like a rosebud. I know a lot of people may think they are rushing things, but when you get to our age, you better rush things.

"He did that!" Myra squealed, the queen of diamonds herself. "Rose-cut rings like that were popular in the 16th and 28th centuries. So, Pick knows his diamonds."

"More like Langston knows diamonds," Pearl corrected her, flashing it in the sun as it glittered all around the kitchen. "He confessed he didn't know what I'd like, but he knew I always loved when he gave me roses, so he asked if they could do something rose-themed. Fred showed Pick a picture of a rose-cut diamond and Pick immediately knew that I would love it. Of course, I would have loved it even if it was just a band."

I had never seen Pearl so happy. Although they hadn't yet picked a date, it warmed my heart to see my best friend engaged and soon to be married.

Myra told her she would take care of the catering and the venue as her wedding gift. I wanted to kill her. She knew I could never give Pearl anything close to that, but Pearl said my friendship was all she needed. I was the sister she never had. I felt the same way.

First, we went from laughing to crying. Our Pearl had finally grown up in her sixties.

I had taken out of the freezer this morning around 5:00 a.m., the rest of a pineapple upside-down cake that June Bug had made for my birthday. It was so big that there was no way in the world we'd be able to eat it all before it went bad, so I had frozen more than half of it for another wonderful event, and I couldn't think of anything more wonderful than Pearl getting engaged.

First, I got up from the table and topped off everyone's coffee cup, and then I brought the cake to the table. Pearl and Myra knew it was the birthday cake that June Bug had made for me. I heard oohs and aahs from them both. I put a pie plate in front of them and cut us three huge chunks of the cake.

We were all eating the cake when I heard a noise in the living room. Apparently, we had awakened the dead. I went into the living room and came back into the kitchen with Chipper on my shoulder. He looked so happy. He was rubbing his face against mine and I have to say it feels so good. And not once has Chipper cursed. It made me wonder if Triston and Arty cursed a lot, too.

The girls went crazy when they saw Chipper on my shoulder. To be honest, I was so happy for him. Bless his heart, he had lost a lot of people recently, and me and Charlie hoped to stop that trend. When I got home yesterday morning, I carried the cage into the house. Charlie asked what in the world I was carrying. I had kept the blue velvet cover over the cage so you couldn't see much, and once the cover was over the cage, Chipper wound down and usually went to sleep. I had taken the cover off the cage, and Charlie's eyes lit up like a Christmas tree.

"Chipper love Thelma, Chipper love Thelma," Chipper said, as I cooed at him, blowing on his feathers like I had seen Arty do. I had to say I was falling in love. Charlie fell in love with him at first sight. He was a handsome boy with those beautiful yellow eyes and the bright red tail. Even when he turned his head 180 degrees to preen the feathers on his neck, it no longer felt like the *Exorcist*. I suppose you get used to it.

"Look at that pretty boy." Myra came over and blew his feathers. He loved the attention. It made me wonder just how much attention he got from Triston or Arty. Lord knows I'm not talking badly about the dead; I just felt sorry for Chipper. Pearl got up and came over. I went over to the table and put his velvet cover on the top and let him stand on the table. I hated when people let cats on their furniture, especially the table, but Chipper had warmed my cold heart.

"Look at him. Chipper, you're a pretty boy," Pearl said, looking down at him on the table. I sat back down and the girls followed.

"Chipper a purty boy," he replied. I really didn't know how many words he could speak, but it was a lot.

"Thelma, it makes me so happy that you and Charlie are going to keep Chipper," Myra said, still cooing at Chipper.

"Chipper ain't going nowhere. Charlie has fallen in love." I watched Chipper walk from Pearl to Myra. Myra was rubbing his head, which he loved.

"Chipper love Myra." He even remembers my name. Myra was surprised. It had been a while since she had seen Chipper, but he hadn't forgotten about her and the love she gave to him.

I told the girls that it was getting time for us to go to the hospital to see June Bug. I also told them that Chipper was coming along with us. They knew that June Bug would love Chipper and Chipper would love June Bug. We just had to make sure that we didn't run into a Nurse Ratched at the hospital. I know that dogs can be brought into the rooms, but I had never heard that about birds. I also haven't ever heard that they couldn't either. One way or another, we would smuggle him into June Bug's room. She needed some love. We all need love. That's what I learned the most from this experience.

Things were looking up for all of us and soon we'd be getting ready to raise money for needy families. Parents would be able to provide Christmas gifts to their children. We also make sure the parents receive gifts. Christmas is the time of year for giving and that's what the Ladies Auxiliary at St Johns Baptist church is all about.

COMING OUT IN 2025

THELMA RUE AND THE BRIDESMAID'S LAST DANCE

ABOUT THE AUTHOR

Wayne Powers, a graduate of USC with a degree in Creative Writing, is a versatile author whose works span children's literature, nonfiction, and beyond. His previous book, **Miracles of Kindness**, captivated readers with its uplifting message, and he's now venturing into the world of mystery with the Ladies Auxiliary Mystery series. When he's not crafting characters or thinking up thrilling plot twists, Wayne enjoys styling hair, spending time with his partner of 26 years, Louis, and playing with their two dogs, Sophie and Sadie. Wayne's latest project, **Thelma Rue and the Bridesmaid's Last Dance**, promises more mystery and intrigue on the horizon.

WAYNE POWERS

Made in the USA
Columbia, SC
09 December 2024

47683386R00159